Praise for Patricia Sprinkle

Guess Who's Coming to Die?

"The writing is captivating, as are the characters."

—Gumshoe

Did You Declare the Corpse?

"Patricia Sprinkle gives her Thoroughly Southern Mystery a charming Scottish accent this time, but everything else is delightfully the same . . . the warm, gentle sense of humor [and] the impeccable classic plotting." —Nancy Pickard

"A leisurely read [that] will have you curled up in an easy chair for the evening." —*Rendezvous*

"[A] primer in how to write a compelling story. Additionally, Jan Karon fans who like mysteries will love Mac!"
—Meritorious Mysteries

Who Killed the Queen of Clubs?

"Time to sit on the veranda with a nice glass of lemonade and enjoy this down-home mystery full of charming characters and sparkling Southern witticisms." —Fresh Fiction

continued . . .

When Will the Dead Lady Sing?

"Patricia Sprinkle takes the reader on a trip to the 'real' South—the South of family traditions, community customs, church-going, and crafty, down-home politics. Reading it is like spending an afternoon in the porch swing on Aunt Dixie's veranda. . . . A delightful book."
> —JoAnna Carl, author of the Chocoholic mysteries

Who Let That Killer in the House?

"Sprinkle's third Thoroughly Southern Mystery is thoroughly absorbing." —*The Orlando Sentinel*

Who Left That Body in the Rain?

"*Who Left That Body in the Rain?* charms, mystifies, and delights. As Southern as Sunday fried chicken and sweet tea. Patricia Sprinkle's Hopemore is as captivating—and as filled with big hearts and big heartaches—as Jan Karon's Mitford."
> —Carolyn Hart, author of the Henry O and
> Death on Demand mysteries

"Authentic and convincing."
> —Tamar Myers, author of *Hell Hath No Curry*

"An heirloom quilt. Each piece of patchwork is unique and with its own history, yet they are deftly stitched together with threads of family love and loyalty, simmering passion, deception and wickedness, but always with optimism imbued with down-home Southern traditions. A novel to be savored while sitting on a creaky swing on the front porch, a pitcher of lemonade nearby, a dog slumbering in the sunlight."
> —Joan Hess, author of *The Goodbye Body*

WHAT ARE YOU WEARING TO DIE?

⊰ A THOROUGHLY SOUTHERN MYSTERY ⊱

Patricia Sprinkle

AN OBSIDIAN MYSTERY

OBSIDIAN
Published by New American Library, a division of
Penguin Group (USA) Inc., 375 Hudson Street,
New York, New York 10014, USA
Penguin Group (Canada), 90 Eglinton Avenue East, Suite 700, Toronto,
Ontario M4P 2Y3, Canada (a division of Pearson Penguin Canada Inc.)
Penguin Books Ltd., 80 Strand, London WC2R 0RL, England
Penguin Ireland, 25 St. Stephen's Green, Dublin 2,
Ireland (a division of Penguin Books Ltd.)
Penguin Group (Australia), 250 Camberwell Road, Camberwell, Victoria 3124,
Australia (a division of Pearson Australia Group Pty. Ltd.)
Penguin Books India Pvt. Ltd., 11 Community Centre, Panchsheel Park,
New Delhi - 110 017, India
Penguin Group (NZ), 67 Apollo Drive, Rosedale, North Shore 0632,
New Zealand (a division of Pearson New Zealand Ltd.)
Penguin Books (South Africa) (Pty.) Ltd., 24 Sturdee Avenue,
Rosebank, Johannesburg 2196, South Africa

Penguin Books Ltd., Registered Offices:
80 Strand, London WC2R 0RL, England

First published by Obsidian, an imprint of New American Library,
a division of Penguin Group (USA) Inc.

First Printing, February 2008
10 9 8 7 6 5 4 3 2 1

PRIMARY CHARACTERS

MacLaren Yarbrough—Hope County magistrate and co-owner, Yarbrough Feed, Seed, and Nursery

Joe Riddley Yarbrough—her husband, co-owner of Yarbrough Feed, Seed, and Nursery

Ridd and Martha Yarbrough—their older son and his wife

Cricket Yarbrough—Ridd and Martha's son (five years old)

Bailey "Buster" Gibbons—sheriff of Hope County and Joe Riddley's best friend

Hubert Spence—the Yarbroughs' former neighbor and old friend

Maynard and Selena Spence—Hubert's son and his wife

Augusta Wainwright—dowager aristocrat who shares house with Hubert

Otis and Lottie Raeburn—couple who care for Hubert and Gusta

Evelyn Finch—manager of Yarbrough Feed, Seed, and Nursery

Trevor Knight—local taxidermist

Starr and Bradley Knight—Trevor's daughter and four-year-old grandson

Wylie Quarles—Trevor's assistant, Starr's former boyfriend

Robin, Natalie, and Anna Emily Parker—Trevor's assistant and her daughters (five and three years old, respectively)

Dan and Kaye Poynter—taxidermists from Virginia

Grady Handley—soldier seeking his wife

Billy Baxter—the Parker girls' "Uncle Billy"

❧ 1 ❧

For months, Joe Riddley had been threatening to shackle me to my desk to keep me from "meddling in murder." I never believed he'd do it.

In fact, when he came into our office that Thursday afternoon in mid-September and set an icy Coca-Cola and a Hershey bar beside my computer keyboard, I was almost ready to nominate him for a sainthood merit badge. What held up his nomination was a look on his face that meant he was up to something. When you've been married nearly forty-five years, you learn to read signs like that.

I hadn't learned to read them well enough.

"Is this a bribe or an apology?" I put one hand over the candy bar so he couldn't take it back.

"Give me space!" That wasn't Joe Riddley. It was Bo, the big scarlet macaw whose rainbow tail feathers streamed down Joe Riddley's back. We had inherited Bo from a man who died in our house a couple of years before,[1] and my husband often took the bird to work, claiming Bo got lonely at home. I didn't complain. I often took Lulu, my three-legged beagle, to work with me for the very same reason. She was lying beside my desk at the moment, worrying a fat

[1]*Who Invited the Dead Man?*

knot of red and brown cloth that she preferred to store-bought toys.

I held the candy bar ready to open as soon as I got Joe Riddley's explanation.

"Neither. I figured those might keep you sending out invoices until quitting time. If you don't want them—"

"I want them, all right. They are probably the only incentives in the world that would keep me working on a day like this." If Joe Riddley wasn't ready to confess, I could wait.

I unwrapped the candy and looked wistfully out our office window. Georgia in mid-September is still hot, but already the air was getting that golden tinge that heralds autumn. While the trees were weeks from changing yet, the breeze rippling the leaves on the triple poplar beyond our parking lot had a lighthearted look, no longer encumbered by the weight of summer humidity. "I envy you, getting to work outside."

"Remind me of that on a rainy day next January, or in July when the thermometer nears a hundred."

Joe Riddley and I co-own Yarbrough Feed, Seed, and Nursery in Hopemore, the seat of Hope County, which is located in that wedge of Georgia between I-20 and I-16. He runs the landscaping part of our business and manages the nursery on the outskirts of town, which sells shrubs and trees to homeowners, developers, and landscaping firms. I keep the books and oversee the store in town, which deals in animal feed, seeds, bedding plants, potting soil, pesticides, fertilizers, and garden equipment.

He peered over my shoulder at the spreadsheet on my computer screen. "We still got money in the bank?"

"Not to worry," Bo advised. I have never known if that bird knows what it's saying or merely gets it right sometimes.

I spoke through a mouthful of chocolate. "Some. The nursery is going to show a nice profit when we collect from those new developments up near I-20, but the store's been losing money since last November. The only thing that's held steady is large-animal feed, and once developers turn pastures into subdivisions, that will go down the drain. We need to consider what we're going to do pretty soon."

In case you are wondering, it wasn't my poor management that had the store running behind; it was what some folks call progress. Back when the federal highway that runs through town was a main drag, it brought right many tourists our way each year. Once I-20 took the traffic, tourism slowed to a trickle, and some folks predicted that Hopemore would shrivel up and die. Of course, the primary business in the county at the time was agriculture, which was great for Yarbrough's.

Like Joe Riddley often says, however, "Land is like gold. They aren't making any more of it." In the past few years, our part of the state had been seeing what the chamber of commerce called "revitalization" and other folks called "the second Yankee invasion": young seniors who wanted to enjoy early retirement free of snow and ice and who were willing to pay ridiculous prices for houses in cookie-cutter subdivisions sprawling over former fields and pastures. Our population used to be a steady thirteen thousand in the Hopemore greater metropolitan area. The next census would show a considerable jump.

Furthermore, while newcomers might be willing to fill our pastures and fields with new neighborhoods in their search for warmth and recreation, they wanted to shop in familiar places. The entire South had broken out in a rash of national chain restaurants, stores, and motels. Hopemore had recently added a Waffle House, and the previous fall a big superstore had opened at the edge of town, to the delight of newcomers—who didn't seem to realize that the small-town charm they had moved south for was headed for extinction. Local merchants were closing their doors at an alarming rate.

Joe Riddley and I were holding on so far, but the superstore had both a garden center and a pet department, so they sold almost everything our store carried, and at lower prices. I couldn't blame people for wanting to save money, but it irked me when somebody bought a plant at the other place and came to us for free advice on where to plant it and how to keep it alive. The superstore's garden center staff knew diddly-squat about horticulture. And while I appreciated my husband's determination not to let employees go until we absolutely had to, we couldn't run the store as a charity indefinitely.

Joe Riddley rattled his keys in his pocket. "You been to the bathroom lately?"

That might seem like a personal question, but when you co-own a business, questions aren't always what they appear. The day before, a small boy had flushed his sister's plastic coin purse down our toilet. I'd had a plumber in there half the morning trying to fish it out.

"Five minutes ago. It's working fine."

"That's good."

He shifted from one foot to the other, unusually restless.

"Sic 'em, boy!" Bo urged.

I reached again for my Coke. "For a nickel, I'd pack up and go down to Ridd and Martha's for a swim. I've been thinking of that pool all afternoon."

A year before, Joe Riddley and I had moved from the old Yarbrough homeplace and turned it over to our older son, Ridd, and his wife, Martha—as Joe Riddley's parents had turned it over to us when we had two boys to raise. Our grandson, Cricket, would be the fifth Joe Riddley Yarbrough to grow up in that place. The thing I missed most was the swimming pool. During warm weather, I went down several times a week to swim.

As I took another swig of Coke, Joe Riddley dropped a coin.

"Is that my nickel?" I was so busy drinking I scarcely noticed him crawling around my desk—until he grabbed my ankle. I smacked him. "Stop that! What if somebody takes a notion to mosey back to look at rakes and hoes?" The top half of our office door was a clear pane of glass, so we were visible to anybody who came to the rear of the store.

"Back off! Give me space!" Bo demanded, trying to take a nip out of my hand.

Something cold circled my shin. I heard a snap. "Hey!" I peered down at my husband's broad back. "What are you doing?" Anklets weren't my style, and this one was heavy.

"What I should have done years ago." I heard another click. "There's been a body found out on the bypass, and I don't want you haring over there to get involved."

I tried to lift my foot, but it moved only a few inches. It was securely fastened to one leg of the oak rolltop that had outlasted three generations of Yarbroughs. I could no more lift that desk than I could lift the courthouse down the street.

Playing along, I tugged at the cuffs—succeeding only in bruising my ankle and snagging my panty hose. "You can't do this. What if I need to leave the office?"

"You've already been to the bathroom."

He climbed to his feet with remarkable agility for a man of sixty-six. That's one benefit of lifting heavy plants and working outdoors his entire life. Then the old hypocrite bent down and kissed the top of my head.

"Let me out of here!" I still thought he was joking. "I'm not going over to the bypass. But what if I have to go down to the sheriff's detention center for a hearing?"

In addition to working at the store, two years ago I became one of three magistrates in Hope County. I hold court each week to hear cases of county ordinance violations, hold traffic court down in the south end of the county a couple of times a month, and may be called by a deputy at any time, day or night, to go down to the detention center (the fancy name for our jail) to hold a bond hearing after an arrest.

Joe Riddley brushed his palms together to get rid of grit that accumulated on our old pine floors no matter how often we swept. "I told them you wouldn't be available for the rest of the afternoon. Judge Stebley is covering for you."

"Which means every law enforcement officer in the county will know about this by nightfall. I will *never* live it down." I was beginning to get cross.

He headed toward the door. "Desperate times require desperate measures. I'll see you in a while. I need to get back to the nursery."

"You can't leave me like this!" I went from not quite cross to furious in one second flat. In that second, I might've had the strength to hoist the desk high enough to slide off the cuff, but the anger surged past and left me with panic. "Don't, Joe Riddley. Anything could happen." I pictured a tornado raging down Oglethorpe Street with me helpless before it.

He lifted the red Yarbrough cap he always wears, smoothed his hair, and settled the cap back on his head. "I've got emergencies covered. Besides, it's only for an hour or so. Then I'll come on back and we can go swim."

"At least tell me who died." I was stalling for time. How could I convince him this joke had gone far enough?

"I have no idea. A truck went over the embankment and was found sitting tail-up in the kudzu."

That didn't help. Practically every family in the county owned a truck.

"Buster got the call while I was driving him back from Rotary Club," he added.

"So that's where you got the cuffs."

Bailey "Buster" Gibbons was not only the sheriff of Hope County but had been Joe Riddley's best friend since kindergarten. When I started school two years later, the two of them were alternately my champions and my tormentors. They would beat up anybody who tried to bother me, then devil me with practical jokes of their own—a tendency they had never outgrown.

"Please, honey?" I was reduced to begging as he put his hand on the doorknob.

"Little Bit, time and time again I have asked you not to meddle with murder. You have nearly scared me to death with how close you have come to getting yourself killed. I still don't know how you got sliced up so bad in Scotland."[2]

Unconsciously I flexed my left hand, which the doctor said would always be stiff from that encounter. He noticed. "See? Next time it could be your neck. I married you so we could grow old together. That means you need to be around. Sit tight until Buster gets this body dealt with and I get an order of sod sent out. Then I'll come back and we'll swim."

"I love you. I surely do," Bo added.

They paused at the door. I had a second's hope that the old coot was going to unlock me. "You reckon the rage for hawthorn will continue this next year? We might need some more," he said.

"You and the sheriff are both going to need new heads once I get out of here." I tugged hard at the cuffs, in case he hadn't really locked them. They held firm. "This isn't funny. I'll put you in jail."

"I'll be back in an hour or so."

With that, he left.

I glared at his back while it receded into shadows as he made his way through the store. "I don't know what I'm gonna do to get you for this," I vowed aloud, "but it is going to be terrible."

I am short, so I keep a stool for my feet under the desk. No matter how I tried, though, I couldn't back far enough away from the desk to get the stool positioned right to keep that cuff from chafing my ankle raw. Lulu was no help, licking my other ankle as I tried to shove the stool into place.

I pulled the phone toward me and called the cell phone of Isaac James, assistant police chief and my good friend. His office was behind the courthouse, less than a block away.

As soon as I heard his bass rumble over the line, I

announced, "This is Judge Yarbrough, and I've got a problem here. I've inadvertently been cuffed to my desk."

Isaac's chuckle filled my ear. "He went through with it, huh? I heard he was threatening to do that."

"How fast can you get over here to let me out? Then you can go to the nursery and arrest the old codger for false imprisonment."

"Sorry, Judge, I'm out on the bypass right now, tied up with a wreck. If you really want to press official charges, though, I'm sure Chief Muggins . . ."

Even Ike was playing dirty. Police chief Charlie Muggins had been trying to pin something on me ever since I got appointed magistrate. I could picture Charlie's smirk as he came through my door—and as he left without helping me at all.

"I thought Sheriff Gibbons went out on that bypass call."

"He's got his wreck and I've got mine. A couple of folks were so busy rubbernecking to see what the sheriff's men were up to, they collided right inside the city limits. It was pretty bad, so I'll be here a while. If you don't want me to tell the chief, I can send one of the deputies. . . ."

He knew good and well I would turn down that offer, too. Ike might laugh and let me out, but if he sent a deputy because I'd requested help, I'd have to press some kind of charges. I might be mad enough to want Joe Riddley and Buster both behind bars for a night, but we'd be the laughingstock of Hopemore once the story hit the weekly *Hopemore Statesman*. There are certain disadvantages to living among people who have known you all your life.

"Who died?" I could at least satisfy my curiosity on that point.

"We don't know yet. They are in the process of winching the vehicle up as we speak. All I know so far is that it's a black Ford Ranger with a blond person in it wearing a white shirt."

I heard somebody speak behind Isaac. His voice went

muffled for a sentence or two. Then he said, "It's Starr Knight, the taxidermist's daughter."

I felt like somebody had stolen all my air.

"Oh, no! First his wife—how long has it been since she died? Six or seven years?"

"Something like that. With her death plus all the stuff Trevor has already gone through with Starr, you'd think he'd had his share of troubles."

"Not to mention what he went through before he ever got married."

Trevor Knight was the best living example I knew of somebody who had been to hell and back. He'd grown up in town and gotten drafted before he finished college. He came home from Vietnam wracked by nightmares and addicted to drugs and alcohol. For ten years he had cut a wild swath through middle Georgia. He had been intimately acquainted with the Hope County jail. But during his last incarceration, thirty years before, Trevor had found faith, which helped him lick his demons. Sober and clean, he had returned to Hopemore and gone to work for our local taxidermist. In the past twenty-five years, he had bought out the business and built it up until he now had two people working for him.

In the process, he had become known for compassion toward people the rest of us might give up on. That very morning he had chaired the breakfast meeting of a committee that helped turn around local teens headed in the wrong direction.

Unfortunately, his own daughter had been one teen he'd been unable to help. After her mother died, Starr had spun out of control. She started wearing a lot of makeup, provocative clothes, and flashy hairdos. At fourteen she was drinking. By fifteen she was a drunk. At sixteen she was pregnant. For a while after the baby came, she had cleaned up her act. She got a job at the Bi-Lo grocery store and was working a rehab progam. However, in recent months she had slid downhill again. I'd seen her several times sashaying down Oglethorpe Street wearing a soiled skimpy top, skintight jeans, and too much makeup—which was unsuccessful at covering the deterioration of her pretty face.

From the speed with which Starr had been losing her looks, I guessed she'd been using methamphetamine. Like many small towns across the United States, we were drowning in meth. Nobody knew where it was coming from or how to stop the deluge.

Her little boy, Bradley, nearly broke my heart, tagging along behind his mama with dirty hands, torn jeans, matted hair, and a bewildered look on his face. Two weeks ago the authorities had taken the child away and placed him with Ridd and Martha, who had completed training to become foster parents. Trevor had petitioned to get the child, and a court date had been set. Meanwhile, Cricket, who was five, had taken the four-year-old Bradley under his wing.

How would Martha explain to the two little boys that Bradley's mother was never coming back? As sorry a mother as Starr had been lately, Bradley still cried for her every night.

I realized Ike was talking again. ". . . must have driven somewhere to get drugs and was too high to make the curve on her way back. Kids picking up trash for community service saw the truck bed sticking out of the kudzu and called the sheriff. Hold on a minute." I heard somebody speaking to him in the background.

While I waited, I wondered what Starr had been doing out on the bypass. She lived in an apartment in town, and her daddy lived in the other direction. And why would she miss a shallow curve she'd been driving all her life?

Isaac came back on the line. "The truck is Robin Parker's and it was reported stolen Monday afternoon. It's totaled. Robin won't be driving it again."

"That's awkward. Robin works for Trevor. What a mess."

"It's gonna get messier before it's over. Ms. Parker claimed her truck was stolen out of Trevor's yard while they were working. His workroom doesn't have any windows out back, where it was parked. Well, I'd better get back to work." Before he hung up, Isaac added, "Oh, Judge? Don't leave town today, okay?"

"That wasn't funny. I'm in pain over here."

I was talking to air. Ike had already gone.

⇥ 2 ⇤

After that conversation, getting out of the cuffs moved down to the second most urgent issue in my life. The most urgent was letting Martha know what had happened.

Ridd answered the phone. Until I heard his clogged "Heddo?" I'd forgotten he was recovering from a bad cold and had taken the day off from teaching math. He didn't even try to hide his disappointment at hearing my voice. "I thought you might be Bethany."

As hard as it was for me to believe, my older son was now forty-two and was normally a well-balanced adult whom folks looked up to. For the past three weeks, he had been an emotional mess. His little girl had gone to college, two hours away. My maternal take on his head cold was that he had gotten run-down from worry.

My own worries made me speak more sharply than I normally would. "No, this is your mother, and I have some very bad news. Starr Knight has been found dead in a car that went over the embankment out on the bypass."

No point in beating around the bush when you have that kind of information to impart.

"Oh, God." From Ridd, that was a prayer. Unlike his younger brother, he didn't swear. "You're sure?"

"What's the matter, Daddy?" I heard Cricket in the background. I had expected him to be at school and Bradley to be in day care.

"Are both boys in earshot?" I asked.

"Yes. Cricket's got my cold, so everybody stayed home today. We're playing Go Fish and they are whaling the tar out of me. Let me take the phone to the kitchen."

In another second he asked softly, "There's no chance this is only a rumor?"

"I had it straight from Isaac James."

"Her poor dad!"

I could appreciate why Ridd would identify with a father who had lost his daughter, but I hauled him back to the other priority on his plate. "I'm wondering what this will mean for Bradley. You all may have the task of telling him. I don't envy you a bit."

There was a long pause. He apparently hadn't considered that part of it. Then he asked, in a falsely cheerful voice, "You guys looking for a snack?"

I heard the boys clamoring for juice and Cricket Dog, Lulu's son, yipping for a treat. I might as well let Ridd discuss his favorite subject until he could get rid of them. "When did you hear from Bethany last?"

"Yesterday. She loves her classes, loves her roommate, hates the food, and was fixing to give some football players a ride to Wal-Mart. Can you believe that? She knows not to give rides to strangers. And football players? You know what they're like."

"Your brother was a football player."

"I wouldn't have trusted my daughter with Walker at that age, either."

I sighed. When you have kids, you think you'll get them into elementary school and your major work will be done. Then you think if you can get them into high school—or into college, or out of college—surely by then they will be grown-up and your worries will be over. Yet there I was with a son old enough to have a daughter in college, and he still expected me to bear his burdens.

"She's a grown-up now," I reminded him, "and she's a sensible girl. Stop worrying and let her enjoy her freedom."

"Easy for you to say." He sounded as gloomy as Eeyore. "You never had a girl. They worry you to death."

"I didn't need a girl for that. I've got your daddy. You will not believe what he's done to me this afternoon."

For the first time since he came on the line, Ridd laughed. "He carried through? I heard what he was threatening to do."

If you live in a city and depend on television, radio, or a newspaper for news, you might wonder how Ridd had heard. If you live in a small town, you take it for granted that news floats on the breeze. All you have to do is cock your ear and listen.

"How fast can you bring a tool over to cut me free?"

"Not on your life. I suspect Daddy could still whup me if he tried."

"Pop can whup anybody!" Cricket boasted in the background.

Martha came on the phone. "What's up, Mac? Why's Pop going to whip Ridd?"

I heard Ridd say, "Hey, boys, would you like to take your snack out onto the porch?"

For a moment I had a wistful longing for that wide screened porch with a table placed to get the best view of the yard. I pushed regret down where it belonged and promised, "I'll tell you about that in a minute. First, Starr Knight has been found dead in a car out on the bypass."

Martha caught a quick breath, and her immediate reaction was the same as mine. "Poor Bradley! How on earth are we going to tell him? And Cricket? He dotes on that child."

We discussed that for a few minutes, and then she asked, "Why was Ridd saying his daddy can still whip him?"

When I told her, she gave a gurgle like a mountain stream. Given the prickles in my left leg, I would have preferred a mountain stream at the moment—preferably an ice-cold one with my foot dangling in it.

"Put some lotion on your ankle," she advised. "That will

help it slide up and down easier." Martha supervises our hospital emergency room, and was at home only because she was working a weekend rotation. "I hate to say it, Mac, but I understand where Pop is coming from. You've put yourself in danger too often lately."

"I don't put myself in danger," I protested. "I do my best to avoid it. It just happens sometimes."

"Like every time you get too close to a murderer."

That stung. "I don't cozy up to them, but I can't sit by when somebody I care about is in danger, or asks me to use what common sense and local knowledge I have. You know good and well I don't thrust myself into investigations out of curiosity. But like Mama used to say, 'We don't have to go looking for trouble. God puts enough trouble in our path to keep life interesting.'"

"If you think God puts murder in your path to keep your life interesting, you're skating on real thin theological ice. The closest I'll come to agreement is that you have been providentially placed sometimes to figure out some stuff the police haven't."

"Why can't Joe Riddley see that?"

"Because he loves you more than life itself, and he doesn't want to lose you."

"He doesn't have to insult me. You should have heard him. 'There's been a body found out on the bypass and I don't want you haring over there to take a look at it.' I don't go haring anywhere simply to look at a body. Besides, Starr wasn't murdered. I'm not going to get involved in investigating her accident."

"Of course not, but cut Pop some slack right now. He's worried about the business, which means he needs you worse than ever."

"I wish he had cut me some slack. My leg is going to sleep. I may have to have an amputation."

She gurgled again. "Like I said, put some lotion on your ankle. He won't leave you there long. You know that as well as—oops! I've got to go. Ridd's gone down to the barn, and

I hear Cricket laying down the law to Bradley about how many cookies he's allowed. Poor Bradley. He must think he's got three parents sometimes."

"Instead, he's got none." That sobered us both. "Are the boys getting along all right otherwise?" I asked.

"Beautifully, most of the time. Cricket's done pretty well at sharing his toys, and Cricket Dog, he doesn't even seem to mind that he's no longer the littlest, but I have to watch him to make sure he doesn't boss Bradley around. I really do need to go. Bye."

The only lotion I had in the office was in the top drawer of a filing cabinet halfway across the office. When something is out of reach, it doesn't matter if it is a mere five feet away or two hours, like Bethany. Having had my philosophical moment and shared a smidgeon of sympathy with Ridd, I punched the buzzer on my phone. Evelyn Finch, the store manager, picked up. "You need something, Mac?"

"Yeah. I need you for a second. Are you busy?"

"I wish. It's deader out here than a bar on Sunday morning." Before I could ask how she knew what a bar was like on Sunday morning, she added, "I'll be right there," and hung up.

Evelyn was nearly as short as me and a little plumper, but she was also twenty years younger and faster. She poked her head through my door in three seconds flat. "What do you need?" Her voice sounded kind of thick, like she was coming down with a cold, too.

I bit my tongue to keep from saying, "I need for you to pick one hair color and stick with it a few weeks so I can get used to it." Evelyn frequently experimented with new shades from the drugstore. She had been born with a bushy head of hair in the shade of red that fades to pink and goes gray early. Recently, she'd been trying every red known to CVS, claiming she was trying to match her freckles. This week's color came close. She looked like she'd shampooed in carrot juice. To avoid mentioning the fact, I said, "Your eyes look pink. Are you sick?"

She brushed one cheek and I realized she'd been crying. "I just heard about Starr Knight She wasn't even twenty. Her whole life was in front of her."

I knew Evelyn was connecting Starr's death to her husband's. Fifteen years before, when Evelyn and Jack Finch were both thirty, he had met a timber truck head-on. We had hired her afterwards in order to help her keep her home until she decided what she wanted to do with the rest of her life. To everybody's surprise, including hers, she had taken to our business like a wasp to molasses. She had a good head for selling and was blessed with a soft heart and a caring nature that brought in a lot of repeat customers. In fact, Evelyn was the main reason Joe Riddley didn't want to close the store. He wanted to hold on until she had enough in her pension fund to give her a decent retirement.

"The accident was awful," I agreed. "I heard who it was from Officer James." To other people Joe Riddley and I called law enforcement officers by their titles, to show respect.

Evelyn blinked back tears. "Was that why you wanted me? To tell me about Starr?"

"Not really." I hated to admit my real reason, but I was in pain. I pointed to my ankle. "Joe Riddley is playing a joke on me. I want you to fetch a crowbar and see if together we can lift this dratted desk high enough to slide the cuff out from under. Ask Gladys to help, too."

Gladys was a part-time employee we'd hired after Bethany went to college. She was roughly the same age as Methuselah and her arms resembled cooked noodles, but I was beyond being choosy.

"I'm sorry, Mac, but the boss said I wasn't to mess with those cuffs unless there was an emergency. I promised I wouldn't."

Fifteen years she'd worked for us and Joe Riddley was still "the boss"?

We'd deal with that later. I had figured out what Joe Riddley had meant when he said he had emergencies covered.

"Dang it, woman, you work for me as much as you do him. I even sign your paycheck. Go get that key he left and let me out of here!"

I spoke loud enough to wake Lulu. She looked up from her snooze, flapped her tail against the floor in protest at being interrupted, then resumed her nap.

I was still waiting for Evelyn to head for the key. Instead, she shook her head. "Can't. You aren't big enough to beat me up. He is. I can stay back here and keep you company, if you like. There's no action up front, and Gladys will be here another hour."

I wanted to yell loud enough to blast the carroty hair off her head, but I spoke as mildly as I could. "Then reach in that top drawer and hand me the lotion. Martha said it might keep the dratted thing from chafing."

Evelyn not only fetched the lotion, but she knelt and rubbed it into my ankle. "I'm ruining your stockings."

"They're ruined already."

She maneuvered the cuff on the leg of the desk up a bit and fixed the stool so it was under both my feet. I sighed. "That feels so much better. Thanks. Do sit down and stay a while. I don't feel like working anyway, and nobody is going to complain if they get their invoice late."

Evelyn started for the small wing chair we keep under the window for guests, thought better of it, and backed up to Joe Riddley's leather desk chair. "Can you see me over here without breaking your neck?" I appreciated her thoughtfulness, considering that her feet didn't reach the floor in that big old chair and would soon be needles and pins. Short people are going to need a lot of compensation in heaven to make up for the discrimination we go through down here. On the other hand, while I appreciated her concern for my neck, it was my leg I was currently concerned about.

"Ignore that old bat's instructions and get me out of

here." I tugged at the cuffs again. All I accomplished was widening the hole in my panty hose.

"I can't. I gave him my word, and I have my reputation to think of."

"What about my reputation?"

She snickered—which I thought was pretty sassy, considering that she depended on my goodwill for her daily bread.

I picked up my Hershey bar and held out what was left. "You want some candy?" I wasn't offering her a bribe. I was obeying Mama's injunction not to eat without offering some to anybody who might be around. As long as I had to endure the cuffs, I might as well finish up the treacherous offerings that had come with them.

"No thanks, he already—" Evelyn's face turned so pink that her freckles blended together.

My jaw dropped. "He brought you candy, too? So much for your blameless reputation. Now that we both know you're amenable to corruption, woman, how about if I let you go home early? You don't even have to come in tomorrow."

I could tell she was tempted. I should be free in two minutes flat.

Unfortunately, Evelyn was made of sterner stuff than I needed at the moment.

"I told you—I promised." She pulled her feet up under her and sat on them. I gave her a stony look for a very long moment.

Eventually I decided we might as well talk. "Did you hear the rest, about the truck Starr was driving?"

"I heard it was Robin Parker's." From the way Evelyn said the woman's name, I could tell she wasn't buying stock in Robin anytime soon.

"You're not a member of the Robin Parker Fan Club?" I took a swig of my Coke, which was getting warm and losing its zing.

Evelyn reversed her legs and wiggled to get more comfortable. "I hardly know her, but she's too goody-goody for me. She never smiles, and she watches over those two girls like we had predators behind every bush. She hardly lets anybody talk to them."

"You can't fault a single mother because she's careful with her daughters. I wish Starr had been more careful with her son. But I wonder why she took Robin's truck."

"Maybe she was jealous of the way Trevor keeps bragging on Robin. Wylie Quarles has worked for Trevor a lot longer, but Trevor never says much about his work."

"Maybe that's because Robin is a better taxidermist. Some women can't help being great."

Evelyn snorted. "Like the person cuffed to her desk at the moment?"

"Don't get personal." I finished the Coke and tossed the bottle toward a recycling bin I kept by my desk. Consistent with the rest of my day, it clattered to the floor and rolled out of reach.

Evelyn sighed as she retrieved it. "Starr had such a tough life."

I've never been one to color a person with sentimentality just because she died, and I was not feeling charitable at the moment. "Starr made a lot of bad choices in her life, and her daddy spoiled her rotten. She might not have turned out the way she did if her parents had reined her in a little."

Evelyn's eyes flashed with indignation. "Her mother reined her in fine, until she got so sick. It was Trevor who spoiled her, and he couldn't help it. Starr wrapped him around her finger the minute she was born."

That's when I remembered that not only did Evelyn and Trevor go to the same church, but they had been dating earlier that summer. For all I knew, they might have started discussing marriage in the near future. Evelyn and I didn't often sit down and discuss our personal lives.

"I'm sorry. I don't know them well enough to make judgments. Did I hear you are dating him?"

"Not anymore. That didn't work out."

In spite of what Joe Riddley might tell you, I have enough tact to curb my curiosity at times. I was doing a pretty good job of it, considering that a widowed man who owned a business ought to look pretty good to Evelyn. Single men in her age bracket were a rarity in Hopemore. Still, I didn't say a word—just sat there trying to get as comfortable as I could with one leg cramping up.

To my relief, she told me before I broke down and asked.

"The main thing Trevor and I had in common was that we'd each lost a spouse and had a big hole in our lives. We knew how that felt. He had known Jack a little, too, and I knew Cathy real well, so we could talk about them without it being awkward. I figured, though, that after a while we'd build something of our own over the holes. Sort of a floor over a basement, you know?"

"Bless your heart, you're a poet. I never knew that."

She gave me a rueful grin. "Trevor and I never made any poetry together. He hasn't gotten over Cathy, and I don't think he ever will. Our relationship—or what I thought could be our relationship—never went beyond talking about Cathy and Jack. There was one more thing, too. You know my dogs?"

"Of course." Two of the ugliest mutts I'd ever seen. They were so ugly they were downright cute, and Evelyn adored them.

"I started noticing how Trevor acted around them. He never played with them, but he'd sit on the couch and stare at them. I got it in my head that he was trying to figure out what pose they would look most natural in if they were stuffed. I might have been wrong, but it still gave me the willies."

I shuddered and glanced over at Lulu. As if sensing my attention, she opened one eye and wagged her tail. I reached in my bottom drawer and tossed her a treat. Joe Riddley claims I love that dog more than I love him. On that particular day, it was a close call. When she died, I wanted her decently buried. The idea of Trevor stuffing her in a "natural pose" didn't bear thinking about.

Since Evelyn wasn't engaged to Trevor, I didn't have to give him a halo for good parenting, either. "I don't know how he treats dogs, but he seems to have made a mess of Starr after her mother died. Just because he looks like a big soft teddy bear doesn't mean he has to act like one. He was a first sergeant in Vietnam, for heaven's sake, and commanded over a hundred men. Why couldn't he rein in one young girl?"

Evelyn scratched her scalp, which cheap dye was drying out terribly. I kept suggesting she go see Phyllis, my hairdresser, and get a really good color job, but so far I hadn't persuaded her. "I think it was because he and Cathy married late and he never got over being astonished that they could produce such a gorgeous child. Remember Starr as a little girl? Blond curls and big blue eyes, with the longest lashes you ever saw? She looked like a princess."

Evelyn sounded so wistful that I wondered if that's how she had wanted to look when she was a child. Maybe it was still how she wanted to look. Mama used to say, "You can be anybody you like, so long as you don't look in the mirror."

I returned to the subject at hand. "You reckon that's why they saddled her with the name Starr?"

"It was worse than that. Her legal name was Starry Knight. The night she was born, Trevor stepped outside and looked up at the heavens to thank God for his miracle. The sky looked so pretty, he got inspired to name the baby after it."

"You've got to be kidding."

"Nope. That's a quote. Starr shortened her name in elementary school, because the other kids started taunting her with 'Sorry, Starry.' She told them they'd be the ones to be sorry, because she was going to be rich and famous someday."

Poor Starr was never going to be anything. That silenced us for a minute.

"But she didn't get wild until after her mother died?" I needed to keep talking to take my mind off my left leg. In spite of the lotion and the stool, it was getting raw.

"Oh, she was always high-spirited, but Cathy kept Starr on a tight leash until she got so sick. Both parents let Cathy be the disciplinarian and Trevor be the sugar daddy. That backfired after Cathy died."

"But Starr seemed to be doing real good for a while there."

"Yeah. When she got pregnant, Trevor sat her down and told her that if she drank while she was pregnant, she would do damage to her baby that nobody could ever fix. He gave her articles on fetal alcohol syndrome and crack babies, and begged her to give up drinking and drugs until the baby was born. And he promised to take care of them both as long as she needed him to. That seemed to work. She finished high school and got a job down at the Bi-Lo, and she and Bradley lived with Trevor. She took good care of her baby, too. At church, we figured that she was like her daddy—had simply needed to sow a few wild oats."

Evelyn stopped and heaved a sigh that seemed bigger than she was. "We were all thrilled when she started showing some interest in Wylie Quarles. He has a good job, sings in our choir, and is a fine young man. They could have made a decent couple." She was silent a moment, regretting what would never be.

"So what happened?" I prodded.

"I don't know. Back last spring, Starr and Trevor had a big blowup and she moved out. Took Bradley with her, and as far as I know, she hadn't been back since."

"She'd started using something again, too."

Evelyn echoed my own fears. "I wondered if she was taking that methylethelene or whatever it's called. She was looking terrible lately. And you know how she'd been neglecting Bradley."

Before we could say anything else, the door was flung open. The office seemed filled with electricity, and I got a whiff of the pungent odor of nervous sweat. Lulu leaped to her feet, barking as only a beagle can.

Trevor stood in the door, his brown fluffy hair standing out in all directions. His stomach strained his red T-shirt and bulged over the waistband of his jeans, racing his beard to see which would be first to get inside the office. Sweat stood in beads on his forehead and had made circles under his arms. I'm not one to see auras around people, but if I could, I'm sure the air around his head would have crackled.

I shushed Lulu sharply, although I don't think Trevor noticed her. "I need you, Judge." His cheeks were wet with tears.

"Oh, Trevor, I am so sorry." I wished language were more adequate. He looked to me like a man holding on to sanity by one skinny thread. "How can I help you?"

"I want my grandson! What's happened to the boy?"

I chewed my lower lip and considered how to reply. In the normal way of things I wouldn't have any idea where the child was. I am a magistrate. It's juvenile judges who handle foster placements, and they generally keep them private, to prevent parents from snatching a child and disappearing. The only reason I knew where to find Bradley was because he was down at Ridd and Martha's.

I decided to answer with the truth, but not the whole truth. "Magistrates don't have anything to do with juvenile court."

"The police chief said you ought to know where the boy is. Do you?"

Faced with a direct question, I wouldn't lie. "Yes, but I can't tell you without permission of the juvenile court."

"Then get them on the phone, dagnabit! I want that boy! It's bad enough I lost my daughter!" He slammed one fist against the doorjamb. The entire office shook. Lulu growled.

"Trevor—," Evelyn started.

"Don't 'Trevor' me, woman. I want my grandson. He's all I got left now. My little girl, my Starr . . ." Tears gushed from his eyes and down onto his beard. He leaned his head against my wall and wept with gusty sobs. "I gotta have my grandbaby, you understand? I gotta have him!"

I reached for the telephone. "Let me call the juvenile judge."

In a city, Trevor might have had to wait several days for a court hearing. In Hope County, the juvenile judge and I had a quick conversation and I was able to tell him, "You go down to my son Ridd's place—the big blue house we used to live in, half a mile down Yarbrough Road. You know where that is?"

He fought for self-control. "Past the Bi-Lo?"

"That's right. It's the last house on the road. Ridd and Martha have been keeping Bradley. The juvenile judge will meet you with papers to sign, and then you can take him home."

"Thank you." He wiped one damp hand on the seat of his pants and held it out to me. "I didn't mean to talk rough, but I got the news about Starr not half an hour ago"—he took a ragged breath—"and I'm pretty shook up." He sniffed back tears.

I handed him a tissue. His courtesy was touching under the circumstances. "I understand, but pull yourself together before you get down there. That child is going to be confused enough without you scaring him half to death."

"Yes, ma'am, I will." He wiped his nose and eyes and took a tremendous breath, pulling calm from somewhere deep inside him. "He's very precious to me. I don't know if you can understand—"

"I've got four grandchildren. I understand. Is there anything you need back at your house—meals or anything?"

"Our church will take food over," Evelyn assured me.

He gave me a considering, bashful look. "You wouldn't like to come down with me, would you? I don't know how I'm gonna tell Bradley about this."

I opened my mouth to say, "Why, sure," but realized I couldn't. "I'm sorry, but I've got something keeping me in the office this afternoon. Ridd and Martha are both there, though. They'll be with you while you tell him. I'll call and tell them to expect you."

When he left, Evelyn and I sat utterly drained. When I summoned the strength, I reached for the phone to call Ridd. "You wouldn't have wanted to live with that man," I told her as I punched in the numbers. "He'd have worn you out in a week."

She was so pale her freckles stood out. "I've never seen him like that. You don't think he'd been drinking, do you?"

"No. He's just learned his child has been killed. That can make anybody crazy."

Forty minutes later, Bo greeted me from Joe Riddley's shoulder. "Hello! Hello!"

"Ready to go home, Little Bit?" My jailer fished in his top pocket for the key and knelt to unlock the cuffs.

I was tempted to kick him good, but there are limits to what you do when you plan to stay married another forty years. Still, I warned as I reached for my pocketbook, "You had better return those cuffs pronto, or you may wake up to find yourself attached to the bed in the morning."

He opened his desk drawer and tossed the cuffs in. "I'll take them over tomorrow."

I hobbled toward the car behind him. "I will get revenge, you know, as soon as I figure out how."

He laughed.

As we drove home, I pointed out, "You realize you wasted this grand gesture, don't you? Starr Knight was in the truck, but she wasn't murdered. She was most likely driving under the influence and didn't make the curve. I have no reason nor inclination to get involved."

Which just goes to show: A judge should never pronounce the verdict until all the evidence is in.

❧ 4 ❧

Friday I holed up in my office and compensated for Thursday's leisure. Since Joe Riddley had a midday meeting, I went home to eat alone. Clarinda, our cook, was at a meeting of her sorority and had left food on the stove. I didn't see a single soul except Gladys until midafternoon, and she was a morose woman, not inclined to chitchat with customers or with me. That's why it was only when a sheriff's deputy came in around two thirty with a warrant she wanted me to sign that I heard the latest dreadful news.

As I handed her warrant back, I noted, "You seem a tad distraught today—or is it distrait? I never can remember the difference."

She rubbed one hand back and forth across her mouth like she was trying to get rid of a bitter taste. "I went to school with Starr, so this has shaken me some."

"It is very sad," I agreed.

"Sad? It's depraved. I mean, who would beat somebody to death like that?"

My jaw dropped.

She took a step back. "You mean you didn't know?"

My stomach felt like somebody had kicked me. "I heard it was an accident."

"It was no accident. It was dark before we got her out of

that truck, but we found that somebody broke her legs, arms, back, and neck. It must have been a madman."

"And he's still walking around out there somewhere?" Walker's two kids were at the age where they liked to roam the town with their friends. How safe were they? How safe were any of us?

"We'll get him. The sheriff is pulling out all the stops. Right now they're going over the truck for evidence and trying to find people who saw her after Monday afternoon, when it was stolen. But you know something odd?"

"What's that?"

"You knew Starr, right? Not what you'd call sedate."

"No, I'd never have called her sedate."

"You know what she was wearing when she died?"

"A white shirt or something?"

"A white button-down oxford-cloth shirt, black polyester slacks—baggy ones, at that—and black low-heeled shoes. I saw her right after they took her out of the truck, and she could have been a nun."

I considered the unlikely outfit. "Could Trevor explain it?"

"Nope. He said he wouldn't have thought Starr would be caught dead looking so respectable. Then he remembered she had."

That curdled my gizzard. "I'll be praying that you find him," I promised.

As she started to leave, I said, "Wait." I opened Joe Riddley's drawer and handed her Buster's cuffs. "Take these back to Sheriff Gibbons. He may need them. And if I see even a shadow of a smile on your face, you are going to be in big trouble."

"No, ma'am. I'm not smiling. I'll deliver them."

She held her snicker until she was out the door.

I couldn't sit there and dwell on routine work. I kept thinking about what Starr must have suffered. "What we need is a walk," I told Lulu. "Want to go to the bank?"

I put her on the leash, stopped by the register to pick up

the pitiful receipts for the day, and turned toward the corner with the light. I had to tug on Lulu's leash to make her follow. The bank is directly across from our store, next to Spence's Appliances, and she preferred to jaywalk.

"As a judge, I need to set a good example," I reminded her. "It's only half a block more each way."

As we waited for the light to change, I glanced over across the street and smiled in anticipation. An ancient navy Cadillac sat in the handicapped space in front of the bank, a Cadillac that used to belong to Pooh DuBose, widow of Lafayette DuBose, before her death. Now Augusta Wainwright, Pooh's oldest friend and our town's leading aristocrat, relied on it and its driver, Otis Raeburn, for her transportation. Gusta might be old, but she was still hardy, and she and the bank security guard had a running feud about her right to park in the bank's handicapped spot without a handicapped tag.

"Good," I told Lulu. "We'll be in time for the matinee."

"Ma'am?" A young man I had never seen before thrust a well-worn wallet-sized photograph under my nose. "I'm sorry to bother you, but have you ever seen this woman? I'm trying to find my wife." His brown eyes were anxious.

Lulu sniffed his cuffs while I took the photograph and studied it. The woman had wide blue eyes, enhanced lashes, enhanced lips, and probably an enhanced bosom. Her bottle-blond hair was arranged in one of those wild, curly styles that always make me think the woman either just got out of bed or ought to belong to a prehistoric cave community. You couldn't have proved by that picture that she had a stitch on.

"I haven't seen her."

"Are you sure?"

He'd have to be crazy to expect somebody like that to blend into Hopemore, but he didn't look crazy, just very ordinary. He was tall and slender, with coppery hair cut close to his head and the erect carriage I associate with military men.

"Somebody that glamorous would stand out a mile

around here. I haven't seen anybody who looks like she ought to be in movies."

"She *is* beautiful." His hand trembled as he stroked the picture. It looked like a familiar gesture. "She went missing a year ago, while I was in Afghanistan. I was with the Tenth Mountain Division, stationed at Fort Drum in upstate New York?"

He made it a question, and waited for me to show some recognition of the base or the division. I hadn't heard of either one, but I nodded, to encourage him. He seemed to need to talk.

"I was short when I went over—due to get out a few months after I got back—but Bertie was real homesick. I guess she couldn't wait. She gave up our apartment and disappeared. I've been looking for her ever since."

"Georgia's a long way from upstate New York."

"I know, but she was from the South. I met her when I was in basic training at Fort Gordon, and one of my buddies thought he saw her in Augusta a month or so ago. I've been looking around there and in all the nearby towns. I'm afraid she might have lost her memory or something."

My guess was that she had decided an ordinary young man wasn't what she wanted, but she wasn't likely to find much excitement in Hopemore. I felt so sorry for him that I offered, "Leave your name and contact information at the feed-and-seed store over there, and if we see her, we'll let you know."

"Here's my card." It had been printed on a computer. His name was Grady Handley, and the area code was the same as ours.

"You're not still stationed in New York?"

"No, ma'am. I got out in June, and I've been looking for Bertie ever since. When I heard she might be down here, I got a temporary place to stay while I look around."

The light changed. He wandered down the sidewalk in search of other highly unlikely leads, and I hurried toward the bank.

Before I went in, I peeped in the open window of Gusta's car. As I had expected, Otis sat behind the wheel, cap pulled down over his eyes so he didn't have to meet the glare of Vern, the bank's security guard, through the double glass doors.

"What you know, Otis?" I greeted him.

He took off his cap and inclined his head, his face creased in a smile. "Hey, Judge, I saw you crossing the street and was hoping you'd stop. Do you have a minute? I got a problem I need to discuss with somebody, and you're the very one I'd choose."

Lots of people confuse magistrates with lawyers or think they can get advice free from a judge when they'd have to pay a lawyer. Otis was no freeloader, though, and I couldn't imagine him breaking the law. We don't tend to arrest people in Hopemore for driving ten miles an hour in a thirty-five-mile zone. "I've got a few minutes. Shall I get in and sit down?"

"Why, sure." He gestured with a hand the same soft dusty brown as pecan shells. "Make yourself to home."

I tied Lulu to the pole of the handicapped parking sign and slid into the passenger seat, the least-used seat in the vehicle since Pooh died. Gusta sat in back, as was fitting for a reigning monarch. "What's on your mind?"

Otis was past eighty, still preached each Sunday in one of the small black churches in town, and was one of the most courtly men I had ever known. Before he got down to his problem, he insisted on observing the formalities. "How you doing, Judge?"

I opined I was doing fine and asked after his wife, Lottie. He opined she was fine, too. "So what's bothering you today?" I asked.

"Two things, actually. I can't seem to get my mind around what's happened to Starr."

I was surprised at his familiar use of her name. "You knew her?" Since Starr and her family lived outside of town,

I couldn't imagine how Otis had gotten acquainted with them.

"Oh, yes, from before the time Starr was born. I used to drive Miss Winifred and Mister Fayette's animals over for Mister Trevor to mount the heads." Otis and Lottie were the only two people in town who ever called Pooh by her given name.

"I knew Pooh and Lafayette were avid hunters, but I hadn't realized they'd mounted the heads of animals they'd shot."

"My, yes. They had a regular competition going to see who could bag the best-looking one. When I took the animals over, Starr would come running. She loved knock-knock jokes."

"What did you do with the heads afterwards?" I'd been in Pooh's house thousands of time, and I never saw a mounted head.

"I'd take them up to the lake house Mister Fayette built for himself and his buddies, and hang them on the wall. I reckon they got twenty buck heads up there by now, plus a couple of boars, and one antelope Miss Winifred bagged out west." He chuckled. "Mister Fayette was some put out that she got an antelope and he didn't. I don't know what Jed will do with the place now. He's not much into hunting or fishing." Jed DuBose, an attorney in town, was Pooh's grandson and heir. "Still, Mister Trevor is an artist at what he does. It would be a shame to throw them away."

That seemed like a good segue back to our original subject. "So you knew Starr pretty well."

"You could say that. We laughed and carried on a lot. I had to rescue her from a tree one afternoon when she climbed higher than she could get down from and didn't like to call her mama. Her mama was right strict on her." He hesitated. "Starr got a little wild after her mama died, but I always figured she'd grow out of that. She was such a sweet-natured child. Children tend to revert to their natures when they grow up. She just didn't get a chance to grow up."

That gave us cause for a minute of silence, but Otis wasn't finished dredging up memories yet. "When Starr was real little, mind how she used to ride with her daddy in his green pickup down Oglethorpe Street? She was like a princess, waving to everybody on both sides." He lifted one hand and gave a regal wave. "Her curls used to shine like sunshine. 'Course, he spoiled her, buying her everything under the sun, but he never let her be rude to another person. One day in the grocery store there was only one Snickers bar left in the box. I was reaching for it when Starr said, 'Daddy, I want that candy bar.' I drew back, like, to let her have it, but Mister Trevor said, 'No, honey. Mister Otis already claimed it. You pick another kind.' And she picked up that candy bar and handed it to me with the prettiest smile, and she said, 'Here, Mister Otis. I like peanut butter cups, too.' Such a sweet child." He closed his eyes, and a tear escaped and rolled to his jaw. "Nobody had cause to be so vicious to that sweet child."

I heartily agreed with him. "You're a preacher. What do you think goes so terribly wrong in a person that he can do cruel things to somebody else? Is that part of some people's makeup from the second they are born? Or do they learn it from cruelty others have shown them?"

"I don't rightly know, Judge, but I do know this. Anybody who doesn't believe in evil hasn't looked around very far. They's something in the universe that feeds on violence, and it's more than human. And it will latch on to and take over any human willing to let it."

"Somebody sure let it take them over this week."

"You got that right. It distresses me mightily to think of Starr dying that way. I will never forget her waving to strangers on the sidewalk and giving up her candy bar so I could have it." He wiped one hand across his face, and his finger glistened with tears.

I felt a lump in my throat. Seemed to me Starr had just had the most heartfelt eulogy she was likely to get.

We sat in silence while a fly buzzed in through my window and out through his.

"You mentioned you had two things bothering you?"

He approached the matter crabwise, from the side. "Well, it's like this. I talked to Jed earlier this *after*noon." He came to a dead stop, as if unsure how to go on.

"What's Jed done now?"

Pooh's grandson might now be one of the best lawyers in Hopemore, but he had been a mischievous boy and was a mischievous man. Otis had been getting him out of scrapes since he could walk. I figured he had gotten himself into another scrape and sent Otis to make things right. I figured wrong.

"He's not done anything. It was Miss Winifried. Seems like when she died" —Otis stopped and swallowed, his Adam's apple bobbing in his skinny throat—"she left Lottie and me what you might call a little windfall. A big windfall, actually." He lowered his head and stared at his clasped hands, which were shaking. "I never expected it from her, but she's left us enough to buy us a house, see some of the world, and keep Lottie comfortable after I'm gone. I can't get over it. I surely can't."

Lottie was nearly twenty years younger than he, so that must be some windfall.

"You took care of Pooh all her married life, and look at all you and Lottie did for her after she got so sick and forgetful. I think that was utterly fair."

Otis spoke what we both knew. "Fair don't generally come into it where money's concerned. You might think Jed would be upset at our getting so much, but he seems pleased as punch about it."

Considering that Pooh had left Jed the controlling interest in the nationwide trucking company her husband had founded, he wasn't going to miss any meals because of Otis's inheritance. Besides, he was married to Augusta Wainwright's only granddaughter. Between them, he and Meriwether could probably buy up several countries and still have pocket change. Otis, however, was as touched by Jed's generosity as he had been by Pooh's.

"He says we can stay right where we are if we want to, until they decide what to do with Miss Winifred's house, but if we find a place we like, he'll handle all the business side of buying it, for nothing. That is one fine family, Judge. One fine family. And Miss Winifred—" He choked and his lips worked. He pressed his knuckles to them and said in a voice clogged with tears, "Seems like I can't get used to her being gone."

My own eyes filled. "I can't either. She was one of the sweetest people this town ever knew."

"I keep seeing her all over the place. Handing out cookies to children from her porch after school, working in the yard in that big floppy hat and giving me what-for if I pruned the bushes too short, looking for her scruffy black pocketbook so she could go down to read to children in the hospital, playing with that big old dog she used to have . . . When she was alive, she stayed in one place. Now, seems like she's all over the house at once. Lottie and I both feel it." He covered his eyes and tears fell between his fingers. I handed him a tissue and pulled out one for myself.

For another couple of minutes we sat grieving together for a very special lady. Otis was a most comfortable person to grieve with.

"So what's the problem?" I didn't want us to be sitting there bawling when Gusta came out and the show began.

"It's Miss Gusta and Mr. Hubert I'm concerned about. They's nowhere for them to go."

Two years before, when Meriwether had inherited a house from her daddy and moved out of her grandmother's antebellum home, Gusta had moved in with Pooh, and they had turned the big yellow Victorian house into a private retirement home. Hubert Spence, who used to live down the road from us, had paid for an elevator to be installed and moved in with them. Hubert was a widower and a heart-attack survivor, so it was no longer wise for him to live alone. And though Pooh and Gusta had both been over eighty and Hubert was in his late sixties, they seemed to get along fine. Hubert boasted that he could walk to Spence's Appliances, and he basked in the attentions of Otis, Lottie, and Gusta's longtime housekeeper, Florine.

Pooh's death in May had left a vacancy at their house as well as a big hole in my heart. I had been wondering what Hubert and Gusta would do. To my shame, it hadn't occurred to me that Otis and Lottie might like to make some changes, too. Typically, Otis was worried about the others.

"You know Florine can't manage that big house by herself, even if she was of a mind to, which she isn't. She's used to mostly doing for Miss Gusta. They's no way she's gonna take on all the cooking and cleaning plus laundry for Mr. Hubert. Lottie could keep working there, of course, even if we had our own place, but I'd kinda like to take her to see some of the world while I'm still able. I'd like to see some of those places Miss Winifred visited and talked about. I'd like to see Mali again, too." His voice was wistful.

Pooh had not been your ordinary world traveler. Her trips generally took her to remote villages where her dollars were at work building schools, clinics, housing, or roads. Now that Otis mentioned it, I recalled that his congregation had held a musical event to help Pooh put a water system in a village in Mali. Afterwards, Pooh had surprised him and Lottie by taking them and two other couples from their congregation to see the finished product.

But Otis would be wise to travel soon if he planned to. His world-wandering days were limited. And while I appreciated his concern for Gusta and Hubert, I doubted that either of them would take Otis and Lottie into consideration when making plans for their own futures. Since I couldn't say that out loud, I asked, "What does Lottie say?"

"I haven't told her yet. She couldn't go with me down to see Jed because she had promised Miss Gusta she'd bake one of her lemon pecan pound cakes for the Magnolia Women's Club meeting this afternoon. When I got home,

Miss Gusta wanted to come to the bank, and I decided I'd like some praying time before I talked to Lottie, anyway. While I was sitting here praying a few minutes ago, I saw you crossing the street, and it seemed like the Lord told me to talk to you before I brought it up with her."

I was so astonished that my name would crop up as the answer to anybody's prayers, I almost missed what he said next.

"I didn't rightly like to discuss all this with Jed, considering that Miss Gusta is Jed's family since he married Miss Meriwether. I'd be grateful if you wouldn't mention it to him."

I noted that Meriwether had become "Miss Meriwether" since she grew up, but Jed would never be anything to Otis but "Jed."

"I thought maybe you would have some notion what I ought to do," Otis concluded in a tentative voice.

"I wish I had a quick answer for you, but I don't. Jed, Meriwether, and little Zach could move in with Gusta and Hubert, but I'm not sure Hubert or Gusta would like living with a baby, and I can't see Jed being happy with that arrangement."

"Besides, Miss Meriwether loves that house her daddy left her, and Miss Gusta tends to like to have the say in her own place."

Mama used to claim, "When two folks understand each other, there's no need to mention aloud the nasty things you are both thinking." Otis and I both knew that Gusta would like to have her say in the whole world if anybody would elect her Supreme Empress.

But I guess I'm as bad as Gusta, in my own way. I never can resist an invitation to give advice. "Give me a day or two. Can I talk it over with Joe Riddley?"

"That will be fine, but please don't tell anybody else. I don't want it to get all over town. If folks hear you've come into some money, seems like relatives you never knew you had come crawling out of the woodwork."

"I won't tell a soul but Joe Riddley. Oh, here comes Gusta now."

"Let the show begin." Otis put on his cap and opened his door.

Gusta stomped out of the bank, leaning heavily on her silver-headed cane. I climbed out of her front seat and said cheerfully, "Hey, Gusta." I didn't bother to open the back door for her to get in. I knew the drill.

She ignored me and, like an actress girding herself for a performance, waited silently on the sidewalk until Otis came around the car. It would never have occurred to her to open the door for herself.

Vern followed her out and started dancing around her on his game leg, looking like he had ants in his baggy gray uniform britches. The whole block could hear his tirade. Lulu, not to be outdone, contributed her share to the chorus.

"By rights, I oughta call the cops and get you arrested! You know you cain't park there 'lessen you get yourself a permit. All you has to do is ask your doctor. He'll give you one, you being so old 'n' decrepit 'n' all."

Gusta drew herself up to her full and considerable height. "You odious little man, those permits are for those who have difficulty walking. I can walk. I simply do not choose to walk any distance to a bank my husband founded. I was parking in that space long before that blue sign went up— before you were born, in fact. I shall continue to do so as long as I live."

"It ain't right!" Vern's voice went up and down the octave of frustration. "They's laws! What if somebody came who needed that spot?"

Gusta lifted her chin and looked down her nose at him. "They'd do exactly what they would do if I had a sticker and parked there. They'd find another space."

She stomped past Vern, her cane ready to swat him if he got too near. She took a distant swipe toward Lulu for good measure, but we all knew she wouldn't hit my dog. Not if she planned to live another day.

She seated herself in the backseat with the grace due her position as the granddaughter of a former governor and the sister of a former U.S. senator—even if both had been dishonest old lechers and, in the senator's case, a drunk. By then a small crowd had gathered and folks were exchanging surreptitious smiles.

As Otis went toward his own door, Gusta deigned to lean out and speak to me. "Do something about that man, will you, MacLaren? Arrest him for obstruction of banking or some such thing. Otis, I am late for women's club. Step on it, please."

He pulled out and headed for the women's club at a brisk twelve miles an hour.

The performance hadn't tickled me like it usually did. I was perturbed by Otis's situation and saddened by his memories of Starr. I hoped the sheriff would find her killer soon.

The only thing I had to offer that case was a casserole. I would take one to Trevor as soon as Joe Riddley and I finished work.

⨾ 5 ⨿

"I hope you are doing this out of the goodness of your heart," Joe Riddley told me as we left town and headed west into a hot late-summer evening.

"Mostly because of Bradley. That's why I made spaghetti." That silenced him. Joe Riddley had grown as fond of the boy as I had in the short time the child had been part of our extended family. "I made enough for us, too," I added, "since we'll miss the buffet at the country club."

Normally I would have been taking one of the frozen casseroles that Clarinda keeps in our freezer for times of bereavement. A frozen casserole is much easier to transport than a hot dish and can be saved in the freezer until all the fresh food is gone. However, Bradley and Cricket had eaten with us one night, and Bradley had liked my spaghetti so much, he ate three helpings. Only for a child would I endure a hot casserole on my lap for three miles on a sweltering evening. I could feel warmth seeping through the thick towel I'd placed under it to keep it from burning me or staining my khaki skirt.

That far out of town, beyond zoning restrictions, folks had enough land around their homes to indulge individuality in the matter of land use. Some had inserted businesses between residences. Some properties were better kept than

others. One of our lawn-service customers lived just west of
Trevor in a two-story brick McMansion that sat on an acre
of landscaped lawn surrounded by a wrought-iron fence. Beyond that was a camouflage clothing store housed in a
Quonset hut.

Since we approached from the east, we passed Trevor's
neighbors on that side: a cluster of three mobile homes nes-
tled like chicks around a baby blue double-wide anchored
by a huge screened porch. The biggest thing on the property
was a barn at the back. A sign out front read SANDERS STA-
BLES. HORSES BOARDED.

I huffed at the sight of their yard, which was filled with a
collection of elderly Volkswagen Beetles hunkered down in
various stages of decay. "Looks like the county would make
them do something about those cars."

Joe Riddley was too busy slowing down and putting on
his turn signal to reply.

A thin stand of pines separated the Sanders property from
a white concrete-block building with a black-and-white sign
at the road: TREVOR KNIGHT, TAXIDERMIST. Joe Riddley turned
into a drive that was nothing more than ruts worn through
the grass. A right fork in the drive led to the white building.
It sat sideways to the highway, so that the front door and display windows faced a grassy parking area with spaces indicated by weathered railroad crossties. The left fork led to a
frame ranch house stained dark brown.

Guests to the house parked wherever they liked. That
evening, the yard was full of cars. Joe Riddley pulled in near
the ditch by the road, which was as close as we could get. I
climbed out, carefully holding the casserole away from my
yellow top, Joe Riddley left his cap in the car, and we
trudged up the drive. We exchanged greetings with a knot of
men smoking under a sycamore and dodged children playing tag. An earlier breeze had disappeared, leaving the air
hot and thick. Distant thunder rumbled. Gnats lit on any
piece of skin they could find. Hopemore is below the Geor-

gia gnat line, and if you think that's a mythological geographical designation, come on down some hot afternoon.

I blew puffs of air to keep the pesky critters at bay while we headed toward a short concrete walk lined with unkempt borders of liriope that had begun to straggle into the weedridden grass. "We could send a crew out here to improve that grass and dig out the liriope."

"We aren't here to drum up business." Joe Riddley steered me by one elbow up the walk. "We are here to take in spaghetti, express our regrets to Trevor, and go home. There's a special about Iwo Jima on television that I want to see."

"For what, the fifteenth time? Or is it the twentieth?"

"A woman who reads the same mysteries over and over can't complain about my movie-watching habits. Come on, Little Bit. Say your piece, hand over the food, and let's leave. The man deserves some privacy in which to grieve."

Joe Riddley wasn't the only grumpy person in Hopemore that evening. The senseless brutality of Starr's death was affecting everybody. In a small town you feel the death of people, even if you don't know them well. When a young person dies, she takes a piece of the whole town's future. And when somebody dies savagely, as Starr had, you take it personally that such a thing has happened where you live.

Robin Parker stood on the stoop outside the front door. Given that she worked with Trevor, I shouldn't have been surprised to see her minding his door, but I was. After all, she'd only been in town since spring. Doorkeepers after a death are usually close friends or family. Were she and Trevor moving toward making her a part of his family? Men have been known to marry women only a few years older than their daughters.

If Trevor married Robin, though, he would certainly be lowering his standards. His first wife had been a pretty woman who fixed herself up and dressed as well as she could afford. Every time I saw Robin, I wondered why she didn't do more with herself.

She wasn't ugly, just plain. Tall and skinny as a rake handle, she could have benefited from mascara and eye shadow to bring out her eyes behind their gold-rimmed granny glasses. A rosy lipstick and a little rouge could have brightened her pale complexion, and if my face had been that thin, I'd have fluffed out my hair and maybe gotten a curly perm or highlights to brighten it. Robin pulled her brown hair back in the crooked-part ponytail favored by so many mothers of small children. I didn't know her well enough to know if she looked the way she did out of religious conviction, because she was a militant feminist who scorned makeup, or because she didn't know what to do with what she had, but that evening at Trevor's, she wasn't even wearing the light pink lipstick she typically favored.

I did notice that in honor of the occasion, she had doffed her usual jeans and oversized shirt and had put on a denim skirt with a light blue T-shirt and a big navy shirt. I wished she had chosen a brighter shade of navy, though. That color made her more drab and shapeless than usual. I was tempted to send her an anonymous subscription to a fashion magazine.

Her smile was wan as she held the door. "Come on in. I'm sorry you had to come under these circumstances, but I know Trevor will be glad to see you. He's in the den."

I couldn't place Robin's accent, but it wasn't Georgian. Some people think all Southern accents are the same, but in fact no two states talk alike. Accents even vary within states. Vowels tend to broaden out and melt, the closer you get to the coast. Hers were crisp.

Beside her stood a man wearing a rumpled camouflage suit in the jungle colors I associate with the Vietnam War and my own children's growing-up years. In fifth grade, Ridd didn't want to wear anything except camouflage pants and T-shirts. This man was too young to be one of Trevor's old army buddies—not more than thirty, I figured—but maybe he was the son of an army buddy.

He had thin yellow hair falling to his shoulders, an

equally yellow mustache, and blue eyes set aslant in his face, and while I couldn't recall ever seeing him before, he looked familiar. I realized why when Robin's older child came running up the steps yelling "Mama! Mama!" as she pushed her way past Joe Riddley and me to clutch Robin's skirt. The child had the same wispy yellow hair and slanted blue eyes. She looked like a wraith, her skin like skim milk. Pale blue veins throbbed at her temples, the same shade as her eyes. As I looked from one to the other, Robin shushed her daughter long enough to say, "Joe Riddley and Judge Yarbrough, I want you to meet my brother, Billy Baxter."

We barely had time to nod at each other, for the little girl was prancing up and down in obvious distress. "Mama! Mama!" She was about five or six, and so hyper that she reminded me of a toy I used to have: a wooden paddle with a rubber ball on an elastic band. The only way to keep it going was to jiggle your arm real fast. That kid jiggled so much she made me dizzy.

"Mind your manners," Robin said, rebuking her. "Tell the Yarbroughs you're sorry you shoved. And where's your sister?"

She threw us a quick and unapologetic "I'm sorry," then turned back to her mother. "That's what I wanted to tell you. Some big boys are going to throw rocks at cars on the road, and Anna Emily is tagging after them. I told her and told her not to, but she won't mind." She danced in impatience to see the reaction to her news.

Robin didn't disappoint her. "Excuse me." She hurried down the steps to the yard, accompanied by the wraithlike jumping bean. I wasn't surprised when Joe Riddley went after them. If anybody could persuade boys to change their ways, he could.

Billy Baxter gave me a halfhearted salute and headed for a dirty green pickup. "See you later," he called to Robin as he swung up into the cab.

I met a wall of noise and heat when I went through the door, for the air conditioner had given up trying to deal with the crowd. The air in the living room was fuggy with mixed perfumes, aftershaves, and warm bodies. I barely had time to see a sofa and a couple of chairs covered in faded sure-don't-fit slipcovers before some woman I didn't know took my arm and dragged me toward the kitchen at the back.

Sweat trickled down inside my shirt as I carried my dish through the crowd, speaking to acquaintances and looking for someplace to set it down. Flushed-faced women cleared a space on the beige Formica counter for me to deposit the spaghetti among a sea of ham, potato salad, sweet potato casseroles, cakes, pies, and vegetables and salads that had probably been growing in local gardens earlier that day.

"That's real nice of you, Judge," a stout woman said.

The way she was eyeing my offering, I could tell she had her suspicions that I'd started with a jar of store-bought sauce and simply added ground beef, garlic, and oregano— and she clearly thought spaghetti a pretty poor offering compared to those of women who had baked, peeled, picked, and prepared food for hours.

I reminded myself that she hadn't sat in an office all day, but there is no way a working woman leaves a kitchen full of homemade food without a load of guilt.

I trotted my sorry self to the den to speak to Trevor.

Loud voices poured out the door before I got there. One—a high, anguished tenor—cried, "If I find him, I'll kill him! So help me, I will."

"Don't talk about killing in here, Wylie," a bass admonished him sharply as I stepped through the door.

I concluded that the intense young man pacing before the cold fireplace must be Wylie Quarles, for as soon as he caught my eye, he got real interested in a hangnail. I knew him slightly, although not by name. He came to the store each spring to buy seeds and starter vegetables for his mother's garden. I remembered Evelyn raving that he sang in their choir, worked for Trevor, and used to date Starr. I wondered if Starr had minded that she was several inches taller than he.

If his threat was anything to go by, he certainly minded that she had been killed. Long dark hair hung in eyes that were pink and bloodshot with unshed tears. Beneath a skimpy black mustache, his mouth was set in an angry, determined line.

The rest of the room was full of men I didn't know, but I'd seen a few in traffic court or before my bench for littering, building-code violations, or dumping furniture in bins designated for household garbage. I saw no indication they were nervous in my presence. Several lifted a hand and called, "Howdy, Judge. Howdy."

Trevor sprawled in a brown recliner that had shaped itself to his bulk. He looked like a dead man breathing. His beard hung listless on his chest, his eyes were fixed on the middle of the tan Berber carpet, vacant and unseeing, and although his friends spoke around him, he gave no sign of hearing.

The most alive part of him was his left arm, which cradled Bradley. The fingers of that hand stroked the boy's arm in a slow, somber rhythm. Bradley's eyes were closed, but I didn't know if he was asleep or trying to avoid looking at the pictures of his mama that sat on the television and hung between animal heads on the pine-paneled walls. Trevor had invested a considerable amount in studio portraits of his daughter over the years. Three of the wall portraits were larger than life: Starr as a lovely infant barely able to sit, as a beautiful ten-year-old with soft curls on her shoulders, and as a teenager in a halter top and too much makeup. She was probably fourteen in that picture, but looked twenty. It was the most recent one he displayed. My guess was that Starr had never again looked good enough for a studio portrait.

"Hey, Trevor, here's Judge Yarbrough come to see you," said a man named Farrell Stokes. Since he'd retired, Farrell did nothing except hunt and fish, so it made sense that he would know Trevor. I wondered if he bugged Trevor to get his animals finished the way he bugged our lawn service about his yard. He was a persnickety little man who could be a pest if things weren't done exactly the way he wanted them.

Trevor lifted his head as if the weight of it was too much to bear, and stared at me without a word. The look in his eyes was one I'd seen in the eyes of a dog pleading with Joe Riddley to put it out of its misery.

"I wanted to say again how sorry I am." I stepped forward and offered my hand.

He clutched it with his free one. "I appreciate it, Judge. I didn't mean to get out of line in your office yesterday."

"You were grieving."

"Grieving a whole lot more today. Did you hear what somebody done to my baby?" His gaze strayed to her teenage picture and his lips trembled.

"I heard."

"They had no cause to do that. And why'd they dress her up like that? Starr never wore that kind of stuff."

"Starr never had cause to steal that truck, neither." Wylie was indignant. "I told her she could use mine. Keys were in it. All she had to do was drive it off."

"The sheriff will find whoever did it," Farrell insisted. "Hang on to that."

Trevor was silent, but Wylie wasn't comforted. "Putting them away won't bring Starr back, or keep her from going through what she did." He made a fist and slammed it down on the mantelpiece. "A trial is too good for whoever did that to Starr."

Farrell gestured toward a glass case that held a tiny fawn peering down at its reflection in a mirror pond. The deer looked alive enough to start nibbling the silk grass around its hooves. "You gonna enter this in competition, Trevor?" It was an obvious attempt to distract Wylie.

Trevor didn't respond.

"Trevor!" Farrell said sharply. "I asked if you're still going to the trade show and if you plan on entering Starr's fawn." He explained to those of us who didn't know, "Starr found that baby dead in the woods last spring and brought it home for her daddy to fix up pretty."

"He finished it last week," Wylie added. "She never even saw it."

"Wylie!" Farrell exclaimed in rebuke.

It had taken that long for Trevor to register what Farrell had asked him. He shook his big head. "I probably won't go to the show. Doesn't much matter anymore."

"I wouldn't cancel yet," Farrell advised. "It's not until February. You might change your mind."

One of the men whose name I didn't know boasted to the others, "I'm hoping to get me a buck this fall that he can enter."

Not to be outdone, Farrell said, "I've about persuaded Robin to put in her fox and rabbit. That girl is good, ain't she, Trevor?"

"Good at getting her own way," Wylie muttered, but Farrell had the floor and no intention of yielding it.

"She can stuff anything. I'm of a mind to take her my wife and ask her to stuff the old bag in a nagging position. That way she'd look real natural."

Everybody laughed until they remembered why we were there. They hushed at once, and gave Trevor quick, embarrassed looks.

Trevor gave no sign of hearing. His head had sunk on his chest and he was staring at the rug again.

"Wylie?" Farrell persisted. "Robin's good, ain't she?"

"I guess." Wylie was still working that hangnail. It would be bleeding soon if he didn't leave it alone.

"Did she ever do taxidermy before, or did you teach her everything she knows?" another man asked. Somebody else snickered. Wylie swung around with fire in his eye.

Farrell made a shushing motion with his hand and spoke as if to a deaf or mentally impaired person. "Trevor, Vic wants to know if you all trained Robin or if she already knew something about taxidermy when she got here."

The words took a while to percolate to Trevor's brain. He

roused himself with a visible effort. "She was trained before she got here. That's why I hired her."

"She's got a natural talent for it," Farrell told the rest of us. "That fox is one of the prettiest things you ever saw. Looks like he could come over and lick your fingers."

"Chew 'em off, more likely," I contributed.

Bradley stirred in his granddaddy's arms at the sound of my voice. I bent to say softly, "Hey, Bradley? I brought you some spaghetti."

Trevor gave the boy a little shake. "You awake, boy?"

Bradley opened drowsy blue eyes. I wondered if somebody had given him something to sedate him. Then he saw me and his eyes flew open. "Me-Mama!" He held out his arms and struggled to climb off his grandfather's lap.

I bent and gathered him into my own arms. He nearly choked me, he held on so tight.

"That's what my grandchildren call me. He learned it from Cricket," I explained over his head to the puzzled men. I didn't bother to add that children in foster care are quick to give foster parents and grandparents family titles, as if trying to establish that they have a right to be there. It always breaks my heart how fast a foster child will call a strange woman Mama.

"You doing okay?" I murmured to Bradley.

"Yes, ma'am." His face was as pretty as his mama's used to be, but that night both face and voice were colorless. "I'm a norphan. Did you know that? Norphans are boys who don't have a mama or daddy, and my mama went to heaven without me."

"I know she did, honey, but she didn't mean to. I'm so sorry." I cuddled him for a while, then put my lips close to his ear and whispered, "I brought you some spaghetti."

"I doesn't want pasketti. I want my mama."

"I know, baby, and I wish I could have brought her to you. But maybe you'll get hungry later." I raised my voice a tad. "Why don't you ask your granddaddy if he'll let you come play with Cricket one afternoon next week?"

His blue eyes shifted from my face to Trevor's with a faint flicker of interest. "Can I, T-daddy?" He snuggled up to me, his breath as sweet and warm as milk.

"We'll see." Trevor sounded wrung out and bone weary.

"I'd better be going for now. I'll see you later, Bradley." I gave him a squeeze, then lowered him into his grandfather's waiting arms. Trevor drew him close.

"Thank you for coming, Judge," he mustered the energy to say. "I appreciate all that Ridd and Martha did for Bradley here."

"They were glad to do it. He's a great kid—aren't you, Bradley?"

"No, ma'am. I'm a norphan."

With a clatter of feet, Robin's older daughter came running in. "Bradley? Bradley!" I got the impression she generally ran, yelling ahead to warn folks she was coming.

Her younger sister sidled in behind her, giving the room a nervous glance. I figured she must be around three, and shy. The hair curling to her shoulders was the color of a penny, her eyes like chocolate. She took a thumb out of her mouth to say something softly to a man by the door.

He looked startled. "Not tonight, honey." He moved uneasily on his feet.

The elder sister shrieked, "Bradley! Missy brought bubbles! Come on!" The air seemed to vibrate with her high little voice. She grabbed at him and danced in impatience beside Trevor's chair. I am generally opposed to medicating children, but that one looked like she could use something to calm her down. I pitied Robin, having to deal with her all day.

The younger sister put a gentle hand on Bradley's. "Come blow bubbles wif us?"

He looked up at this granddaddy uncertainly. "I like bubbles."

Trevor asked Robin's older girl, "Will Missy be watching out for you all?"

"Mama's out there." She pranced in her eagerness to be off.

"Then go find the bubbles." Trevor set Bradley down. The older girl tugged his hand, pulling him in her wake. The other sister trotted behind. I was glad I didn't have the raising of them.

Trevor's eyes followed the children.

I touched his shoulder. "I'll be going now, but you know how sorry we are."

He put his hand over mine and pressed it. "Thank you for coming. Take care, now."

"You take care." I slipped away. As soon as I was out of the room, I heard Wylie's voice raised in anger again.

Joe Riddley was munching a sandwich in the small living room while talking with Maynard and Selena Spence, Hubert's son and daughter-in-law. Maynard had abandoned a rising career as an art historian in New York City to come home and take care of his daddy when Hubert had his heart attack. Afterwards, Maynard had stayed in town, revived our tiny Hopemore historical museum, bought and restored a lovely Victorian home, and eventually bought Gusta's antebellum house and started an antique business that was building a nationwide reputation. He had married Selena, a newcomer who worked as a nurse with Martha, and they seemed settled in Hopemore for at least the rest of his daddy's life.

I was surprised to see them at Trevor's, though. Maynard didn't hunt or fish, and he was a good ten years older than Starr, so I couldn't imagine how he knew the Knights.

"You find Trevor in there?" Joe Riddley asked. When I nodded, he went to pay his respects.

I turned to Selena and Maynard. "Where have you been keeping yourselves? Haven't seen you all for at least a week." Having helped to raise Maynard and gotten them out of a spot of trouble on their honeymoon,[3] I loved them almost like my own.

Maynard was his usual good-looking self, his blond

[3]*Who Left That Body in the Rain?*

ponytail confined by a black ribbon that matched a black shirt he wore with gray pants. I doubted that he had dressed for the occasion. Having lived in New York, he tended to wear arty clothes. Selena, like Robin's younger daughter, had red curls, but hers looked dimmed that evening and her freckled face was pale beneath them. "I've been puny this week, so Maynard has been looking after me."

Without thinking, I glanced down at her stomach.

"No, I am not pregnant. People have been asking me that all day. I had a stomach virus, that's all." She turned on her heel and marched toward the kitchen.

I gave Maynard an apologetic shrug. "I'm sorry. I guess we're all waiting for an announcement from you two." Since Maynard grew up eating cookies in my kitchen, I felt I could talk to him like a son.

He colored up. "You may be waiting for a long time. We're not having any luck in that department, and it's got Selena on edge."

I changed the subject. We chatted until I saw Joe Riddley headed my way. "Please tell Selena how sorry I am," I requested. "I didn't mean to upset her."

Joe Riddley hooked me around the neck. "You got anybody else you want to upset, or are you ready to go?"

The children were on the front walk, blowing bubbles under the supervision of a tall, sturdy woman with thick glasses and black hair that flowed over her shoulders in an unruly mane. She must be at least twenty, but had the unfinished look of a young teenager.

Robin sat on the bottom step, watching them. As we passed her, I said, "I'm sorry about your truck."

She swiped back a tendril of loose hair behind her ear. "Me, too. I had a six-year loan on that thing, and the folks down in Dublin say I'll have to pay it off, even though the truck was totaled. They say I owe five thousand dollars more than they're allowing me on it. Can they really make me pay on a truck I no longer have?"

"I'm afraid they can. Those six-year loans are nothing except one more way to lure folks into buying what they can't afford."

Joe Riddley put a hand on my elbow to remind me not to get on a soapbox and preach at somebody who was already converted. "Go talk to Laura MacDonald over at MacDonald Motors," he suggested to Robin. "She might have something on her used-car lot she can let you have at a reasonable price."

Robin sighed. "I sure hate to pay for something I'm not getting to use."

I felt a tug on my pants leg and looked down into the pleading face of her three-year-old. "I like you. Can I go home with you?"

I gently detached her hand. "You don't even know me, honey, and you'd miss your mama and your sister."

She flicked a glance toward her mother, then turned back to me. "Can I come play at your house for a little while?"

"Not tonight. Maybe another time."

What made me say that? If I took one child, I'd have to invite them both, and I wasn't sure our house could survive her hyperactive sister.

Neither Joe Riddley nor I slept well that night. We tossed, turned, and lay awake discussing how dreadful it would be to lose a child or a grandchild and how much our hearts went out to Trevor. My pillow was wet and soggy by the time we'd finished. When I shifted my head over onto Joe Riddley's, it was damp, too.

I got up and fetched fresh ones from the guest room bed, then went to the kitchen and got myself a glass of cold water. As I climbed back between the sheets, I noticed the clock. "It's five—hardly worth trying to sleep. We'll have to get up in a couple of hours."

Joe Riddley was already snoring.

I lay there with my thoughts going round and round. Why had Starr left her daddy's house when they had been getting along so well? Was that before or after she went off the wagon? Why had she gone off the wagon, anyway, after so many years of staying clean? Where had she been going, dressed like that?

Knowing that thoughts, like the sky, are apt to be darkest in the hour before dawn, I forced myself to stop thinking and belatedly kept my promise to the deputy. I prayed that Buster and his deputies would find whoever did that dreadful deed. I prayed for Trevor, and for Bradley. Remembering a police sergeant I'd once met who said she always prayed for the safety of her city when she was in charge of the homicide squad for the night—and that the city had never had a murder on her watch—I prayed for the safety of everybody in Hope County. And I prayed the prayer I often had—which had sometimes gotten me into trouble in my marriage: "If there's something I ought to be doing, show me what it is."

Instead of a blinding revelation, all I could think of was Starr's clothes. Why on earth had she been dressed so somberly when she died? Who might know?

I couldn't ask Trevor, but Evelyn might remember who Starr's friends had been. I fell asleep in the middle of telling myself that Joe Riddley couldn't accuse me of meddling if I was simply asking about the victim's clothes.

❧ 6 ❧

The news about how Starr died spread like flies. Hopemore was terrified. By Saturday morning, foot traffic in town was nil. I heard from the few customers who came by that parents weren't letting their children go to friends' houses and were setting up parent patrols at soccer and football games. Young mothers gave up jogging or riding bikes with infants in three-wheeled rickshaws. Few women played golf or tennis that weekend. Deputies reported that law enforcement phone lines were clogged with calls from people who heard noises outside their homes or noticed somebody acting strange.

As you might imagine, Joe Riddley kept a close eye on me. Autumn Saturdays are busy down at the nursery, with homeowners coming by for plants to put in over the weekend. Usually he works there while I pay bills and catch up on paperwork. That morning he stuck around the office reading seed catalogs with the same passion I bring to a good mystery. I was impatient for him to leave, so I could call Evelyn in to talk to her about Starr's friends.

Lulu dozed at my feet. Bo stalked along the top of the curtain rod, darting looks to see if I was watching. "You poop on that curtain, you are dead meat," I warned.

"I love you. I truly do," he replied.

I was fantasizing about an appropriate revenge for Joe
Riddley's Thursday prank when Hubert Spence came in,
beaming like he had won the Georgia lottery. Behind him,
Evelyn was clutching fistfuls of hair and shaking her head to
signify "I tried to keep him from bothering you, but I
couldn't."

I motioned her back to work. Nobody can stop Hubert.

He bounced into the office with his hand outstretched,
and the way he pumped Joe Riddley's, you'd have thought
they hadn't seen each other for years instead of at Rotary a
few days before. "Hey, ole buddy. How ya doin'?" Without
waiting for a reply, he turned to me. "And how you doin,'
Judge? Is that a new outfit?"

"Relatively." I had treated myself to a celery green
pantsuit at the end-of-summer sales. It was possible Hubert
hadn't seen it.

"You're looking good. Real good."

He looked pretty good himself. Not as handsome as Joe
Riddley, of course, who inherited high cheekbones, straight
dark hair, and an olive complexion with a tinge of red under
the skin from his Cherokee grandmother. Still, Hubert was
more than passably good-looking. Before Gusta had agreed
to let him live in the same house with her, she had insisted
that he bathe regularly, a habit he'd given up after his wife
died. Once he got cleaned up, he started paying attention to
what he wore and how he cut his hair. He had squired a con-
gressman's sister around the year before, and that past
month I had heard a couple of widows talking like Hubert
was worth a second look.

"The world treatin' you all right?" he asked me, still
beaming.

"World's treating me fine." I eyed him warily. I couldn't
think of a single reason for him to leave his store and come
see us at work. Although we had been good neighbors for
thirty-five years—Joe Riddley had harvested Hubert's watermelons and fed his cows while he was laid up with his
heart attack several years back, and Hubert and his son,

Maynard, had been real helpful to me in the weeks after Joe
Riddley got shot[4]—we had never been drop-in friends. The
men had serious differences that were only partially due to
the fact that Joe Riddley went to Georgia and Hubert to
Georgia Tech. They had yet to agree on football, religion, or
politics.

Hubert started toward the wing chair, then aimed a suspi-
cious look at the curtain rod, which was directly over the
chair.

"Back off! Give me space!" Bo taunted him.

"Come," Joe Riddley commanded, holding out his arm.
Bo flew down to perch on it, then sidestepped up to Joe Riddley's shoulder and sat bobbing his head, waiting to be en-
tertained.

Hubert sat down on the front edge of the chair, a man
with something important to say. If he'd smiled any wider
he'd have split his jaw.

"You want a Coke?" Joe Riddley offered.

"No, thanks, I'm fine." He rubbed his palms together.
"You all likin' your new house and all? Don't miss the old
place?"

He was talking about the small brick house we'd bought
in town when we'd deeded the old place to Ridd. Moving
after all those years takes a while to get used to, so Joe Riddley ignored the questions. "Why don't you let us in on the
secret of what brings you to our office on this fine day?"

Hubert crossed one stubby calf over the other thigh and
beamed from one of us to the other. "I have made a momentous decision, and I wanted you folks to be the first to
know."

Joe Riddley and I both swiveled our chairs around so we
could see him more easily.

"You gonna marry Gusta?" Joe Riddley hazarded.

Since Gusta was nearly twenty years older than Hubert, I

[4]*But Why Shoot the Magistrate?*

figured that wasn't likely. "You gonna sell your store and retire?" I guessed.

Spence's Appliances had been hit even harder than we had by the opening of the big-box superstore on the edge of town. Folks in small towns don't need a lot of major appliances, so most of Hubert's business had come from selling radios, televisions, razors, blenders, and the like. He didn't have the volume to be able to compete with big-box prices.

"Nope and nope." He wore the smug smile of somebody who knows the right answer. His voice dropped a notch, into the realm of his normal grumble. "I'd rather marry a mosquito than Gusta. They have a lot in common, now that I think about it. Both drive you crazy and go straight for the jugular. And who'd want to buy my store? So I'm not getting married and I'm not retiring—not exactly. I've decided to go into another line of business." He looked from one of us to the other, priming our pumps for the revelation. "I am going to run for mayor. And since you now live inside the city limits, you can vote for me."

He sat back in the wing chair and waited for applause—or maybe a campaign contribution.

It took all the self-discipline I possessed not to shriek, "You are what? Of all the tomfool notions I ever heard, that's the dumbest."

I don't want to distress those who might belong to Hubert's party, but Hubert's politics were 90 percent rant and 10 percent rave. No government ever did anything right as far as he was concerned, and his solutions were generally predicated not on what was best for the majority of citizens but entirely on what was best for Hubert.

"What led you to this momentous decision?" Joe Riddley spoke in a milder voice than I could have managed.

Hubert scrunched up his eyes, a sign he was about to get serious and hateful—which, with Hubert, was often the same thing. "That damfool woman talking about running. She wasn't raised in Hopemore. What does she know about being mayor of the place?"

"Which woman is that?" Joe Riddley's voice was still mild as sweet milk.

"Nancy Jensen. She ain't never been anything but a housewife, and she was born and raised in Waycross. She ain't been in town more than ten years." Hubert thought it cute to talk like a hick at times, even though he had an engineering degree and had made straight As in English all through school.

"She was a chemistry teacher for years before she married Horace," I pointed out, "and she's been here at least fifteen years. Their son, Race, is fourteen."

"Okay, fifteen. That doesn't make her an expert on the place. What does she know about running a town?"

I knew I ought to show the same restraint Joe Riddley had, but I figured Nancy knew at least as much about running Hopemore as Hubert did. She had chaired every club in town, was an elder in the First Presbyterian Church, and had put on the golf club dance the previous summer. I had served with her on several committees, and felt she had perfectly good administrative skills.

However, while I would certainly vote for Nancy over Hubert, I had better manners than to tell him so—until he added, "She couldn't even keep her husband at home, and now she's trying to take everything he's worked all his life to build." His voice was full of spite.

Hubert's take on the facts was close enough to make trouble for Nancy in an election.[5] Her husband *had* run off with another woman back in July—although it was a woman he'd been involved with, off and on, since he was fifteen—and in the divorce Nancy *was* being represented by an excellent lawyer who argued that a corporate executive's wife who gave up her career in order to help advance his deserved more than half of their joint assets. The lawyer argued that Nancy had sacrificed her own earning potential to increase Horace's, so his ability to earn more was an intangible family asset that needed to be factored into the final financial settlement. I agreed with the reasoning, although in this particular case, Horace's ability to earn money came from the fact that his granddaddy founded Middle Georgia Kaolin, which Horace now ran.

In any case, I was not willing to hear Hubert bad-mouth a woman because her husband had abandoned her. "The divorce needn't keep her from being a good mayor," I said. "In fact, it could make her a better one, since she will have plenty of time to devote to the job."

"She got arrested a while back, too, didn't she?" he demanded. "Shootin' up a motel? We don't need criminals running this town."

"Those charges were dropped. Don't you go bringing them up in your campaign."

Hubert was turning pinker by the second.

"Which makes you madder?" Joe Riddley asked him, still keeping calm. "That she wasn't born here or that she's a woman?"

"Both. No offense, Mac, but you get a woman in power? Next thing you know, everything's gone all touchy-feely. As you both know, I ain't one for touchy-feely, so I've decided if you want something done right, maybe you'd better do it yourself."

The scary thing was, Hubert might have a chance. Our incumbent had said he wouldn't run again, and we had never elected a woman mayor. Also against Nancy was that she was a middle-aged woman who thought things through before she spoke. Hubert had that shallow friendliness that has been the hallmark of too many Southern politicians who get elected decade after decade not on the strength of their intelligence but on connections, a handshake, and a smile. He would have another advantage, too. While it shames me to admit it, we still have a lot of voters in Hope County who can't read. When they got to the polls and saw "Spence" on the ballot, they might simply vote for a combination of letters they recognized from the sign on his store.

For the moment, I had said my say. Joe Riddley could have the last word. "It's a mighty big decision," he said. "You sure you want to do this? You know how the newspapers are. They'll dig up every bit of dirt they can find."

Hubert waved that away with one pudgy hand. "I ain't worried about the paper. Slade Rutherford can dig all he likes. He won't find anything in my past worse than a little watermelon stealing when we were boys."

I abandoned my vow of silence. "And water tower painting in high school."

"Well, yeah, boys will be boys."

I was fixing to point out that that particular boy had painted Joe Riddley's name and mine inside a four-foot heart for the whole town to read, but Joe Riddley beat me off the mark. "Are you sure you want the responsibility for running this town? There's not much money in it. What's the salary, six or seven thousand dollars?"

"Something like that."

"And you'd have to give up the store and spend a lot of time listening to people's gripes."

"The store is gonna die on its feet anyway, and I figure it's better to listen to other people's gripes and do things right for a change, than spend my time griping that other folks are doing them wrong." Hubert had given the decision at least half an hour's thought.

When Joe Riddley nodded, I knew he wasn't endorsing Hubert, merely agreeing with his sentiment. "Have you talked to Maynard about it?" he asked.

I suspected Maynard would not be pleased if his daddy jeopardized his hard-won health by getting het up about a political campaign—especially since Hubert and Maynard perched on opposite sides of the political fence.

"I haven't mentioned it to him quite yet. I wanted to test the idea out on you folks first."

If he hoped we'd reconcile Maynard to the idea, he had another think coming. However, Joe Riddley said in a voice as quiet as the day outside, "I wish you luck. You got yourself a manager and the campaign all mapped out?"

"It's early days. I'll bet that Jensen woman won't start campaigning till mid-October."

Why should she? A candidate could easily reach our entire electorate in three weeks.

Hubert slicked back his hair. "I don't think I'll need a manager. I'm a pretty good manager myself. I do need a catchy slogan, though. If you think of something, let me know."

Joe Riddley nodded again. "We sure will." An awkward silence fell. No way we were going to promise Hubert we'd vote for him or write him a check.

He bounced to his feet. "Well, I wanted you all to know. I'll be getting back to you when I've got signs printed and all. Remember, with Hubert at the helm, this town will return to decency and old-time values." He shook our hands like we were perfect strangers, then bounced out in search of new victims.

"Sic 'em!" Bo called after him.

I waited until Hubert was out of earshot before I asked, "Can you think of anything worse for this town than Hubert at the helm? It would be like turning the clock back fifty years."

"A hundred, more like. Let's hope somebody runs against him who actually has a chance of winning."

"You don't think Nancy has a chance?"

"Afraid not. Hubert has her image pegged nicely. In spite of the fact that Horace has been playing around and the shooting charges against her were dropped, during an election all folks will remember is that she got arrested and couldn't hold on to her husband. Besides, who would want to get on the bad side of Horace? He can be a tad abrasive."

That was as critical as Joe Riddley would get, but the fact was, Horace had about as much charm as a wild boar. He also had more money than three-fourths of the town put together, and he knew how to use it to control people.

"It's not fair," I complained.

"When has politics ever been fair?"

"It would be if you decided to run." I couldn't think of a better mayor for the town.

He reached for his cap. "Only running I'm gonna do is down to the nursery, to check on that new shipment of sod. Last batch we got was full of weeds."

Before he reached the door, Evelyn came through it, pink-faced and breathless. "Isn't it exciting? Mr. Spence says he's gonna run for mayor!"

"So he says," Joe Riddley agreed.

"Isn't that amazing?" Her freckled face was lit up like somebody had turned on a bulb.

"Amazing." I looked at my computer screen so I didn't have to meet her eye. In all the years she had worked for us, Evelyn and I had never discussed politics. For all I knew, our old neighbor represented exactly what Evelyn wanted in a mayor. I wasn't about to risk losing a good store manager over Hubert Spence.

❧ 7 ❧

Joe Riddley must have felt the same way, for Evelyn's arrival accomplished what all my wishing had not. He got up, put on his cap, and said, "I'll be back by dinnertime. You want to go to Myrtle's?" I nodded. We always did on Saturdays.

As soon as he and Bo left, I motioned Evelyn to the wing chair. "I've been wondering about something. Do you know who Starr Knight's friends were?"

Evelyn wrinkled her forehead. "You aren't going to start poking around in that, are you? Because if you do, and if I help you, the boss—"

"I am the boss," I interrupted. "At least, one of them. And no, I'm not going to start 'poking around in that.' I've merely been wondering why Starr was wearing those clothes, and whether somebody might know."

That got Evelyn's attention. "I've wondered that, too. I mean, they weren't like anything she ever wore before. More like Missy than Starr."

"Who's Missy?" The name sounded familiar, but I couldn't place it.

"Missy Sanders, the youngest of the family that lives next to Trevor. She and Starr were best friends through middle school. I don't know if they've been friendly lately, though."

Now I remembered. Missy was the girl who had brought bubbles to the children the night before. "Does she live in the Volkswagen memorial trailer park?"

Evelyn laughed. "Don't let her granddaddy hear you criticizing those cars. He came from Germany and he loves every one of them."

"He must. Is he a mechanic?" You might think I ought to know everybody in Hope County, but thirteen thousand people is too many to know personally.

"No, they farm and board horses."

"And buy cotton seed and animal feed from us." The name was beginning to register, although I'd only seen it on invoices. I could probably have identified members of the family by sight, but their orders always came by phone and requested delivery.

"They have a couple of horses of their own, too," Evelyn informed me. "Missy gives riding lessons to kids evenings and weekends. During the day, she works as an assistant to the vet where I take my dogs, and at work Missy always wears a white shirt and black pants."

"Do you reckon she might know why Starr was dressed like that when she died?"

"The sheriff could ask her, I suppose." Evelyn's emphasis on the second word could not be missed. "But like I said, I don't know how friendly she and Starr have been lately. They were inseparable before they went to high school. Starr used to help Missy groom and exercise the horses when owners couldn't get out, and Missy used to come with Starr to church."

"Maybe I'll suggest that the *sheriff* talk with her, then."

"Good idea. You wouldn't want to go out there yourself. The family is funny about strangers. Only folks they allow on the property are those going up to the barn to take riding lessons or exercise their own horses, and riders have to stay in the big pasture or the adjoining wood. The rest of the farm is *verboten*."

"You speak German?"

"Just that one word. I was following Trevor's pup over there one afternoon and the old man yelled it at me. Trevor told me what it meant. He said the Sanders are real clannish and keep to themselves. Old man Sanders lives in the double-wide with the big porch, and his two sons and his daughter all live next to him, like bees in a hive."

"None of them ever married?"

"All of them married, but I guess a condition of marrying into the family is that you have to live on the property—I don't know. I do know that they don't take kindly to people trespassing on their land. Another time when Trevor's pup got loose and wandered over there, they took a shot at it. Said they thought it was a rabbit, when it was a half-grown Lab."

"I'll tell the sheriff to take his gun."

When I passed through the store with my pocketbook half an hour later and said I was going to make a trip to the drugstore, I don't think Evelyn believed me. I cannot imagine why. "They are having a two-for-one sale," I told her, "and Bethany needs a few things."

I bought toothpaste and shampoo to send with Ridd and Martha the next time they went to visit, because college girls don't need to be wasting their money on toothpaste and they can never have too much shampoo. I also bought her a couple of perky lipsticks, to spruce up the mundane gifts, and four candy bars. At the last minute, I added Hershey bars for myself to the pile.

After that, since it was a nice day and our store was in good hands, I took a short ride to enjoy the weather while I munched my chocolate. I did not deliberately set out to visit Missy until I looked up and found myself near Trevor's place. That's what I told Joe Riddley, and I'm sticking to it.

A well-graded driveway led past the trailer enclave toward the barn at the back, while a rutted, uninviting drive-way, best suited to trucks, led toward the trailers themselves. The only person I saw, however, was a man working on a VW Beetle that had started out life green, so I turned my

wheels into the ruts and jounced up the track with some trepidation. The trepidation deepened as the man stood up,
looked my way, and started wiping his hands on a dirty orange rag. He was as wide as a bull on hind legs, his arms as
thick as my thighs. I got a good look at them, because he
wore his stained overalls without a shirt. Sweat shone on his
face and dampened his grizzled mane.

I seldom feel nervous anywhere in the county. Not only
am I a magistrate, but Joe Riddley was a judge for thirty
years before I became one, so most folks in town recognize
us even if we don't know them. And since I was six years
old, folks have known that if they harmed a hair on my head,
they'd have Joe Riddley and Buster to deal with. You can get
accustomed to taking that kind of protection for granted.

That morning, I remembered there were a few pockets of
folks in the county who had managed to never deal with the
law, seldom came to town, and who neither knew who I was
nor cared. From the look on that hefty red face, I realized I
had slid into one of those pockets.

Unblinking blue eyes stared at me as I climbed from my
poor jolted car. "I'm MacLaren Yarbrough, from Yarbrough
Feed, Seed, and Nursery." It did not seem the place or time
to mention that I was a judge. "I'm looking for Missy
Sanders."

"Whut fer?" This was obviously not the old man. His
drawl was pure Georgia cracker. He continued to wipe his
hands on the dirty rag as if cleaning them for his own brand
of surgery.

"I need to talk to her. My older grandson likes to ride." If
he chose to connect those two truths, that was his business.
I saw no reason to add that Tad's mother, Cindy, owned one
of the finest horses in the county and let him ride whenever
he wanted to.

He took his time assessing my statement, then jerked his
head toward the smoother road. "Up at the barn."

"Thanks. I'll look for her there." I saw no place to turn
around, so I backed up. The only thing that kept it from

being one of the crookedest backing jobs ever performed by woman was the fact that my wheels couldn't leave the ruts. My whitewalls would never be the same.

Finally I reached the graded drive. No horse ever headed for a barn with greater relief.

The structure, big enough to house ten horses and their feed, sat near the edge of the thin pine forest that separated the Sanders property from Trevor's workshop. Through the pines I had a clear view of the back of the workshop, which included wide double doors through which, presumably, he took animals to be worked on.

Near the barn were a parking area, a makeshift training ring, and a small feedlot. The feedlot's ground had been churned by hooves into an even brown. Beyond that, a large green pasture stretched to distant trees. A white SUV and a silver BMW were parked in the lot. Three riders cantered across the pasture, while a tiny figure perched on a tall gray horse was being led around the ring by a woman I recognized by her flyaway black hair and the glint of sun on her glasses.

I pulled to a stop beside the BMW and lowered my windows to be comfortable while I waited for the woman and child to complete their lesson.

"She's doing well, isn't she?" asked a voice from the BMW.

A mother with anxious eyes watched the little girl on the big horse.

"Seems to be doing fine," I replied.

The woman lowered her voice, even though nobody could hear us. "The rest of the family may be trash, but Missy is good with children. Dana was terrified the first time, but this is only her second lesson, and already she doesn't seem afraid, does she?"

Not half as afraid as her mother. I wondered if the mother was afraid the child would fall, fail, or be contaminated by Missy's "trashiness."

"She's doing beautifully. Next thing you know she'll be

out there riding with the best of them." I pointed toward the riders in the pasture.

The mother nodded. "It's so important for a child to be exposed to a variety of experiences, don't you think? Things like horseback riding, ballet, soccer, and violin. Of course, they all take up a good bit of time. We have a soccer game at one." She looked at her watch and I did the same. It was half past eleven. We let the conversation die from lack of interest.

"Oh, gross!" she exclaimed a few minutes later.

I first thought she was staring at me with that sick look on her face, then realized she was looking at something on the far side of my car. From where we were parked, through the thin forest separating the Sanders property from Trevor's business, we watched as Trevor and one of his assistants wrestled an enormous head from a garbage bag in the back of a tan pickup. "Looks good," Trevor boomed. He held the head up for his assistant to admire. I couldn't tell at that distance whether his helper was Wylie or Robin. A short, thick man standing to one side talked excitedly, speaking so loudly that some of his words wafted our way. ". . . all day to get him . . . straight through a marsh." I wondered where he'd been. Hunting season didn't start for several weeks.

Shrieks from the other side of our cars distracted us. The child had finished her lesson and was running toward the car, calling, "I did it, Mommy. Did you see me? I did it!"

In record speed the mother gathered the little girl into the protective cocoon of the car, shielding her from the sights next door, and hustled her off to their next activity. I hoped the child would get lunch on the way.

I climbed out and went toward Missy, who was already wiping down the horse. Close up, the beast looked as old as me. Dana had little to fear from that animal.

"Missy Sanders?"

She gave me the courtesy to pause in her grooming. "Yes, ma'am. You wanting riding lessons?" Her voice was high and nasal, unexpected in a woman that thick and strong, but her tone made me want to climb up on that horse and gallop across the pasture to show her I could—if the old horse still could.

However, Mama raised me to be polite. "No, hon. I started riding before I could walk, on my daddy's farm horse." We exchanged the smiles of women who learned to ride because it was necessary. "I'm MacLaren Yarbrough, from Yarbrough Feed, Seed, and Nursery."

Magnified by their lenses, her eyes flickered. "The judge. I know. Didn't Daddy send the check for our last feed bill?"

"This isn't about money. It's about Starr Knight. Evelyn Finch, who works with me, said you were a friend of hers."

She turned back to the horse and started rubbing him down double-time.

"I'm not here with questions about her death. I want to ask about something that puzzles me: the way Starr was dressed when she died."

Missy finished wiping down the horse's forelegs before she spoke. I got the feeling she'd been planning her answer. "Starr ain't been out this way for months. Not since she got a place of her own in town."

I'd walked close to the edge of truth in my lifetime. I knew how to read between her lines. "But you *had* been seeing her somewhere else, right? At her apartment?"

"She never let me go to her place. Said it was real trashy."

Trash is relative. Dana's mother considered Missy's family trash, but that woman must have led a sheltered life. There were hovels in Hope County that made the Sanders clan look downright middle class. Most of our slum housing had been built—thrown together, to be more exact—by Gusta's husband and passed on, unimproved, to his widow. Gusta considered herself a benefactress of the poor because she charged so little rent. She neither knew nor cared that the low rent attracted mostly the desperate—those who scraped together all the pennies they could find to buy drugs.

I pressed Missy again for the truth. "So where *did* you meet her?"

With a huff of defeat, she capitulated. "Hardee's. We'd go get a burger and talk. She was real sick lately."

If Missy suspected the truth about Starr's "illness," I respected her desire to protect her friend. If she didn't, I wasn't about to enlighten her.

"Was she going to see a doctor? Was that why she left town last week?"

When Missy didn't answer my question, I tried another. "Do you know why she was dressed like she was?"

When she still didn't answer, I warned, "You don't have to tell me, Missy, but you will have to tell the sheriff. I'll have to report that you know something and are holding back. He is determined to find whoever killed Starr."

She jerked back a step and blazed back at me. "Do you know what happened to her?" She barely gave me time to nod. "Leave them alone!" she shouted. "You'd do better to put your hand in a nest of rattlers. You ain't got a notion who you're meddling with!"

Her use of Joe Riddley's favorite word stung me into also speaking louder than I intended. "I've got only one notion: locking up whoever killed her and throwing away the key. You'd do well to have the same notion yourself."

Her jaw clenched. "You have to catch them first. And you heard what they done to Starr. That's what they're like!"

I lowered my voice. "Do you know who they are?"

She shook her head and followed my lead. I had to step closer to hear. "If I did, I'd tell. I swear I would. But I don't know. And I'm scared they might think I do." Her eyes, magnified by the thick lenses, were huge and scared. She licked her lips and her gaze flickered to the right and left, as if she feared that a horde of Starr's enemies might be lurking behind a fence post or over behind the truck at Trevor's back door. Trevor and his helper were still talking to the hunter beside his truck.

I had better things to do than watch other people chat. "Why would they hurt Starr? Do you know that?" I asked.

Missy hesitated. "She planned to turn them in. They

musta found out and got her—just like she was scared they would. Leave it alone, or they'll get you, too!"

"The sheriff isn't about to leave it alone, and you know it. He's going to scour this county, and the whole state of Georgia, if necessary, to bring them in. And so help me God, if you are protecting them—"

Her voice rose again. "I ain't protecting nobody! I tried to help. I even loaned her my clothes, but look what they did to her!" She stomped around to the other side of the horse and pressed her forehead against its neck, not even pretending to groom the beast any longer, merely using it for support. It stood and twitched, offering what comfort it could.

"Do you know who she was going to talk to?"

She took her time about it, but finally she nodded. "She had a secret meeting all set up with the DEA, over in Augusta. She said that now that Bradley was safe, she could talk. She thought they might help her get clean again and put her in a protection program somewhere. It like to killed her to think about leaving Bradley even for a little while, but once D-Facs took him, she made up her mind. 'I'm gonna clean up my act and get him back,' she told me, 'and then I'm gonna ask them to put us in that witness protection program and send us far away from here.' It like to killed me to think about losing her like that, but now . . . she's gone for good." The last words were a wail. Missy laid her head on the horse's neck and bawled.

I gave her time to recover. The sun was warm on my shoulders, the air fragrant with scents I grew up with: horses, pasture, barn. Two horses nuzzled each other by the feedlot fence. The three riders were headed back our way from far across the pasture. The only discordant note in the pastoral scene was over at Trevor's, where—barely screened by the skimpy forest—the head of the big animal was finally being carried through the double doors.

"Do they often unload them outside like that?" I asked, trying to introduce a more neutral subject.

Missy looked over her shoulder as if she hadn't noticed

the activity next door. Her shrug confirmed that it was a common occurrence. "They have to. Can't drive a truck into the shop. They even butcher deer out there, if somebody wants the meat for eating. Too many chemicals inside, Mr. Knight says."

"I don't guess any of you saw Starr take Robin's truck that day, did you?"

She blinked and fumbled in her jeans pocket for a tissue. "Starr wouldn't take Robin's truck. She hated that woman."

"Why?"

"She never said." Missy sniffed. "My mom claimed Starr was afraid Robin would marry Trevor and they'd get custody of Bradley. That might have been it. I know she wouldn't let him play with Robin's girls, and they're sweet kids."

"Maybe if she hated Robin, that's why she took Robin's truck—to hassle her." I was fumbling in the dark and we both knew it.

Missy shook her head. "Starr wouldn't drive a vehicle with an automatic transmission. She had a big thing about that. Said they were for wimps and sissies. Besides, Uncle Jacob saw two men at her truck—"

She broke off and gave me the glare of somebody who'd been tricked into saying more than she had intended. "He won't talk to the sheriff. You'd be wasting your time sending him out here to try to talk to any of my family. We stay clear of the sheriff and he stays clear of us."

"You could at least go tell him where Starr was headed. Was she wearing your clothes?"

She gave me a grudging nod. "I told her she needed to look respectable for them to take her serious."

Without meaning to, I glanced down her muscular torso, which was several sizes larger than Starr's. Correctly reading my expression, she added hotly, "The pants had an elastic waist. They were a tad big, but they didn't fall off her."

I remembered that the deputy had said the pants were baggy. I wondered if either the sheriff or the coroner—both males—had considered the significance of the fact that Starr's clothes were too big.

Missy had another concern. "Don't tell Trevor. I don't want him to pay for them, or nothing."

"I won't tell Trevor, but you do need to tell the sheriff."

I had spoken in the process of leaving, so my words were louder than usual. A voice called from the barn, "You haff trouble, Missy?" The accent was heavily German.

I looked up and saw the double of the man around front—except this man's hair was silver. He stood in the shadows that filled the doorway, carrying a pitchfork in one beefy hand. He stepped into the light like Goliath, broad of back and thick of thigh. David's taunt echoed in my brain:

> *You come to me with a shield and a sword*
> *But I come to you in the name of the Lord.*

I didn't feel real confident at the moment that I did come in the name of the Lord. Maybe I came in the name of my own curiosity. Maybe this giant German had been sent by God to drive me away. Maybe Sheriff Gibbons had everything under control. Maybe I ought to get on my horse and ride into the sunset.

I couldn't leave without a low warning. "Tell the sheriff what you know. It's the only protection you've got."

Her glasses reflected the light of the sun so I couldn't see her eyes. "I don't know nothing! You got that? I don't know a dad-blamed thing." She grabbed the reins of the old horse and led it away.

⟩8⟨

The rest of the weekend I wondered if Missy had called the sheriff, or if my visit had accomplished nothing except ruining my whitewalls.

Sunday afternoon I said to Joe Riddley, "How about we invite Buster to join us at Dad's Bar-be-que tonight?"

"You planning to interrogate him about Starr's murder investigation?"

"Don't be silly. We haven't had a chance to enjoy a good meal together for weeks, and it's finally cool enough to eat outdoors again."

A stiff breeze had even driven off the gnats and mosquitoes, so when we got our plates, I suggested we eat at a distant table under the trees. I congratulated myself on finagling it so we were out of earshot of other diners without arousing Joe Riddley's suspicions—until he set his tray on the table. "Okay, Buster, fill us in. Little Bit's ears are flapping."

Buster's bloodhound face looked as mournful as I'd ever seen it. He swung his long legs across the bench and settled himself on one side of the picnic table. He poked at the coleslaw on his plate with a white plastic fork, looking for all the world like he was hunting clues in its mayonnaise. He took a bite and chewed it slowly. He snailed a handout for his sliced-beef sandwich and unwrapped it as carefully as if it were fine crystal. I expected us all to die of old age before he said a word.

I attacked my pulled-pork sandwich to keep from smacking him.

He swallowed, took a swig of Coke, and said, "Forensics folks think Starr was killed on Monday or Tuesday, although with the car windows rolled up in that heat, it was hard to tell. Nobody has come forward to admit they were walking out on the bypass last week before the cleanup crew found her on Thursday, and the vehicle wasn't visible to drivers. It could have been there all that time. My hunch is that she met up with somebody who provided her with drugs, that she reneged on paying him, he followed her home, managed to get her to stop, and killed her."

I gave him a minute to take another bite before I asked, "Have you talked to Missy Sanders?"

Joe Riddley stopped chewing and fixed me with a stare that used to make defendants before his bench quiver in their boots. "What does Missy Sanders have to do with anything?"

Fortunately, I've known him too long to quiver, and I was wearing sandals. "I ran into her yesterday, and she said Starr had borrowed her clothes just before she was killed, and that Starr was going to talk with some Drug Enforcement Agency people." That got their attention. I filled them in on what Missy had said. "I told her to go talk to you, Buster, but I guess she didn't."

"Not that I've heard, but I've been fishing all weekend. I had just gotten home when you called to ask me to supper." He frowned. "I sure wish Starr had talked to me. We suspect there's a meth lab somewhere in the area, but haven't a clue where to look. Nobody's buying any supplies they shouldn't, and every lead we've gotten has fizzled out."

"Maybe Missy can help you."

"Not if all she knows is where Starr was going and why she dressed the way she did the day she died."

"It's a beginning, Buster. She was probably killed by whoever was supplying her with drugs. Now if we—"

Joe Riddley slammed one fist down on the table and roared. "Stay out of it, Little Bit!" I think he was as astonished as we were, because he swallowed and said in a normal voice, "The sheriff can take it from here." He stood. "I'm getting some more tea. Anybody else need some?" I held up my paper cup and he strode off.

"He's really worried, you know," Buster said unnecessarily. "Those boys are dangerous. He doesn't want you to get hurt again."

"I'm not going to get hurt, because I'm not getting involved. The only thing I want to know from you is whether or not you've found anything that points to a suspect."

He didn't say a word, just sat there eating his sandwich.

I gave him plenty of time to speak. Finally I said, "I wonder why Starr was out on the bypass. She wouldn't have used it to drive to Augusta, either from her house or from Trevor's. How did anybody lure her out there to kill her?"

"She wasn't killed out on the bypass." Buster finished his sandwich, wiped sauce off his hands and chin, and took a swig of his drink before he followed up on that bombshell. "We've been over every inch of the dirt on that roadside, and there wasn't a speck of blood. None at her place, either, so she wasn't killed there."

"Was she killed in the truck?" When I was a child, some slaughterers had fetched my favorite calf from Daddy's farm and beat it to death with the head of an axe in the back of their truck, while my little brother, Jake, and I watched. Daddy never used them again, but that didn't erase the memory. It still made me sick to my stomach to remember. I pushed my plate away.

"She wasn't killed in the truck and she wasn't killed out at her place. Both of them were clean. We have no idea where he killed her." Buster tore open the wet wipe that Dad thoughtfully provides with sandwiches just as Joe Riddley came back with our tea.

"Did you solve it while I was gone?" he asked.

"Nope," I griped. "Buster just mentioned some 'he' who killed her, but he's being as close as a clam."

Joe Riddley sat down, took a swig of tea, and said, "You might as well tell us, Buster, or she'll keep us here all night. I heard a couple of mosquitoes on my way back out."

I was dying to press him: *So who is it, Buster? How'd you find him? Anybody we know?* I settled for a harmless question: "Why haven't I seen a warrant?"

Before he got around to answering, he had to finish his drink and neatly fold up all his paper. Sometimes Buster is too finicky to live. At last he said, "Judge Stebley was down at the detention center for a bond hearing Friday when the word came in, so I asked him to issue the warrant. The alleged perp is a kid of nineteen from Hall County, who was arrested up there a year ago for possession with intent to sell. He got probation, but he must have moved on to bigger stuff, because his conviction was for marijuana and Starr had been using meth. She was nearly eaten up with it. We identified him because he left some prints that matched up. His name is Roddy Howell."

That didn't answer all my questions, by a long shot. "Have you talked to the guy?"

"Nope. We're still looking for him."

I pinched one of Joe Riddley's fries, hoping salt might help settle my stomach, which was still queasy from remembering the slaughter of Daddy's calf. "It's great that you've identified him, though."

He sighed. "Yeah, but all we can get him on is accessory to murder. He left enough prints on her body to show he lifted her into the truck, and some in the truck as well, but there's nothing to tie him to the actual beating."

"What about the weapon?" As I spoke, I saw a glower in Joe Riddley's eyes. "I'm not investigating," I protested. "I'm expressing interest in what Buster has to say. Given the kind of thug this kid probably is, I have no inclination to get any closer to him than the other side of my bench."

Joe Riddley sucked up the last of his drink in that noisy way he knows annoys the dickens out of me. "You might as well tell the rest of it, Buster. Have you got any leads on the weapon?"

He might act like Mr. Cool, but I suspected he was as interested as I was.

"Not yet. There's evidence the weapon was in the back of the vehicle for a time—behind the front seat where the jump seats are, not in the bed—but it wasn't there when we hauled the danged thing up."

"They could have thrown it into the kudzu before pushing the car over," I suggested.

Buster gave an unfunny laugh. "You know how long it would take to search that much kudzu? Not to mention how many snakes we'd meet in the process."

Joe Riddley had finished his ribs and was positioning a slice of lemon icebox pie as his next victim. With fork poised, he paused long enough to point out, "The stuff's deciduous. They might not have thought about that." Having said all he planned to say, he turned his full attention to his pie and changed the subject to Georgia's chances in the current football season.

I reached under the table and patted his knee to thank him for helping Buster solve the case. Until he did, folks would keep jumping at every noise and looking over their shoulder half the time, expecting a baseball-bat murderer.

❧ 9 ❧

When Starr's body was released, we turned out in force to pack Trevor's church for the funeral. Two odd things happened that morning. First, Robin and her girls sat in the pew with Trevor and Bradley. Second, Wylie glared at me off and on during the whole service.

It occurred to me that if I could hear Trevor from Missy's place, folks down at Trevor's might have heard Missy. Had that been Wylie out in the yard with Trevor, carrying in the big animal? Had he overheard what Missy shouted at me? An ex-boyfriend turned out to be the killer in a whole lot of cases. Had he known the kid the sheriff was trying to find? I considered his anger and grief over at Trevor's, and wondered if he'd ever done any acting.

At the reception in the fellowship hall afterwards, I overheard two women talking. One said, in a gravelly voice, "I saw that pitiful man and his grandson wandering the aisles of the Bi-Lo yesterday, and I ached for them both."

The second voice was sweet and high. "Why on earth would they need groceries? Folks are keeping their larder stocked."

"Yes, but who takes a gallon of milk or a dozen eggs to a grieving family? You can eat only so much ham and potato salad."

They glanced across the room to where Trevor was shaking hands and trying to be pleasant to people when he would obviously have preferred to be alone with his grief. The first woman heaved a sigh. "I wonder if Trevor is eating at all. He seems to have fallen off considerably since Starr died."

The other reached over and patted her arm. "Go talk to him, honey. You know what they say: The best way to catch a husband is to wear your prettiest hat to his wife's funeral. You're looking fetching today. Go on, now. Give him a smile."

Poor Trevor. It wasn't Starr whom the vultures were circling.

The next morning I had enough distractions to forget Starr's murder for a time. Lulu and I arrived at the store to find Evelyn so excited that her face was bright pink. "Look!" She sported a big button that featured a beaming Hubert encircled by a red doughnut with white words: SPENCE MAKES SENSE.

I bit my tongue to keep from retorting, "Spence makes nonsense."

"Aren't they the cutest things?" She craned her neck, trying to read her own chest.

"Cutest thing I've seen all day," I allowed, "but I'm not sure we need a cute mayor."

"Oh, but Mr. Spence really does know how to run things. He's run that store for—how many years? And he's got great plans for Hopemore." She was breathless, giddy. Sounded to me like Hubert had been handing out charm with his buttons. I also suspected that this was the closest Evelyn had ever come to hobnobbing with a celebrity.

"Running a store isn't exactly the same as running a town." I glanced out the front door. "Speaking of running a store, shouldn't you put the bedding plants on the sidewalk? It's almost nine o'clock."

"Oh!" She hurried to pick up a tray of asters. "I was fixing to put them out when Mr. Spence stopped by. He left a whole box of buttons for us to give out to folks."

I hated to disappoint her, but it was time she remembered the facts of life. "We can't endorse Hubert. I'm a judge. I can't endorse any candidate."

She looked confused. "Will the poster be all right?"

"What poster?" I had come in the side door from the parking lot, as usual. When she made a helpless motion toward the front, I made tracks out onto the sidewalk. In our front window was Hubert's face, big as life and twice as ugly, beaming above his SPENCE MAKES SENSE slogan.

Lulu must have recognized him, because she climbed up on her hind legs and tried to lick him through the glass.

"Sorry, but the poster has to go. I'll get a rag to clean off the dog spit."

Evelyn's only response was to carry out another flat of asters and slam them onto the sidewalk in a manner calculated to do permanent damage to their roots.

"Why don't you take it home and put it in your window?" I suggested as I wiped down the glass and discouraged Lulu from making another attempt at reaching Hubert. "Politicians kiss babies and dogs," I informed her. "Not the other way around."

I was inside removing the first piece of tape when I saw Hubert bouncing down the sidewalk. That's the only word I can think of to describe how he was walking. He could have been traveling on air cushions. His eyes, of course, went straight to the poster—and me removing it. His face flipped from surprised to mad in two seconds flat. Hubert's temper was legendary in town.

He stormed into the store. "What you taking my poster down for? I paid good money for that sign."

I spoke as calmly as I could. Hubert's temper, coupled with his blood pressure, had already been catastrophic to his health once. "I'm a judge. You know I can't endorse a candidate."

That didn't mollify him in the least. "You ain't endorsing

me. You can put up a poster for that housewife, too, if she ever manages to get her act together and print up some. We can face off over the flowers." He motioned toward a new display Evelyn had created Saturday, a green wheelbarrow full of mums in bronze, yellow, and white.

I shook my head. "Sorry, Hubert. I would if I could, but I can't." I'd heard that line in a song when I was a child, and it had stuck with me ever since.

He slicked back his hair and let out a huff of frustration. "You're as bad as Maynard. He won't let me put a sign in his window, either. Says it's bad for business to endorse one candidate over another. But folks gotta stand up for what they believe! We can't be wishy-washy in these perilous times!" He smacked one fist into the other palm.

Lulu yipped and danced in delight. This was more exciting than the store generally was.

Underneath Hubert's anger and bluster, I saw the hurt. "Evelyn could take it home and put it in her window," I told him. "She lives out on the far end of Oglethorpe Street, right near the superstore. You'd get a lot of traffic past there."

Why was I trying to help Hubert, when I wouldn't vote for him unless he was the only candidate running against Hitler? Because friendship is one of the strangest relationships in the world. It makes us do all sorts of things we would never do for either strangers or family. If it had been my brother running (and if Jake were as obstreperous as Hubert), I'd have done all in my power to talk him out of running, and I'd have told him exactly what I thought of his capacity to administer the town. Yet here I was trying to help Hubert with his campaign because I hated to hurt his feelings.

"I'll be glad to put the poster in my window," Evelyn told him as she came in from arranging the sidewalk display. "And if you've got signs on sticks, I'll put one in my yard. If you have bumper stickers, I'll take one of those, too."

He snatched the poster from me and trotted over to thrust it toward her. "Here. If you want more, let me know. I hadn't thought of bumper stickers."

Evelyn looked up at him earnestly. "Don't get the permanent ones—they hurt the paint. Get the kind that peel on and off, or work with magnets. I'll bet lots of people would take one. I'll be glad to help you distribute them. I think it's wonderful that you're running, Mr. Spence."

He turned pink and stretched to his full five-foot-six. "Call me Hubert," he said gruffly. "I'll bring over a sign later. And I'll think about the bumper stickers."

Evelyn raked both hands through her hair—which was a lot more attractive mahogany than it had been carrot orange. Then she realized what she was doing, patted it down, and blushed.

Hubert looked over his shoulder at me. "I guess you won't be handing out my buttons, either?"

"Nope. Sorry. Evelyn can wear hers, though." I was hazy about whether that was legal, but we would presume it was until somebody told me otherwise.

"I'm planning to run to the superstore during my lunch break," Evelyn told him. "I could stand on the sidewalk out there and hand out buttons for half an hour. And bring me a trunk full of signs. I'll go out after work and put them on the right-of-way of every road into town. You can't put up too much publicity."

Sounded to me like Hubert was quickly getting himself a campaign manager. He could do a whole lot worse.

An hour later Slade Rutherford, editor of the weekly *Hopemore Statesman*, strolled into my office, notepad and pen in hand. "Hubert Spence has charged that while judges aren't supposed to endorse candidates, you are showing partiality to—and I quote—'that housewife who thinks she knows how to run Hopemore.' You got any rebuttal to make?"

I exhaled a long breath of relief and disgust. "None that's fit for the printed page. But let me say for the record that I'm not showing partiality to anybody. I told Hubert I can't put his campaign poster in our window because I'm a judge. He suggested I put one for both candidates, and I turned that down for the same reason. End of story. You'd better get that right, after the story you wrote last summer on the investment club murder, or I'll hang you up by the fingernails and let Ridd's pig nibble your toes."

"Ouch." His loafers bulged as he curled his toes under. "I take it Hubert is referring to Nancy Jensen?"

"Right. And between us, the paper might do worse than endorse her."

He tapped his pen on his notebook. "I'm between a rock and a hard place. Last summer, Horace Jensen and Middle Georgia Kaolin contributed more than half the cost of the summer camp our paper sponsored for needy kids. We want to run another camp this summer, so I don't like to rile Horace, and he's not feeling too charitable toward Nancy right now. Have you heard she's suing him for more than half their financial worth?"

"I believe the argument her lawyer is putting forth is that his ability to make more money than she can is an 'intangible asset' he is taking out of the marriage, so she deserves more cash."

"Horace isn't going to like that."

"Horace doesn't like much of anything, or anybody— except someone we don't need to name. That's not for publication, either. I'd be willing to bet, though, that the reason his company contributed to your summer camp was because Nancy told him to, so you'd better think about where your donations are likely to be coming from in the future before you decide who to endorse."

Slade shifted in his chair, a sign he was thinking about what I was saying, so I pressed on. "At least get to know Nancy better. She's an intelligent woman with a number of interests, and I think she's going to bloom once she's divorced. Besides, if you don't endorse her, who are you going to endorse? Hubert?"

"It's a tough call," he conceded.

⊰ 10 ⊱

Not one thing happened in the Starr Knight case for another month.

Sheriff Gibbons called one Friday afternoon toward the end of October. "We've found the weapon. It *was* a bat!" He was crowing like he used to crow as a kid when he correctly identified a sneaker print on the playground.

"That's great! Where was it?"

"In the kudzu, like Joe Riddley suggested."

I considered pointing out it was me who had suggested the kudzu, but I let it pass. Like the Bible says, there are times to make war and times to make peace. Besides, Buster was still crowing. "I noticed this morning that the leaves were off, so I sent somebody out there with binoculars. It took him a couple of hours, but he found it, stuck in the vines. Getting to it was a trick, but we managed to lower a man on a rope to retrieve it. And I know you and Joe Riddley have been cursing the drought, but it has its uses. The bat still shows bloodstains and prints."

"You are a painstaking and patient man. Do the prints match the others you found?"

"We're working on that."

"Did you ever talk to Missy?"

"Yeah, and to the DEA, too. Starr called them in early

September from a throwaway cell phone and said she had information about drug dealing in middle Georgia, but she would need to meet them somewhere, because she was afraid for her child. They made an appointment with her for the following Monday evening in Augusta. That would have been four days before we found her. However, she never showed. They figured she'd gotten cold feet."

"The coldest," I said soberly.

After we hung up, I couldn't sit still, so I headed out front to check our inventory. Lately I had been of two minds about buying products. On the one hand, it could be likened to pouring money down the drain. On the other hand, we had to have something on the shelves if we stayed open. The big question was, what could we buy that we wouldn't eventually have to mark down below cost to get rid of?

Garden clogs—the plastic kind—had been real popular that year, and ours were superior in quality to those at the superstore and not much more expensive. I was behind a rack debating whether to order more when I heard Robin Parker greet Evelyn.

"Hey. We've come to get pansies for the girls to plant beside our front steps. I'm glad we got here before closing time."

The older girl—I couldn't remember their names—begged, "Can we buy a pot for Uncle Billy? Can we, Mama? He likes flowers." Her high voice carried so well, they probably heard it across the street at the bank.

"I don't know." Robin sounded like a woman who was about to say no.

"You have family here?" Whatever her personal feelings toward Robin, Evelyn was, first and foremost, a merchandiser, and that friendly manner sold a lot of goods.

"Is Uncle Billy family? Is he, Mama?" the child demanded.

Robin answered in the resigned tone of a mother who spent her day answering questions. "Yes, honey, he's my brother. That's why he's your uncle." She added, to Evelyn,

"He lives down near Tennille, but he gets up here every week or two."

"He brings me candy, and they cook when we go to bed," announced the older one importantly.

I was wondering whether Billy was indeed Robin's brother, and whether "cook" was a euphemism for something else, but Robin said irritably, "You don't like spicy food."

"Yuck," the child answered.

The little one asked in a soft voice, "Can I go home with you?"

I knew she was addressing Evelyn even before I heard Evelyn's puzzled reply. "Not today. I'm not going home for a while yet."

Robin had better break that child of the habit of asking to go home with strangers. Even in Hopemore, it could be dangerous.

"She asks everybody that," said the older child in a voice full of scorn. "Can we buy him some flowers, Mama?"

"One pot from the two of you together."

Almost any single mother's finances are tight, and Robin was still paying off that truck. If I'd been at the register, I'd have given her that last pot for free. Evelyn could have, too, and she knew it. She didn't offer.

"Come on, Anna Emily, let's pick the very prettiest ones!" Two pairs of feet scampered toward the display at the front.

While they were occupied, Evelyn asked, "How's Trevor doing?"

"Not good. I would have thought he'd get over Starr's death by now, but he still hasn't."

"I doubt he ever will. That child was his life. Last time I saw him, he looked like he was being eaten up inside."

"I know. I do what I can for him and Bradley, but—"

"Look, Mama!" The girls clattered back.

"I picked them, because I'm five," the larger girl told

Evelyn. "Anna Emily isn't big enough to pick good yet. She's just three."

Robin spoke sharply. "That's enough chatter." I agreed that her daughter was a chatterbox, but I hated to hear a mother use that tone with a child.

Not that I hadn't been overheard using it with my own a time or two . . .

Evelyn concluded the sale and wrapped each pot in brown paper to keep it from messing up Robin's car. That's one of the services smaller merchants offer that big ones don't, but it doesn't bring in customers in droves.

When the Parkers had gone, Evelyn called, "You can come out, Mac. They've gone."

"I wasn't hiding," I informed her with dignity. "I was counting clogs."

"Next time I'll count clogs and you can wait on Miss Robin. Do you think she's set her cap for Trevor?"

I had a chance to evaluate that possibility the following Saturday.

Bradley had spent the night with Cricket, and Ridd brought them Saturday morning to the Trick-or-Treat Morning thrown by the downtown merchants. Around eleven, Ridd mentioned to me that they needed to leave soon, because his family was going to the football game at Bethany's college.

"Why don't I take Bradley home, since Trevor lives in the opposite direction?"

Ridd gladly accepted.

On the way, the child grew quieter and quieter.

"You're mighty silent back there," I joked over my shoulder when we were about a mile from his place.

His voice was so soft I almost couldn't hear it. "I wish I could go to your house. My house isn't any fun." In my rearview mirror I saw that his eyes were wide and anxious.

When we pulled in the drive, it looked like the yard hadn't been mowed since Starr's death. Oaks, poplars, and hickories had shed on the unkempt grass, while unopened newspapers lay on the leaves like discarded loaves of bread. I wondered why Trevor didn't cancel his subscription, but figured he couldn't even summon the will to do that.

"Will your granddaddy be here?" I asked as I pulled in the drive.

"He'll be working." Bradley struggled with his seat belt. "He's always working. I'll color at his desk."

"Shall I walk you in?" I had no idea what I'd find in a taxidermist's shop, or whether I'd have the stomach for it, but if Bradley could stand it, surely I could.

"Yes, please." He tucked his hand into mine and we shuffled our feet in the leaves, making a satisfactory crunch and crinkle. It may be heresy for a woman in the lawn maintenance business to admit it, but I have a fondness for places where leaves have not been raked.

Bradley pushed open the door, setting a bell overhead to jingling. "T-daddy? I'm home. Me-Mama brought me."

I followed him into a large room with a desk in the far corner and a number of what I presumed were samples of Trevor's work and customer orders waiting to be picked up. Buck heads gazed down at me from all four walls. A large-mouth bass affixed to a plaque was chasing realistic-looking minnows past water grasses. Turkey feathers hung in a fan over the front door. A member of the cat family lurked in the far corner. An elegant pheasant stood in tall grass under a glass case. On a low oak pedestal, a fox crouched in a circle of fake mud, contemplating a rabbit. The fake mud even had tiny paw prints, and not only did the fox look alive, but he had a grin and a gleam in his eye like he'd spotted dinner.

"Hey, Bradley." Trevor came through a door in the back wall and ruffled Bradley's hair. In spite of what Robin and Evelyn had said, I had not imagined such a change in the man.

His weight had melted off like chocolate in August. He wore a long-sleeved shirt open over a white T-shirt, and the outer shirt hung around him in folds. His jeans, cinched in by his belt, bunched around his body like a gathered skirt. His hair—once fluffy and electric—hung lank and untrimmed. His hair and beard had gone gray.

"I appreciate your bringing Bradley." Even suffering, Trevor didn't lose his old courtesy or fondness for the child. He pulled the boy close to him as if drawing life from the warm little body.

"No trouble at all." I gestured toward the fox. "How do you get the eyes to look so real?"

"Buy best quality." He nodded toward a buck head. "Cheap deer eyes, for instance, don't have a white rim, so they don't look realistic. The eyes need to match the live animal's eyes." He jutted his beard toward the fox. "But that's Robin's work. She's real good."

I spoke on impulse. "If it's not off-limits, could I see what you all do? I've never been in a taxidermy shop."

He stepped aside and waved. "Sure, come on back. We knock off at one most Saturdays, anyway. Just let me get the boy settled first. Children are not allowed in the workroom. Too many chemicals and sharp objects."

He pulled open a drawer of the desk and took out a bedraggled coloring book and some well-used crayons. Bradley moved over to stroke the ratty-looking member of the cat family that had been banished to the darkest corner. "This is my favorite. I call him Bucky."

Trevor grimaced in embarrassment. "Poor Bucky came in for some restoration work, but his owner died."

"Pooh DuBose?"

He nodded. "She was a fine shot. Got that lynx out west somewhere years and years ago. He's past repair, and I'd throw him out, but Bradley loves that beast." He tousled the child's hair. "Okay, Bradley, I'm going to show the judge what T-daddy does, and then we'll go get us some lunch."

I steeled myself for the sight and stench of blood, but what I noticed first was the scent of salt. Next, I noticed the cleanliness of the room. The concrete floor was as clean as any kitchen, and I did not see blood anywhere except on a large white table at the back of the room, where Robin, wearing rubber gloves, was skinning something on a sheet of plastic. To one side of her work space were the double doors I had seen from outside while I was at Missy's.

Trevor gestured toward what looked like a pile of stiff rugs in the middle of the floor. "Those are hides that have already been salted and dried to kill all the bacteria, and then rehydrated in a saltwater bath and air-dried in front of that fan to make them pliable. We use a wet tanning process, because we want the skin to draw up tight and show every muscle detail."

From the size of the pile, it looked like he wasn't going to run out of work anytime soon.

From the back, his two helpers looked exactly alike, for they were about the same size and both wore long-sleeved shirts with the tail hanging down over jeans. The main difference was that Robin wore her brown ponytail higher than Wylie wore his.

Wylie sat at a high bench on one side of the workroom, plying a strange S-curved needle threaded with what looked like dental floss. He chewed on his tongue as he sewed something that looked like a piece of suede with a short hairy mane, like a zebra's. His eyes smoldered as they looked up and met mine briefly. I wondered what I'd done to anger him, but then I remembered he was probably still grieving for Starr, too, in his own volatile way.

"He's stitching up an elk someone got in Idaho back in September," Trevor explained when Wylie didn't speak.

That must be the animal Missy and I had seen them unloading. I didn't see any reason to mention that fact.

"The needle has three sharp edges and the nylon thread is waxed, so they go through the hide more easily." Trevor leaned over and murmured something too soft for me to hear. Wylie swore and started taking out some stitches. I saw then that the elk hide was wrong side out. What I had taken for a mane was simply the hair on the other side.

"Do you cut the animal up the stomach?" I asked, ambling closer.

"Along the back." Wylie spoke curtly, annoyed at having to correct whatever Trevor had mentioned.

"Robin is skinning a bobcat." Trevor led me toward the back of the room, where she was meticulously pulling skin off a carcass, using a knife to cut the tissue that connected them. It was a homely, rather than gruesome, process, not unlike a cook skinning a chicken breast. As I watched, she carefully pulled one paw free. "The tail's the hardest part," she informed me.

I saw Wylie give her a burning, angry look. Could he possibly be jealous of Robin's skill? The telephone rang, and he answered it above his table. "It's for you, Trevor. The sheriff."

If Buster was just getting around to telling him about the bat, I hated for Trevor to have to hear it.

❧ 11 ❧

Trevor excused himself and went to the front room.

I moved closer to Wylie and spoke softly. "I'm real sorry about Starr. Evelyn told me you all had been dating."

He gave a short, rude laugh. "Not lately."

I would have stopped right there, except there was something that had been bothering me. "What did you mean at Trevor's that night, about offering to lend her your truck? When was that?"

"The Monday before they found her. She called here that morning saying she wanted to go up to Augusta, but she wasn't sure the pile of junk she was driving would make it. I told her to come on by and borrow my truck. Trevor would have run me home." He inched up one shoulder in a slight shrug. "Guess it's a good thing for me she took the wrong one, huh? But not so good for Miss Robin over there. Not so good at all." He snickered as he bent over his work. Our chat was over.

I moved down toward Robin, who had been working steadily and ignoring the rest of us. "Looks like you're working on a freezer in somebody's kitchen." I nodded at the white chest she was using for a table. "We used to have a freezer that looked a lot like that down at our big house, except yours is about three times its size."

"It is a freezer." She started cutting the tissue around one eye socket. "We freeze the animals until we're ready to put them in the salt water."

I gestured toward the pile of dry hides Trevor had already shown me. "Are they ready now to . . ." I stopped. I didn't know what the next word was.

Robin gave them a cursory glance, then resumed her work. "Next they go into an acid bath. After that, they're neutralized with baking soda, and when that's done, we use the fleshing machine over there"—she jerked her head in the direction of a big piece of equipment like a meat slicer—"to remove any membranes, fat, and muscle that remain, and to thin down the skin a bit—but not too thin. Finally, we put each hide in a tanning bath for twenty-four hours. When it's done, we put it back in the freezer again until we're ready to work it."

Robin was a natural teacher, and she knew her business. I remembered Trevor saying she had been experienced before he hired her. "Where did you learn all that?"

She shrugged. "I've been doing this for a long time."

Considering that she wasn't twenty-five yet, how long could it have been?

Wylie shot her another angry look.

Robin didn't seem to notice. She picked up the bobcat again. It hung limp and glistening from her hand.

"What do you do with the carcass?"

She nodded toward a box of garbage bags. "Put it in the Dumpster to go to the landfill."

It wasn't illegal, but I wondered if it ought to be. On the other hand, carcasses would decay. Not like plastic bags, which would be around for my great-great-great-grandchildren.

"Now you know everything we know," Trevor joked, coming back into the workroom. "You ready to come work for me, Judge?" In spite of his jovial words, his face was ashen. I wondered how soon this nightmare of getting information in dribbles would end.

I tried to echo his words rather than his face. "Must be nice to work in jeans all day." I moseyed over to peer up at some large white shapes hanging from the ceiling. Most were labeled with a number. A couple had names on them. "What are those?"

"Forms. Each animal is unique, just like people. Take deer, for instance. Some have long snouts and some short, some have big heads, some small. We measure each one and order a form most like it in size and shape, but even then we have to work on the form to get the shape right—muscle it up a little, or take a bit off the snout—before we can mount the skin."

Wylie gave a bitter laugh. "They bring in Bambi and want it to look like Conan."

I was startled. "So you don't actually stuff them? My granddaddy had a deer head on his wall that used to ooze something I presume was sawdust."

Trevor shook his head. "Nowadays we use foam, and glue the hide to the form."

I would have liked to ask about the pruning shears hanging on a Peg-Board at the back of the room along with a hair dryer and some wire cutters, but we heard a horn toot outside. When the doorbell jangled, Robin looked toward the front with a frown. "Is it already noon? I thought I'd be done with this before they got here."

"Mama? Mama!" That was the piercing voice of her older daughter. "We made dough and I made a long worm. Look!"

She and her sister toed the sill of the doorway, obeying with obvious reluctance Trevor's dictum that children were not allowed in the workroom. The big one held up a long piece of green dough that, with a good bit of imagination, might resemble an overfed snake.

The little one edged a tentative toe over the sill, but at a frown from Trevor she drew it back. "I made a turtle." She held out a green blob with five blobs attached at random.

When I bent down to admire it, she said softly, "Can I go home with you?"

Robin didn't look up from where she was gently cutting the skin from around the bobcat's second eye. "We're going home in a little while, as soon as I finish this," she said. "Go color with Bradley until I'm done." They obeyed, obviously unhappy. As Robin bent back to her work, she asked Trevor over her shoulder, "You want me to take Bradley for a few hours? They can watch TV."

Maybe Evelyn was right. Was Robin taking care of Bradley, hoping to eventually take care of his grandfather?

"That would be helpful. I could use the afternoon to work." He gestured with his head toward a bench where a drab fish lay. "I promised Farrell I'd have that bass ready early next week, and I haven't started painting it yet." He added, to me, "I guess I'm getting old. Things seem to take longer than they used to."

"You paint it?" I peered down at the dried brown fish.

"Have to, to make it look natural." He waved toward a piece of cardboard attached to the wall where somebody had been practicing color combinations. "For hogs and bears, the paint hides the white where the form shows through, but we airbrush all the animals, to even out the color and make them more vibrant."

To keep them from looking dead was what he meant, but nobody in that room had mentioned death in my hearing. Apparently taxidermists treated death with as much respect—and avoidance—as undertakers did.

Bradley appeared in the door, the girls in tow. "Can we go play in the sandbox?"

"Yay!" The larger girl clapped her hands, flattening her snake. "Can we, Mama?"

"I'm only going to be a minute," Robin objected. "No point in dragging off the cover."

"Let them go." Trevor waved one hand. "I'll put the cover back on when you've gone."

Before Robin nodded, her older child was halfway to the

front door, dropping her snake on the floor without a thought. The little one put her hand out to me. "Come see the sandbox." She'd left her turtle somewhere, but her palm was still sticky from the dough.

Robin looked up and frowned at the child. "Don't bother the judge, Anna Emily. I won't be more than a few minutes."

"It's okay." I didn't want to disappoint the tug of that little hand. "I'm a big fan of sandboxes. I'll inspect this one until you're ready to go. Thanks for the tour of the business."

The two older children were already hauling a plywood cover off a big wooden sandbox made from railroad crossties. It looked old. I wondered if it used to be Starr's. If so, Bradley and Robin's older girl had inherited it with gusto.

As we walked across the leaf-strewn yard toward it, Anna Emily said with a shy smile, "I like you. Can I go home with you?"

"You have to go to your house," I reminded her. "Your mother is cooking lunch."

"Mama doesn't cook," she said in a mournful voice. "Just with Uncle Billy. After we go to bed."

I had learned years before to take anything children say about their parents with a grain of salt. At eight, our son Walker told his Sunday school teacher with an earnest face that his mama whaled the life out of him if he didn't do his homework. I had not paddled that child since he was five.

Anna Emily's older sister, however, was not so tolerant. "Anna Emily!" She propped both fists on her skinny hips. "I'm gonna tell. You aren't supposed to say that. You know good and well Mama cooks. She fixes applesauce and peanut butter." I could hear Robin's exasperated voice in the child's.

Having never been fond of cooking, I could appreciate that Robin probably made simple meals after a day at work, but neither of her girls looked like they were being raised on peanut butter and applesauce. Anna Emily had bright pink cheeks beneath her freckles.

"I'll bet she makes your breakfast, and dinner, too. But don't tattle," I told the older sister. "Anna Emily was making conversation. Now, show me what you can do with this sandbox." I bent and dribbled sand between my fingers. "I don't think I ever learned your name."

"I'm Natalie, and that's Anna Emily, and that's Bradley. I'll make you some dinner." Mollified by the attention, she proceeded to "cook" me a four-course meal of sand, which she identified as fried chicken, ice cream, noodle soup, and doughnuts. Bradley ran a small bulldozer up and down a miniature mountain. Anna Emily sat on her corner seat and worked one toe in the sand, never taking anxious eyes off me. I had the feeling she thought I might sneak off if she looked away.

Robin came out, pulling a big purse onto her shoulder. "You all ready to go? I thought we'd stop by Hardee's."

"Hardee's! Hardee's!" The older one jumped up and down. Bradley caught her excitement and joined in jumping.

Anna Emily reached for my hand, and tears filled her eyes. "I want to go home with her."

"Anna Emily!" Her mother rebuked her.

I knelt beside her and put my arm around her shoulders. "I have to go back to work right now, honey. I took time out to bring Bradley back from playing at Cricket's."

"Is Cricket your boy?" demanded Natalie.

"I'm his grandmother."

She heaved a sigh bigger than she was. "We don't have grandmothers. They all died." The way she said it, you'd have thought she'd once had a dozen.

I was picturing a field littered with dead grandmothers when Anna Emily said, "I want to go play at Cricket's." When I started to shake my head, her lower lip quivered and tears started down her cheeks.

Robin grabbed her hand and gave me a rueful smile. "I'm sorry. We haven't been here long enough for them to make many friends."

"I'm honored to be chosen as one of them." I climbed to my feet, mindful of my creaking knees.

I walked with Robin and the children toward a Honda Civic parked in the shade. The car didn't look new, but it wasn't real old, either.

"I see you got transportation," I said, congratulating her.

Busy buckling Anna Emily into her car seat, Robin said over her shoulder, "Thanks to Trevor. He paid off the truck and gave me the down payment on this. He said since Starr was the one who wrecked mine, he owed it to me. I didn't think that at all, but I was real grateful."

I figured Trevor was not simply being nice. He knew Robin couldn't get to work if she didn't have wheels. Taking care of employees, even when it seems expensive at the time, is good business practice in the end.

Before he climbed in, Bradley turned and called, "Good-bye, Me-Mama."

Not to be outdone, the girls turned and waved. "Good-bye, Me-Mama!"

As I watched Robin carefully pull onto the highway, it occurred to me that all three Parkers could use friends in Hopemore. I'd ask Martha if I could invite them down for hamburgers with our family one Saturday night.

Joe Riddley claims I love to run other people's lives, and that one of his primary jobs as a husband is to keep me running other people's lives so I don't have time to run his, but there are times when we have to step in and help other folks. That's all I had in mind.

First, I needed to check on my husband.

I pulled my cell phone out of my pocket and called him.

"Where the dickens are you?" he demanded. "I'm at Myrtle's starving, and the game starts in an hour."

Each fall, Joe Riddley brought a television to our office on Saturdays so he could watch Georgia play ball while he pretended to work.

"I'm over at Trevor's. I brought Bradley home, but I

ought to be back in town in fifteen minutes. Why don't you go on and order me the meat loaf dinner?"

"With green beans and mashed potatoes?"

Oh, that man knows me well. For an instant I was tempted to order okra with macaroni and cheese, just to put him off his stride, but I've been eating meat loaf with green beans and mashed potatoes all my life. No need to get radical at the moment.

As I headed back to say good-bye to Trevor, Wylie was pulling out of the yard in a black Ford Ranger. He didn't see me as he peeled out of the drive.

Back in the workroom, Trevor was delicately moving an airbrush over the fish. Looked like he'd decided to skip lunch since he didn't have to feed Bradley.

"I don't mean to bother you—just want to say good-bye and thanks for the tour," I said.

He left his work to walk me to my car.

"It's hard to work with little people to look after," I said sympathetically.

"Yeah, but it's easier now that we have all three kids in the same day-care home down the road. Bradley went there from the time he was a baby—until Starr pulled him out last spring, when she moved. But he loves Marianne, so I've put him back with her, since—" He broke off, and a frown creased his forehead. "I sure hope his being there is going to help Anna Emily settle down. She's already been kicked out of two day-care centers. I suggested to Robin that she try Marianne's when Bradley started back, but Marianne says she's nearly at her wits' end."

I was surprised. "I'd have thought it would be Natalie who would give trouble. Anna Emily seems so quiet."

"Yeah, but she keeps getting out the door and wandering off, or asking delivery people if she can go home with them. It's a real problem. Still, the girls like Bradley and he likes them, so I hope his being there will make a difference."

Trevor swiped one hand over the lower part of his face. "Starr would have a fit about my putting Bradley in with the girls. I don't know if you've heard, but she had a conniption when I hired Robin, and she didn't want Bradley to have a thing to do with those girls." His mouth curved in the ghost of a grin. "I think she was jealous, dumb as that sounds. Starr was used to being the only female on the premises, and used to running my life. To tell the truth, I wasn't crazy about the idea of hiring a woman, either, but Robin was too good to pass up."

"Is Wylie equally good?"

"No, but he's not bad if he could learn to stitch a straight seam."

"He seems real cut up about Starr."

"They'd been dating some. I wish . . ."

He didn't finish the sentence, or need to. I was sure he had a number of regrets. Anybody who has lost a loved one does.

I laid a hand on his arm. "The sheriff is going to find the perpetrator, Trevor. I know it's been a long time from your perspective, but he's going to get him."

In the distance, we heard a flock of geese. We both craned our necks and watched until they appeared. They flew directly overhead, startling a flock of birds that burst into the sky like confetti.

"Good-bye." I started my engine. He didn't say a word.

As I pulled away, Trevor was still watching the geese— mere specks by then—with a look of longing on his face.

❧ 12 ❧

Martha claims that what happened next was an act of God. If so, it only goes to show that God can use anything, even greed and pride, to accomplish good.

All I had on my mind was getting to Myrtle's Restaurant before Joe Riddley ate my meat loaf. There were two ways to Myrtle's from Trevor's, but downtown would still be full of people from the Halloween revelry. I chose the back way, down by the railroad tracks, to avoid what my eleven-year-old grandson calls "Hopemore's rush minute."

As I approached the water tank down near the tracks, I slowed to admire it. It was freshly painted white, with HOPE-MORE stenciled on it in big red letters. Privately, I took credit for the improvement.

The water tank stands in the middle of an asphalt parking lot that used to serve several businesses down by the tracks. As the businesses closed, the tank and its lot were ignored, until the tank, which had gradually faded to soft blue, sat surrounded by an out-of-control privet hedge, broken asphalt, and high weeds. A year before, Lulu and I had found the body of a homeless person under that tank,[6] and for a brief time the Hopemore water tank dominated national

---

[6]*When Will the Dead Lady Sing?*

news. After city leaders noticed how pathetic that tank looked, they authorized funds to paint it and replace the hedge with a chain-link fence and a padlocked gate. In the unlikely event that the water tank ever got its picture on national news again, it would accurately represent our fine town.

I drove along with my windows down to enjoy the cooler October air and the sight of the spruced-up tank. In spite of the padlock and fence, however, somebody had gotten inside the gate and littered. A heap of white lay crumpled at the base of the ladder.

As I got nearer, I heard shouting.

"Help! Please! Somebody, help!" That's when I noticed Evelyn, halfway up the narrow ladder leading to the base of the tank. She stood with both arms extended, leaning far back. Between her and the ladder was something I took for a full feed sack. Not until I drove as close as I could get did I realize the sack was Hubert.

I grabbed my cell phone and dialed 911. "Send somebody to the water tank, pronto," I told the emergency operator. "Somebody's climbed up the ladder and gotten into difficulties."

"Right away, Judge. We'll get you down. Don't worry."

I didn't notice until after I hung up what she had said. Not only did she think it was me up that tank, but she hadn't sounded the least bit surprised.

The gate stood open. I hurried through it and called up to Evelyn, "Help's on the way. Has he fainted?"

"Of course I ain't fainted," Hubert raged. "I'm just a mite dizzy, that's all. Can't seem to make my feet and hands work right."

"I've called for help," I yelled. "What were you doing up there?"

"None of your dadgum bidness."

"Please, help me." Evelyn sounded like she was at the end of her tether—or the end of her arms. I saw now that the reason she was leaning out so far was that she was pinning Hubert to the ladder so he wouldn't fall.

"Hubert," I called sternly, "can you come down one rung?"

"I can't move at all," he bawled. "Everything is going round and round."

"It may be his heart," Evelyn cried.

"Or a wide streak of yellow up his spine. Hubert Spence, you listen to me. Evelyn's about to fall off that ladder holding on to you, and she's running out of strength. You've got to help her. You hear me? Now, Evelyn, I want you to ease down one step. Hubert, when she starts to move, you ease with her. Can you do that?"

"Mac's down there if we fall," Evelyn added.

I backed away. I had no intention of getting squashed. Besides, I felt dizzy myself, craning my neck like that.

Evelyn's foot felt for a lower rung. As she started to descend, Hubert whimpered, but I saw his foot leave the safety of its rung and begin to feel for the one below.

One foot, one hand, at an excruciatingly slow pace, the two of them descended. I could hear Hubert's labored breathing and worried about his heart in spite of what I'd said. He had no business being up that ladder.

They were halfway down when we heard a siren approaching.

"What's that?" Hubert's voice was full of panic.

"They are coming to help," I called up. "But you all are doing fine."

"I'm gonna fall," he cried.

I got an inspiration.

"Hang on one minute more, and they'll be here with a net. You can jump. It can't be more than fifteen feet now. Maybe ten."

"I ain't jumping into any net. Get out of my way, Evelyn. I can come down by myself."

Evelyn climbed the rest of the way down, keeping a careful watch on Hubert. With renewed vigor he made his way down the last few feet. By the time the rescue crew pulled to a stop at the fence, they were both back to earth, but they were trembling and his face was a terrible shade of gray. I wasn't sure how long he could stand.

"You okay, Judge?" called one of the crew members, hurrying my way with a stretcher. "We got word you were up the water tank."

"Not me. Hubert. I think he could use a check-over at the hospital. Evelyn, too."

"I'm okay," Hubert insisted, but he could hardly breathe. Within seconds, the techs had him safely in the back of their vehicle.

I put one arm around Evelyn to steady her. "What on earth made Hubert climb that tank?"

She bent and picked up one end of the dropped cloth. "This." She shook it out and I saw it was a long banner, designed to hang from the top of the ladder and cascade down like a waterfall. At the top, Hubert's face would have beamed over the town while large red letters proclaimed, SPENCE MAKES SENSE.

Evelyn rode with Hubert to the hospital. I called Maynard. He and Selena were at an antique show down in Dublin, but he said they'd come to the hospital as fast as they could. Given how long it would take to process Hubert and Evelyn in the emergency room, I figured I might as well go eat my dinner.

When I walked in, folks started laughing, clapping, and shouting, "What-a-go, Mac! You go, Judge!"

When I slid into the booth across from Joe Riddley, he asked, "What were you *doing* up that tank? You said you were coming straight here."

"Who told everybody I was up that tank?" I took an angry swallow of tea and glared around at the other patrons.

One of the deputies raised a sheepish hand. "That would be me. I was near the operator's desk when you called."

"You owe me an apology and my dinner. I called to say

that somebody else was up the tank." I spoke loudly enough
to be heard by everybody there. "It wasn't me."

I could tell from the way folks bent over their plates that
they didn't believe me. I would never get that story straight
in some people's minds.

"Here's your dinner." Myrtle slid a plate in front of me.
"Joe Riddley asked me to keep it warm. We figured you'd
need something hot in your stomach after the shock."

I was torn between being grateful for their thoughtfulness
and mad that they thought I was dumb enough to climb the
tank. I was so hungry, I decided to go with grateful.

Martha was down visiting Bethany with Ridd and
Cricket, but when we went by the hospital after lunch, we
spoke to an emergency room nurse named Kate. She told us,
"Hubert's heart is fine. He simply had a panic attack, but the
doctor wants to keep him overnight for observation. It's
Evelyn who is in pain. She sprained both arms somehow."

When I explained what Evelyn had done, Kate stared.
"She held him up all that time? No wonder she's sore! The
doctor told her to go home, take painkillers, and rest, but she
insists on staying with Hubert until Maynard gets here, and
she says she has to work this afternoon." That nurse had
known us all her life, but she looked at Joe Riddley and me
like we were monsters who kept employees locked in a win-
dowless sweatshop and let them out only at night.

"When will Maynard get here?" Joe Riddley asked.

Kate checked her watch. "He ought to be here in another
half hour at the most."

"Tell Evelyn I said she's to take today and Monday off,
and see how she feels then. We'll manage without her. She
did a very brave thing."

I asked permission to go back and see Evelyn briefly in
the cubicle where Hubert was waiting for a room. He was
snoring. She was sitting in a straight chair with both arms in
slings, propped on pillows on her lap. Her face was so pale
that her freckles stood out like constellations. Sweat beaded
her upper lip.

When she saw me, her eyes filled with tears. "It was all my fault!"

I laid a hand on one shoulder, but took it off when she winced. "You weren't the one starting up that ladder with a banner."

"No, but I suggested that a banner hanging from the water tank would get a lot of attention. I even called my sister and got permission to hang it."

Evelyn's sister was somebody important down at the water company.

"She told me that Hubert could put up a banner, but that if other candidates requested equal time, we'd have to work out a schedule. And she gave me the key to the gate." She started to put one hand up to rake it through her hair, then winced again and dropped her arm.

"Have you taken anything for pain?"

"No. They gave me a prescription, but I wouldn't let them give me a shot. I can't drive all woozy. I'll get the prescription filled later, after Hubert's son comes. I don't like to leave him alone. I sure would like some water, though."

I went and fetched her some, then held the cup while she drank. "Hubert is feeling no pain. He won't care whether somebody is here or not."

"I don't like to leave him. He might wake up and not remember where he is."

Never try to discourage martyrs. It makes them more adamant. "Have you had lunch?"

"I'm not hungry." It was a lie. We could both hear her stomach growling.

"How do you plan to get home when you can leave?" If she and Hubert had walked down to the water tank from our store, her car must still be in our parking lot.

"I'll walk to the store and get my car."

"No way you are going to walk nearly a mile with those sore arms. Give me your keys and call when you're ready to leave. I'll send somebody over to get you, and if you'll give me the prescription, I'll get it filled. You stay home until you are no longer in pain. You hear me?"

"But we'd planned to put up yard signs this evening." She cast Hubert an anguished glance. "Do you think he'll be up to running after this?"

I reached over to catch one of her hands and squeeze it, but had second thoughts and stroked Hubert's sheet instead. "I don't know, but he's a tough old bird. We'll have to see how he feels when he's had time to recover. He never should have gone up that water tank."

She sniffed and grabbed a tissue from a box on Hubert's nightstand. "I know. I told him I'd do it, but he said he'd climbed that tank a hundred times as a kid."

"He lied. We weren't allowed to climb that tank as kids. The only time I know of that he went up that ladder was when he painted a big heart on the tank at the end of his and Joe Riddley's senior year in high school, with 'Joe Riddley loves MacLaren' in the middle."

"Really?" Her eyes kindled with misplaced adoration.

"Yeah, but I didn't know it was Hubert until last year, or he wouldn't have lived this long. Now, give me that prescription so I can send somebody back with pain pills. You look like you need them." As I closed the curtain to the cubicle, I saw her watching Hubert with tenderness.

I stopped by the nurses' desk and asked if they could get her a milk shake and something to eat. "Put it on Hubert's bill. She's working on his campaign."

When I got back to where Joe Riddley was waiting, I said, "You know, Evelyn's probably twenty years younger than Hubert, but both of them could do a whole lot worse. And if they got married, she could move in with Hubert and solve Otis's problem."

Joe Riddley draped an arm around my shoulders. "I can't see Evelyn taking care of Gusta, can you? So why don't we let them recover from this present crisis before you precipitate another one."

⇥ 13 ⇤

As soon as the Halloween festival weekend was over, all the downtown lampposts sprouted gold wreaths with red bows. The sheriff called me around ten on Monday morning.

"I've got an important question, Judge. Is Joe Riddley gonna boycott the lighting ceremony tonight? I was at a breakfast meeting this morning, and folks were laying bets about when he'll turn them on. I want to know how safe my money is."

At six p.m., Hopemore would have our traditional turning on of the lights, when downtown merchants flipped switches to outline all their roofs so the town looked like a toy village. For the past five years, however—since the chamber had voted to kick off Christmas right after Halloween instead of after Thanksgiving—Joe Riddley had refused to start the Christmas season that early, making our store stand out like a six-year-old's missing tooth.

"We'll turn them on tonight. I've argued him down this year. I want to celebrate this Christmas as long as we can."

The sheriff had known me too long not to know what I was thinking. "You afraid it may be your last one in the store?"

I had to swallow a lump in my throat before I could answer. "Four generations of Yarbroughs have managed to keep some sort of business going in this location, but we are speedily losing ground. I cannot bear to think of this old building turned into another dollar store, real estate office, or shop carrying antiques no older than we are."

He laughed. "Sounds like my money is safe, then. I knew you'd bring the old coot around. We could use some bright lights this winter. The place has been a bit gloomy."

"Folks who kill other folks with baseball bats have that effect on people."

The whole town was getting more and more nervous as the weeks dragged on and nobody was caught in the Starr Knight murder case. I'd started sticking closer to the office, took Lulu with me everywhere, and made sure my doors were locked before I started my car. When a friend tapped on my car window while I was stopped for the red light, I jumped halfway out of my skin.

As far as I was concerned, one bright spot lit the dreariness, though. Hubert came out of the hospital Wednesday so embarrassed at what had happened that he decided to withdraw from the upcoming election.

He also put a big banner over his store: GOING OUT OF BUSINESS SALE. EVERYTHING MUST GO. CLOSING CHRISTMAS EVE.

Lulu and I popped over Thursday morning to see what all he had to sell. "Appliances, shelves, light fixtures. You all in the market for a new refrigerator?"

"We got new appliances when we moved in, but we might be interested in a freezer. We left ours with Martha." I moseyed over and checked out the one upright he had left. "What kind of price can you give me?"

"Half off." He trotted over and started extolling the features of that particular model as if he had several for me to choose from. I stepped back slightly and noticed the price on the side. It was a hundred dollars higher than it had been the last time I'd checked it.

I wanted to grab him by the neck and throttle him, but restrained myself. "I'll talk to Joe Riddley," I said with admirable politeness.

"You might want to take some of those lights up there. They're better than the ones you all have."

"The ones we have are fine. What are you planning to do once you sell out?"

"I'll find something. You don't have to worry about that."

That afternoon, Maynard dropped by my office, doing enough worrying for everybody. "If Daddy sits around, he'll have another heart attack, but what else is there for him to do? I didn't want him elected mayor, but at least he'd have had something to occupy his time and his mind."

I turned my chair to face him more comfortably. "Didn't I hear you're remodeling the upstairs of Gusta's house into an apartment? Could Hubert live there and help you out with the business? He could wait on customers while you are out scouting for merchandise."

I thought that was brilliant. If I could only think of something to do with Gusta, Otis and Lottie's problem would be solved.

Maynard shook his head. "You know as well as I do that Daddy and I get along better if we aren't under each other's feet. Besides, he likes where he is and I like the fact that somebody's looking after him."

Poor Otis and Lottie weren't fine, stuck taking care of Hubert, but I couldn't say that. In spite of what Joe Riddley might tell you, I do have a modicum of tact at times.

A second bright spot lit my horizon the second Monday in November. Joe Riddley had gone into Augusta for a meeting, and I was working at my desk when the sheriff called. "Hey, Judge, you busy?"

"Busy sitting here trying to think up some way to pay Joe Riddley back for that prank two months ago. I haven't come up with the perfect revenge yet, but when I do, it is going to be terrible. You're coming in for your share, too, don't forget."

"I'm shaking in my boots. Will it lessen my punishment if I tell you I have some progress to report on the Starr

Knight case? We got back lab reports on the bat, and I've sent a deputy up your way with a warrant for arrest. The blood on the bat was definitely hers, and they found a match for the prints."

"Was it the kid you're already looking for?"

"No. They belong to Slick Redmond, who has been up twice for battery—a real nasty customer. He's currently on probation down in Laurens County, so they had his present address. The sheriff down there is standing by to pick him up as soon as I get a warrant."

"I have my pen in hand."

Buster called again later. "Doubleheader, Judge! When the Laurens County sheriff went looking for Redmond, he found Howell, too—the other one we've been looking for. They've been living together. The sheriff pulled them both in, and my man is on his way to pick them up. Will you stand by to come down when they get here, to hold a bond hearing?"

"It will be my pleasure. I'm still trying to figure out, though, why Starr took Robin's truck instead of Wylie's for her trip. He says he offered to lend it to her, and Missy says Starr would never have taken a truck with an automatic transmission."

"You know Joe Riddley wants you to stay out of this."

"I am out of it. I'm just mulling it over. Haven't even left my seat."

"Don't, until I call you."

I didn't need to leave my seat to find out how similar Robin's truck had been to Wylie's. A couple of well-placed phone calls elicited the information that Starr had moved out of her daddy's house with a three-year-old Chevy truck, which she had sold for cash a few weeks later. That could have bought a lot of drugs. She'd gotten a decrepit Toyota pickup soon after she sold the Chevy, but after they found her body, the Toyota had been found in front of her apartment with two slashed tires. Apparently Robin's truck and Wylie's were the same make, model, and color, but Wylie's was three years older, with a standard transmission. Starr would never have mistaken one for the other. Women around here know trucks like New York women know Prada. So had she deliberately taken Robin's as one more dig at a woman she disliked? Or had the two guys that Missy's Uncle Jacob saw over there that day taken the truck? And how had they or Starr gotten the keys? Had Robin left them in the truck?

I called her and asked.

"Yeah," she said in a puzzled tone, obviously wondering why I was asking. Since I hadn't come up with a good excuse, I hadn't bothered to use one. Instead, I'd asked her straight out. "We all leave our keys under the seat when we're working. It makes it easier to move vehicles if somebody needs to bring in a large animal. Whoever is at the best stopping place goes out and moves them all. We've never had any problems except that one time."

I tried to put the rest of Starr's afternoon in some kind of order, but couldn't—not so it made sense. If she was going to Augusta, she didn't need to head back to town or use the bypass. There was a shorter way to I-20 from Trevor's house. So when and where did she meet up with the men who killed her? Was it the afternoon she took the truck? If not, why hadn't she gone to her meeting? Where was she from Monday until she was killed? Had she been down in Dublin, where Redmond and Howell lived? Or were those guys dealing drugs somewhere in Hope County? Why did they dispose of her over the side of our bypass?

When I saw Joe Riddley's shape looming outside our door, I quickly turned back to my computer screen. I wasn't investigating, I reminded myself. I was simply mulling things over.

Buster called around eight, and I went to the detention center to confront two of the sorriest specimens of humanity it has ever been my misfortune to meet. To look at them, you'd have thought Georgia's water shortage was desperate. Their nails were rimmed in black. Their hands were grimy.

The parts of their faces not covered in pimples were dingy with a greasy sheen. The odor rising from their clothes was so pungent I almost suggested we move the hearing outdoors. Slick was twenty and Roddy nineteen. I grieved to think how few years it had been since each had left the hospital as a clean pink baby.

Detention center hearings were held behind a U-shaped counter in the foyer of the building. After I was appointed magistrate, the county had ordered a box for me to stand on when I had a hearing down at the detention center because that counter had been built to accommodate Joe Riddley, who was over six feet, and our chief magistrate, who was six-three. Often, though, I dispensed with the box and came out from behind the bench. Most times I didn't even bother to put on my robe. I am pretty informal as judges go.

That evening I put on my robes, climbed up on my box, and peered down at the defendants. "Stand and state your full names for the record, please."

They slouched to their feet, the crotches of their jeans hanging to their knees. "Pull up your pants," I snapped, "and stand erect in this courtroom." I didn't feel the least bit lenient. I kept seeing those two swinging a baseball bat hard enough to break a young woman's bones and kill her.

Slick sniggered, probably having only one context for the term *erect*.

Roddy looked around, puzzled. With the bench in the middle of the front hall, he apparently hadn't realized he was in court, or that court, like church, is not so much a matter of place as a state of mind and the right personnel.

I glared down at Slick. "If you laugh again, you will be in contempt of court. Do you understand me?"

He sobered up enough to give me a sullen nod. The deputy blinked. The sheriff coughed to cover his smile at how tough the magistrate had gotten all of a sudden.

Roddy looked at the floor while Sheriff Gibbons advised them of their rights and read the charges against them. Slick looked straight ahead without a flicker of emotion on his face. I thought that odd, since the evidence was stronger against him. Roddy had left his prints on Starr's body and shoes, but Slick had left the prints on the bat.

Because this was a murder charge, I couldn't have set bond if I had wanted to. I advised them that a letter would be sent to the superior court and a judge would come down to hold a bond hearing at a later date. Everybody in that courtroom knew the superior court would deny it. There was no way a judge was going to let those two loose on the world. Even if they didn't manage to beat up somebody else before they came to trial, they might meet up with Wylie or Trevor and get themselves killed.

Slick gave me a contemptuous look as I sent them back to the cells, but Roddy looked at the ground as he shuffled after the deputy. "Be sure they bathe before bed," I called after them. Roddy's head jerked around. Slick gave no sign he heard.

After I took off my robe, I borrowed the sheriff's private restroom to wash my hands. "I feel like we ought to disinfect the whole place," I said with a shudder when I returned to his office.

"Scum," he replied. "Absolute scum."

"Have they given any reason for what they are alleged to have done?"

"Slick denies it completely. Roddy won't say a word, not even to his lawyer."

"Slick seemed amazingly cool. Did you tell them what evidence you have against them?"

"Not yet. They got here right before you did, and I decided to leave that up to their attorneys. I frankly don't want to have more to do with either one of them than I have to."

I sighed. "I hope Trevor doesn't attend the trial. The sight of those two could break his heart again."

I wish I could report that Nancy Jensen got elected mayor the following day. Instead, a man who had declared at the last minute, the manager of a video store down near the Bi-Lo, beat her by a narrow margin—primarily because he was a man.

Without the election to talk about, Hubert stopped coming over. For two weeks, Evelyn drooped around the store like wash that's been left in the rain. She didn't even color her hair. Gradually it began to turn the color of a rusted tin roof—gray with streaks of muddy brown.

"You're gonna scare off what few customers we have if you don't perk up a bit," I told her the Monday before Thanksgiving. "Call Phyllis and see if she can take you this afternoon. Tell her I said to make you beautiful. Get your nails done while you're at it, then call Hubert and invite him to dinner tonight. He loves home-cooked meals."

She cut her eyes my way and turned bright pink. "I couldn't! What if he wouldn't come? I'd feel like a fool."

"Make beef stew and I promise you he'll come. Now go call Phyllis, and if she has an opening, take the rest of the afternoon off. If we get a sudden throng, I'll draft Joe Riddley to work the register."

The next day Evelyn came in with a really nice haircut, her hair the color of autumn leaves, perky polish on her nails, and a glow on her face.

"I take it Hubert came to dinner." I was dying for details, but determined not to beg. "How did it go?"

She gave a shrug and turned away. "Okay."

"I see that blush. Did he invite you to eat Thanksgiving dinner with him and Gusta?"

"No." She let my heart go down a few notches before she added, "I'm going to eat with some folks from my church, Hubert is eating with Selena and Maynard, and Miss Gusta is going over to Meriwether and Jed's. Friday evening, though, he's bringing barbecue over and we're gonna watch the game."

I trotted back to my office, planning what I'd get them for a wedding present.

⸰ 14 ⸰

Martha called to say she had invited Trevor and Bradley and Robin Parker and her girls to share Thanksgiving dinner with us.

"Would you consider inviting the Spences, too? I've been wanting Robin to meet some people her own age, and Maynard and Selena are close."

Thanksgiving in our family has always been a holiday when we put all the leaves in the table and invite anybody we think would enjoy coming.

"That would be good. Selena already knows Bradley. He was in the hospital last summer with a broken arm, and she took care of him."

That must explain why she and Maynard had gone to Trevor's after Starr died.

Martha was still talking. ". . . not sure how I'm going to do the tables this year. You heard, didn't you, that Walker and Cindy are going up to her parents' for dinner? That means we won't have their big kids to ride herd on the little ones, and with Robin and Trevor, that will make four kids under five. I can't let them eat in the kitchen by themselves."

"And Ridd would have a fit if you suggested that Bethany eat out there."

"You got that right. He's already complaining that she'll

only be home four days. Besides, she's bringing a friend with her."

"I'll make the supreme sacrifice. I'll send Joe Riddley to eat with the kids."

I could hear Martha counting. "That works. We can fit ten at the table if folks get close."

We drifted into a discussion of Bethany's friend and from there to a discussion of food. As I hung up, I couldn't help thinking how nice it was that my children had gotten to be the grown-ups and all I had to do was show up with a few dishes.

Thanksgiving Day the temperature soared to seventy-two and the sky was a clear, deep blue that seemed to go all the way to heaven. I was delighted. That meant we could sit out on the porch after dinner.

We arrived, later than we had planned, to discover a minor problem. Bethany had showed up with two friends, having found somebody else who wasn't going anywhere for the holiday and continued the family tradition of inviting her along. "I'll need one more grown-up to eat with the children," Martha told me, thinking we were speaking privately.

There is no such thing as privacy with four small people around. I had opened my mouth to unwillingly volunteer when Bradley announced, "I want Miss Selena at my table."

"Miss Selena! Miss Selena!" Natalie chanted, jumping up and down.

Anna Emily joined in. She'd been clinging to Selena's hand ever since we got there, but I hadn't paid much attention until then.

"You sure made a new friend fast," I joked, hoping she'd accept the invitation.

Joe Riddley clapped Maynard on the shoulder. "Why don't you come, too, to help us ride herd on these cowboys and Indians?"

Maynard looked startled. He'd had little experience of being a child, much less taking care of them. He'd been too young for our boys to play with, and while he was growing up, we had no other children down our road and his mama tended to keep him home helping her rather than encouraging him to join other children's activities. After his initial hesitation, however, he said with a show of enthusiasm, "That will be fun." He did enjoy Joe Riddley, so I hoped his meal wouldn't be a total waste.

From the giggles and squeals we kept hearing, the children's table had a better time than ours.

I cannot say that the adult table was a success. Robin had put on her denim skirt and dark navy shirt in honor of the occasion, but she said no more than the turkey and kept looking toward the kitchen door and tightening her lips in a way I couldn't interpret. She left the table three times to check on her girls. Martha and I exchanged a look that said if Robin wasn't careful, she'd wind up as overprotective as Maynard's mother. We both felt that children deserve stretches of independence from their parents. How else will they learn to live in the world without us?

Trevor wasn't lively, either; in fact, he was sunk in gloom. And Hubert was downright testy about "being forced to close the doors on a perfectly good store."

If it hadn't been for Bethany and her two guests, we'd have had a pretty thin time. Fortunately, they were at that self-absorbed age when they presumed everybody wanted to hear about their lives, and they had lots of funny stories to tell about their first weeks at college.

After dinner, Bethany and her friends offered to clean the kitchen. Joe Riddley, Ridd, and Hubert went to watch football on TV. Robin, Maynard, and Selena stayed with Martha and me on the porch, and the children went out to play in the yard.

"Aren't the woods pretty?" Selena was holding her husband's hand, but addressing us all. "All gold and green. And look at that Bradford pear up by the road. It's green, gold, burgundy, and peach, all at once."

"My favorite is that dogwood." Maynard pointed to a

small tree covered in deep plum leaves. "I used to climb that thing."

"Joe Riddley planted it the year we moved into this house," I told them. Before we could continue our praise of the gorgeous day, Robin's girls came pelting back in terror.

"There's dogs!" Natalie made them sound like man-eating beasts.

"The big ones are penned and cannot get out," Martha assured her. "The only two in the yard are Me-Mama's beagle, Lulu, and Lulu's son, Cricket Dog. Both of them are very friendly. If they jump on you, say, 'Down,' and they'll obey."

"I want to stay with Mama," Natalie whined.

Anna Emily buried her face in her mother's skirt. "I doesn't like dogs."

"They eat you up," Natalie explained.

Martha gave a reassuring laugh. "Not those two. The worst they'd do is lick you some. Come on, let me introduce you." She held out a hand.

Natalie edged closer to Robin and Anna Emily clung to her mother. "No!"

Anybody could see that the girls were truly terrified.

I started to get up. "Let me put them in the pen. It will only take a minute."

"I'll do it," Maynard offered. The rest of the afternoon was punctuated by an indignant beagle duet.

Once the dogs were penned, Selena was able to persuade the girls to walk back outside with her and play with the others. Maynard stayed out, too. Anna Emily clung to Selena's hand for the rest of the afternoon, and several times I saw her give the barn and the dog pen an anxious look, but Natalie played happily with Bradley, Cricket, and Maynard. As I watched Maynard giving piggyback rides and pushing kids on the swing, I wondered if he was making up for his isolated childhood.

After a while, Bethany and her friends came out and joined Maynard and the children in throwing Frisbees and playing keep-away. I was delighted to hear children's voices echoing up and down our road again.

It wasn't long before Trevor left the men and joined us. As he sank into a wicker chair next to Robin, he muttered, "Can't seem to get interested in football these days." He seemed content to sit without talking, watching the children play and listening to us women chatting. Martha and I tried not to let on that he had cramped our style.

Anna Emily pitched a fit when her mother said she couldn't go home with Selena or stay with Cricket and his parents. Tears streaming down her cheeks, she held up her arms to Maynard. "I want to go home with *you*!"

Poor Maynard didn't know how to respond.

"She says that to everybody." Natalie clued him in. "Come on, Anna Emily. I'll race you to the car."

Obediently, Anna Emily turned and ran.

When the guests had gone, the dogs were let out of jail and Bethany took her friends over to visit with some of her high school buddies. Martha and I finished up a few last chores in the kitchen. "Do you think Trevor is interested in Robin?" I asked her. Martha is one of the wisest women I know.

"Not romantically. They treat each other more like father and daughter. Did you notice how he kept making sure she had what she needed, and how she told him a couple of times that he needed to eat? My guess is that Robin is becoming the daughter Trevor always wanted Starr to be—thoughtful, hardworking, clean of drugs. Maybe Trevor is a father figure Robin is lacking. She seems woefully short of family."

"She has a brother over near Tennille, but I've only seen him once. I think it could be good for both their kids to have something like a normal family, don't you?"

Martha didn't answer for such a long minute, I thought she hadn't heard me. Then she stood from putting bits of turkey into her cat's bowl. "If I didn't know better, I'd think Anna Emily had reactive attachment disorder. But that's something Starr's child ought to have had, not Robin's. If anything, Robin smothers those children. I never see them away from her."

"What's re—whatever it is?"

"Reactive attachment disorder? It's what happens to a child who fails to bond with somebody in the first couple of years. One of two things can happen. Either they don't bond with anybody, or they bond casually with everybody, like Anna Emily tends to do."

"Couldn't it be a habit, sort of testing the waters to see what she can get? Or a way of getting attention from her mother?"

"I hope so." Martha didn't sound convinced.

Around three the following Wednesday afternoon, Evelyn came in to say Gladys had everything under control out front and she was going home early because she and Hubert were going to Dublin to eat dinner and see a movie. I started thinking about them—whether they were really suited or whether she'd be borrowing trouble marrying a man that old with a tricky heart. Gradually it dawned on me that I wasn't going to get any work done with all that on my mind.

"I'm going down to Myrtle's for some pie," I informed Lulu. "Hold the fort."

Myrtle still made chocolate pie like my mama used to, rich and dark, with three-inch meringue. The kind of pie that is good for anything that ails you.

The beautiful weather we'd had for Thanksgiving had been blown away by a stiff, steady breeze that brought clouds in on Sunday and a chill on Monday that lingered. Winter was definitely coming. The wind wasn't what folks up north might call cold, but it was chilly enough for me to wrap my coat around me as I walked and decide to order coffee with my pie instead of iced tea.

When I entered the restaurant, I thought at first that I was the only person there. Midafternoon is Myrtle's dead time, especially when school is in session. I was delighted to spot Selena's bright head over in a far booth.

"You having a pie break, too?" I called as I walked across the restaurant.

The face she turned toward me was pink and wet with tears.

"Oh, honey! What's wrong?" I slid into the booth across from her and handed her a tissue from my purse.

She sniffed and dabbed her eyes, but she would need several tissues before that flood was mopped up. I pulled out a whole pack and set it on the table beside her black coffee. Before we could say another word, Myrtle called from the kitchen door, "You want your usual, Mac?"

"Yeah, and bring a piece for Selena, too."

Selena lifted a limp hand. "I don't need . . ." Then she dropped her hand, pulled out a fresh tissue, and held it to her nose as she fought back tears.

"You okay?" Myrtle asked as she set our pie and my coffee before us.

"We're fine." I waved her away after she'd heated up Selena's cup. Myrtle had a tendency to hover if she thought a good conversation was in progress.

I started to eat my pie. Selena would speak when she was good and ready.

I've heard you can tell a lot about a person by where she starts to eat her pie—from the tip or from the back. I don't know what it says about me, but when it comes to Myrtle's pie, I start with whichever part she has set down nearest my mouth. I had taken two good-sized bites before Selena poked a tentative fork into the point of hers. She took a tiny nibble, then another. Her third bite was of a decent size, her fourth rivaled one of my own.

We did not say a single word until our plates were scraped clean and our cups were empty. I slid out of the booth and went to the employees' door, which led to the kitchen and Myrtle's office. "Could we have some more coffee in here?"

Myrtle slouched out of her office and reached for the pot. "Aren't you going to complain about my floor today?"

"Nah, I'm gonna let somebody trip on one of those holes in the tile and sue your pants off. Hand me the coffeepot and go back to your smoke."

"I don't—"

"Don't lie to me. I can smell it from here. I don't mind you smoking. It's the lying I can't tolerate."

Before you think I'm hard on Myrtle, you need to know that we go way back. In first grade, she used to steal cookies my mama put in my lunchbox and replace them with little boxes of raisins her mama put in hers. That wouldn't have been a bad swap, except she told me after I'd been eating raisins for half a year that raisins were dead baby roaches. That set the tone for our lifelong relationship.

I carried the coffee back to our table, poured us each a fresh cup, and slid into my side of the booth. "I don't want to pry, but do you want to tell me about whatever has you watering the earth? Not that we can't use the moisture, mind you, but you are wasting it on those tissues. I've got some pansies that could use a drink."

Selena sniffed. "I'm okay now."

"You sure?"

She started to nod, then flung her arms down on the table and laid her head on them. "No! I'm not fine. I can't . . . I can't . . ." She gasped for air and got it out. "I can't have a baby! I've got endometriosis too bad." She started to bawl.

"Oh, honey!" There are no words sufficient for that tragedy in a woman's life. I let her sob. That whole time, I was informing the Boss upstairs that when I arrive in heaven, one of our first conversations is going to be about why foolish fourteen-year-olds can get pregnant and a married woman who would make a great mother can't.

When her sobs had slacked off, I asked, "Does Maynard know?"

She sniffed. "No. I just saw the doctor this afternoon. He

won't mind as much as I do, though. He's already said"—
she hiccupped—"he prefers an adult household."

I knew as well as she did that was because he was an only
child who had never been around children growing up. Maynard would make a terrific dad once he got used to the idea.

As if she had read my thoughts, Selena swiped her nose
with another tissue and wailed, "But he's so *good* with children. And they adore him. You saw him down at Ridd and
Martha's. All I wanted was one child who looked like him."
Her fountains gushed forth again.

It took nearly ten minutes before she took a deep breath
and sat erect. "I guess it wasn't meant to be." She didn't
sound resigned. She sounded as bleak as if somebody had
condemned her to a life in solitary confinement.

Which could have been how she felt.

Lots of things I could say flitted through my head, things
like "Lots of couples are happy without kids," or "Why
don't you all consider adopting?" None of them were appropriate at the moment. I winged a quick prayer for wisdom,
hoping I'd get an inspiration that would turn me into a good
counselor. Instead, the first thing that popped into my head
was that new apartment Maynard had been talking about.
Maybe it was as good a distraction as any.

"I hear you all are turning the upstairs of Gusta's house
into an apartment."

She nodded as she gave her nose a final wipe. "It got finished Saturday. Maynard thinks it will be good security to
have somebody living on the premises, and he doesn't need
the upstairs for display. It's lovely. Would you like to see it?"
She stuffed all the soggy tissues into her pocketbook and
gave me the first hopeful look I'd seen from her all afternoon.

I had half a dozen things I ought to be doing, but none of
them were all that important right that minute. I gathered up
my pocketbook. "I'd love to see what you've done with it."

She had her car, so we drove the short distance and
parked in the driveway of the big antebellum house with the
discreet sign out front: WAINWRIGHT HOUSE ANTIQUES. Gusta

had agreed to sell her home only if Maynard would use her name. He had kept the feel of the place as well. Bright pansies bordered the walk, and porch rockers invited you to sit a spell on a warmer afternoon.

"The first time I ever came to this house was nearly sixty years ago, for Gusta's bridesmaids' luncheon," I ruminated. "I was not quite six, and Gusta had asked me to be her flower girl. Mama was worried sick I'd spill something on my white organdy dress at the luncheon, but all I could think about was that I had on new ruffled panties and I was going to lunch in the castle where the princess lived."

Selena gave a watery laugh. "She sure grew up to be a queen. You ought to hear her when she stops by. Says she's coming 'to visit my old house,' but she's really coming to snoop. She tells Maynard how to display every item, and she even made him get rid of one set of dishes. Said they were trash and she didn't want them in *her* house."

"How does Maynard deal with that?"

"He adores her, and says she is almost always right."

As I followed Selena up the drive I'd used so often, I knew why Gusta kept coming back. Times change and age must make way for youth, but it is hard to turn a house you have loved over to other people. Martha's den furniture was much nicer than the old recliners Joe Riddley and I put up with, but I still missed our decor. What I missed most was being able to sit out on the wide screened porch after a hard day at work and let the peace of the countryside seep into my bones. What did Gusta miss most about her house? I would have to ask.

We climbed a new fire escape/entrance staircase on the side of the house and opened a new door where a hall window used to be. I couldn't remember ever being upstairs at Gusta's except once, when she was sick and I took her a potted cyclamen.

"He sealed off the front stairs with that wall." She pointed. I would never have guessed that the wide curved staircase was beyond the wall. "And he sealed off the back two bedrooms and the attic rooms to use for storage." She led me through a wide hall, where heart pine floorboards were polished to a gleam, to the front room where Gusta used to sleep, overlooking the courthouse square. The room had been pale gray, for Gusta was fond of gray, especially after her hair went silver. Now it was a soft butter yellow.

"This will be the living room, with the dining room behind it. See? Maynard had a door opened up that used to be there anyway."

"I like the color you used. It brightens the place up considerably."

She led me to what used to be a storeroom at the back. "This is the kitchen."

It wasn't large, but seemed larger because it had white appliances, white cabinets, and a white floor. "I like a white kitchen," said Selena-the-nurse. "If it's dirty, I want to know it. The tenants can put up curtains and accessories in whatever color they like."

Across the hall were a large front bedroom with a full bath and a smaller bedroom with a shower-only bath.

"That's it." Selena concluded the tour. "I hope somebody is going to want it."

"Folks will be beating down your door to rent it. Are you sure Hubert couldn't live here?"

Even as Selena shook her head, I knew it wouldn't work. Hubert could never climb all those stairs, and he'd already paid to put an elevator in Pooh's house as his "entrance fee." I doubted he'd pay again to put one in Maynard's. Besides, as Maynard had pointed out, the two of them got along better when they weren't living in each other's pockets.

"You'll find somebody," I said again as we clumped downstairs. "Now, you go talk to Maynard. I need to get back to the office, and I'll walk. I need the exercise."

She gave me a quick hug. "Thanks. I'm glad you were there."

"Always at your service," I told her. "Especially for pie."

* * *

As I walked the short distance to the store, my mood was as somber as the scudding clouds overhead—and as fruitless. Just as they could not seem to bring us rain, I could not think of easy solutions for any of the problems my friends faced. I couldn't figure out how to help Selena in her sorrow, how to advise Otis and Lottie about getting out of their situation with Gusta and Hubert, how Trevor would ever emerge from his deep pool of bone-numbing grief, or what any of us would do with Hubert once he didn't have that store to go to every morning.

I walked along in such a deep funk that I didn't notice Robin and her girls until I heard Natalie's piping voice. "Anna Emily! Come on!"

On the sidewalk ahead, Robin and Natalie were heading toward their car, down the block. As usual, Natalie was prancing around, talking a mile a minute, while Anna Emily lagged behind. Robin was so busy listening to Natalie, she didn't notice that Anna Emily had paused at the doorway to an empty storefront that used to house a children's boutique.[7]

I saw the child look up at somebody in the doorway and speak, and I knew exactly what she was asking: "Can I go home with you?"

Not until Robin reached her car did she miss the child. "Anna Emily, get over here!" The child reluctantly followed the others to the car.

Robin smacked her sharply on the bottom before fastening her into her car seat, but I suspected it was going to take more than smacks on the bottom to cure Anna Emily of that habit.

By the time Robin drove away, I was abreast of the doorway. The man standing there looked familiar, but I couldn't identify him until I saw the photograph he was holding. He was staring after Robin's car with a bewildered look on his face.

[7]*Who Let That Killer in the House?*

"She asks everybody that," I said, greeting him. "The little girl. She has this habit of asking to go home with anybody she meets."

It took him a moment to register that I was speaking to him. "That was really weird."

He was thinner than he had been, and slightly unkempt. His face was so gaunt, and his skull showed clearly beneath the skin. His hair was growing out into a crop of curls. His clothes were crumpled, like he'd left them in the dryer too long. I wondered how much eating or sleeping he had been doing since I ran into him at the corner back in September, and whether he was running out of money to support his search.

The look in his eyes disturbed me enough that I looked around to make sure there were other folks on the sidewalk before I continued the conversation. Even knowing that the killers of Starr were behind bars didn't break a weeks-long habit of distrusting strange young men.

"Did you ever find your wife?" I gestured toward the photograph.

He looked down at it like he had forgotten he held it. His hand was shaking.

Impulsively, I caught his wrist. "You look like you need something to eat. Down that next side street is a great local restaurant, with the best chocolate pie in the world. Go get yourself something to fill your stomach, and tell Myrtle that Judge Yarbrough sent you. She'll put it on my tab."

"I'm not—" He started to protest, then nodded. "That would be great. Thanks."

He set off down the sidewalk at a rangy lope.

❧ 15 ❧

The whole town was edgy, knowing that the alleged murderers of Starr Knight were in the detention center. That was especially true after Slick went berserk and raised such a ruckus that he injured two guards. By nightfall, everyone knew he had been put into solitary confinement, but I'm sure a lot of folks slept uneasily, knowing he was breathing the same air they were.

The sheriff came by the next morning to tell me about it. "He jumped his attorney and would have throttled him if the guards hadn't intervened. As it was, he left one guard with a broken arm and one with a broken nose. It took five men to wrestle him down and get him into solitary. He fought them tooth and nail, and his vocabulary gave us all an education."

"What on earth set him off?"

"The bat. He didn't know we had it. Therefore, he thought the prosecutor didn't have any concrete evidence against him except somebody who might have seen him with Starr. From what he said—or shouted—Roddy was supposed to have gotten rid of it, and Roddy thought kudzu would do the trick. Could have, too, if Joe Riddley hadn't reminded me that the stuff is deciduous. Slick started yelling that he'd kill Roddy for that. He is now utterly out of control. We slammed him into solitary, but that hasn't settled it, not by a long shot. He yelled and screamed half the night. Our deputies are wary of him, the guards are scared to take him his food, and all the inmates are restless. Roddy was shaking so bad, the doctor gave him something to calm him down."

"Have you tried working on Roddy? Maybe he'll do a plea bargain and testify against Slick." As soon as I said that, I could hear Joe Riddley inside my head: *Don't tell the sheriff how to do his job, Little Bit.*

Fortunately, Buster is sometimes more lenient with me than my husband.

"We tried that, but Roddy isn't talking. Won't say a thing, either to us or, apparently, to his attorney. Just shrugs when he's asked a direct question. But I'll be glad when this trial is over. The detention center is beginning to feel like one of the lower circles of hell."

As soon as he left, I called Judge Stebley, our chief magistrate. We consulted; then he called up to Augusta and requested a speedy trial. When a slot opened up in the Superior Court calendar, the two of us pulled in a couple of favors and got the trial set for the third week of December. We needed to get that case over and those guys shipped out of town.

Business was slow enough that Evelyn and I left Gladys in charge and attended the proceedings.

Slick was shackled, cuffed, and heavily guarded, but if looks could have killed, we would all have been lying on the floor and poor Roddy would have been pulverized.

Roddy reminded me of a child: contrite, bewildered, and resigned to punishment. His main fear seemed to be of Slick.

Slick was like a cornered tiger, tensed and ready to pounce. It was clear he had never expected a case to be built against him. His primary response to concrete evidence was not remorse but rage.

Wylie disturbed the court as much as Slick did. He boohooed when the prosecutor introduced the photographs of Starr's body, and called Slick such filthy names that the judge threw him out.

Trevor sat like a man of stone. Evelyn whispered to me, "Everybody who knows him begged him not to come, but he shook us off like a horse shakes flies."

I had expected Robin to be there to support him, if nothing else. She did not appear. I tried to tell myself that maybe she was squeamish, that maybe somebody had to keep the business open, but a voice inside my head kept saying, *She ought to have come for Trevor, after all he's done for her.*

Then I discovered she was a subpoenaed witness for the defense. She took the stand nervously, spoke inaudibly, and never looked at the defendants, but she testified that the bat could have been in her truck when Starr took it. I reminded myself not to judge people until all the evidence is in, and then only in my courtroom, where rules are predetermined and clear.

Trevor sat up front, close enough to get a good look at every photograph and every scrap of evidence. Most of the time, he stared at the backs of those boys' heads so hard it was a wonder he didn't bore holes in their skulls.

That week's *Hopemore Statesman* reported, "At the end of each day, Trevor Knight rose and walked alone from the courtroom through a crowd that parted like the Red Sea to let him pass."

Proceedings were mercifully short. Neither of the defendants testified, and the only pieces of evidence introduced were photographs, the prints from the bat and Starr's body, and lab results that indicated the blood on the bat was Starr's, the prints were Slick's and Roddy's, and the bat fit Starr's wounds.

The verdict was predictable. As my son Walker phrased it, "Guilty as hell."

Roddy stiffened for an instant as the verdict was read; then his shoulders slumped.

Slick turned to his attorney and shouted a stream of profanities, the gist of which was, "What good are you? He said you'd get me off!" He lifted his cuffed arms and would have slammed the man if a guard hadn't stepped between them and held him.

The day of the sentencing, it finally rained. The courtroom was full of dripping umbrellas and pungent with the smell of wet coats.

The judge asked Trevor if he had anything to say before he sentenced them.

Trevor walked heavily up to the witness chair, but when he got there he simply sat for a long time, looking at each boy. Roddy looked down at his hands and shuffled his feet. Slick lifted his chin and glared.

Trevor heaved a sigh. "You don't deserve to live and you don't deserve to die before you've lived long enough to realize what you've done. I hope you both experience some regret, but neither your regret nor anything they do to you will ease my pain." He turned to the judge. "Whatever you decide is fine with me."

He lumbered out of the courtroom, his shoulders hunched, his beard resting on his chest. Not one soul spoke to him. It would have been a gross impertinence to interfere with such cataclysmic grief.

By then the rain was coming down in slanting silver lines. I heard more than one person claim that the heavens were weeping for Trevor. Knowing what I do of God, I suspected the heavens were also weeping for Starr and those two young men. Every child starts out with the possibility of a brighter future than the ones they had chosen.

Because no evidence was presented to show premeditation—their attorney had done his best for them, in spite of Slick, and had produced Robin's testimony to indicate that the bat could have been readily available and used in a fit of anger—the defendants got life in prison. Slick got no possibility of parole. Roddy could get out in fifteen years or so if he behaved.

Some thought that was better than either of them

deserved, but Slick raised his cuffed hands and lunged at Roddy. "I'll kill you! So help me, if it is the last thing I ever do, I will kill you!"

It took three guards to wrestle him down. Not a soul doubted he was serious, especially Roddy. The judge recommended that the two of them be sent to different facilities.

However, as usual, Georgia penitentiaries were crowded. Hope County was informed we'd have to retain the prisoners for a number of weeks.

Hopemore looked forward to Christmas with mixed feelings—nervousness that the two killers were still in our community, but a sigh of relief that the nightmare was over.

Unfortunately, it wasn't.

᪥ 16 ᪥

In the new year, our recent troubles were temporarily eclipsed by a momentous event: The Georgia Taxidermist Association was fixing to hold its annual winter convention in Hopemore. It wouldn't be until the end of February, but starting in January, the whole populace was being urged by our chamber of commerce to "Make Hopemore the Best It Can Be!"

Elementary school children contributed bulletin board art to the Bi-Lo and the library. Middle schoolers formed teams to pick up litter around town each week. Senior high service clubs came around to downtown merchants offering to wash plate-glass windows or do touch-up exterior painting in return for a donation to their latest cause. The garden club pruned and weeded public areas and planted pansies in new urns up and down Oglethorpe Street and around the courthouse square. Joe Riddley and I donated the urns; then the Garden Club bought the pansies from the superstore. The new president had the nerve to call and say, "We knew you wouldn't mind, since we could get them a few cents cheaper per pot."

As far as I could tell, the only people not out making Hopemore better were members of the chamber of commerce and the city council. You couldn't really blame them.

This was the first statewide convention to be held in our
new community center, and our city fathers had worked
hard to make that happen. First they'd had to convince tax-
payers we needed a big community center more than we
needed better schools or better housing for our poorer citizens. That took more than two years, and involved a lot of
talking, eating, and drinking. Then they'd had to convince
the state taxidermist association that Hopemore could provide the same amenities as Macon or Tifton, where they'd
held conventions before. That had also involved a lot of
talking, eating, and drinking. By now, the officers of the
town were exhausted.

"They lied to the GTA," I pointed out to Joe Riddley at
breakfast one morning. "We aren't anywhere in the same
league as Macon or Tifton. We have one motel, two bed-
and-breakfast places, and two motels up at I-20. And we
only have three restaurants."

"Four, since the Waffle House opened up."

"Even so, with that many people looking for beds and
meals, the place is going to be a madhouse. We can't come
close to accommodating a crowd."

Joe Riddley sipped his coffee and mulled that over.
"We'll learn how the Romans felt when they got overrun by
the Goths and Vandals. At least the motel is decent."

That was one thing we had to give the city fathers credit
for. The Magnolia Inn used to be charming—an old-
fashioned place painted white with three stories, deep balconies with rocking chairs in front of all the rooms, and
thick white columns holding up the balconies. Live oak
trees shaded it, and its dining room was the best place in
town for elegant dinners. However, once I-20 opened up
and tourists stopped coming through Hopemore, the inn
had deteriorated badly. In recent years, it had become little
more than a magnet for vagrants and rats. Once the community center was in the works, however, the city powers-that-
be used that as leverage to persuade a national chain to buy
the motel and upgrade it. The work had been finished in

November, and it sat out on the federal highway in newly refurbished splendor.

Lest you think I am telling you more about a motel than you want to know, bear in mind that it plays an important part in this story.

With the community center completed, the motel fancied up, a superstore on the outskirts of town, and a new four-lane road up to I-20—providing access to two more motels—our civic leaders were boasting that Hopemore's tourist tide was about to turn. Their heads were so big at the moment, their necks could hardly bear the weight.

They managed to overlook all the empty stores along Oglethorpe Street, and produced blank stares when I pointed out that most of the profits from those tourist hoards were unlikely to flow into Hopemore pockets. After all, the superstore, the motel, and two of our four restaurants were not locally owned. The primary source of income for Hopemore was going to be the fee that the conference paid for using the community center, and all that money would have to go toward the center's enormous mortgage. The rest of our income would come in the form of whatever money visitors spent on meals and tips at Myrtle's and Casa Mas Esperanza, our Mexican restaurant. Since neither Myrtle nor Humberto Garcia was likely to raise wages for the weekend, I figured the primary benefit Hopemore would reap from the convention was that Myrtle would extend her annual five-day cruise to seven.

Have you ever wondered how much better off our society would be if decision makers were all required to take one class in basic accounting?

The main topic of conversation in town was not the convention but two new elevators the motel had installed. Except for the one Hubert had added to Pooh's house, those were the first elevators Hopemore had ever had—or needed. They had been built into new towers at each end of the front balconies, and a hexagonal cupola decorated each tower. From the way people carried on about those elevators, you could have deduced they were the eighth wonder of the world.

"No more lugging bags up two flights of stairs," Hubert boasted, making me wonder when and why he had ever stayed there to suffer that experience.

As far as I was concerned, the best thing about the upcoming convention was that it had persuaded Myrtle to replace her floor. In fact, perhaps envisioning the world beating a path to her door, she had elected to spruce up her whole establishment. She closed down in January and covered her plate-glass windows with brown paper so nobody could peek. She reopened two weeks later with black vinyl booths, red Formica tabletops, a black-and-white-checked vinyl floor, and red-checked curtains at the windows. When she handed me one of her new red-bound menus, I saw that the price of everything, especially chocolate pie, had gone up. One thing that wasn't going to be in the red around the place was Myrtle's bank account.

Everybody else fixed up a bit, too—even us, although I doubted that many taxidermists were going to stop by Yarbrough's to buy seeds or fertilizer. Still, we were selling a lot of plants and potted flowers to decorate the center during the event, so washing our windows and setting up pretty displays seemed the least we could do.

I noticed Evelyn humming while she worked one afternoon. "You still seeing Hubert?" I teased.

She turned as red as the poinsettia she was putting in our half-price sale. "I've been meaning to talk to you about that."

"You don't need my permission, honey. I was his neighbor, not his mother."

She huffed. "Not about seeing him. It's—well, he wants to go down to New Orleans for Mardi Gras and wants me to go with him. Could I have time off? I've always wanted to see it."

I couldn't say a word to save my soul. The notion of two people as straitlaced as Evelyn and Hubert partying their way through a New Orleans Mardi Gras plumb cooked my bacon.

She misunderstood my silence. "I know I already used last year's vacation, and we aren't far enough along yet in this year for me to have accrued much—"

"It's not the time off, hon. You deserve it. You haven't had a real vacation in all the years you've worked for us. Just a night or two at a bed-and-breakfast somewhere and the rest of the time catching up at home."

"I love bed-and-breakfast places, but I'd love to go to Mardi Gras, too."

Mardi Gras with Hubert wasn't the way I'd choose to spend my vacation, but I told her, "If it tickles your gizzard, go right ahead. Take all the time you want. How long were you all planning on being gone?"

"A week, from Thursday until Wednesday." She was blushing so bright I could have turned off the lights. "The problem is, that's the same weekend the taxidermists are coming."

"We'll survive without you. You take all the time your heart desires. Just don't let Hubert break it."

"He won't. If I've learned anything in the years since I've been alone, it's how to take care of myself."

Still, the woman skipped as she headed to the phone. Then she turned her back and lowered her voice while she talked, so I didn't hear a word she said.

Next thing we knew she was waving airplane tickets around, boasting about the great bargains she'd gotten on clothes, and reading travel books from the library over her lunch hour. You'd have thought she was heading to China.

Of course, I was so green with envy that somebody could have stuck me in a pot and sold me. I'd been trying to get Joe Riddley to take me somewhere exciting for years, and the idea that stick-in-the-mud Hubert was going instead galled me no end.

They left on an incredible Thursday. The landscape was a symphony of gold, brown, and green. The sky was clear

and blue. Daffodils were up and fattening for blossom.
Hellebores were creating a show of cream and mauve bells.
The breeze held only a slight reminder of winter. Robins
were thick on the ground.

Evelyn looked downright pretty in a new tailored green
suit. Phyllis had persuaded her to get a short haircut that
tamed her unruly locks and flattered her face, and had used
a color on it that brought out the tawny color of her eyes. If
I hadn't known better, the way she was glowing, I'd have
thought the woman was going on her honeymoon.

With its usual winter capriciousness, the temperature
plunged overnight from the midseventies to forty. A drizzle
descended. My breath rose like smoke, and a damp chill assaulted my face when I stepped out Friday morning to get
the paper. I paused to take a deep breath of the daphnes I'd
planted by the walk, for the clusters of tiny pink trumpets
were sending out an odor so sweet it was cloying. I wished
I could dilute it and spread it all over town. Birds called back
and forth, gossiping about the rain and the temperature,
while moisture fell from the trees in a constant *drip, drip,
drip.*

The mercury continued to plummet. By noon, the thermometer outside our window read thirty-three. "You reckon
the roads will ice?" I asked Joe Riddley as we prepared to go
home for our midday dinner.

"This is as cold as it's supposed to get." He shrugged into
a parka, wrapped a scarf around his neck, and pulled gloves
from his pocket. His joints stiffened if he didn't bundle up.

"We won't do any business this afternoon," I predicted.

When we came back from dinner, we saw a swarm of
taxidermists buzzing around the community center, but sure
enough, our store was as dull as an abandoned hive. Around
three, I looked up and grumbled, "Anybody with a lick of
sense is holed up by the fire with a good book."

Joe Riddley put down his catalog. "You wanna mosey
down and look at the convention exhibits?"

"Are we allowed?"

"Trevor said the exhibits are open to the public. He offered to show us around."

"He decided to go after all?"

"I understand that both he and Robin have entered pieces in competition."

I reached for my pocketbook. "So why are we hanging around here?"

"Thank you very much," Bo squawked from the curtain rod.

"Not you, buddy." Joe Riddley stroked the scarlet breast with one forefinger. "I'd be afraid somebody might decide to stuff and mount you." He lifted the macaw and set him on his desk, then littered the surface with nuts and seeds from a tin in his bottom drawer.

I couldn't help remembering what Evelyn had said about how Trevor looked at her dogs. "Not you, either," I told Lulu, who was already at the door. "Stay."

She gave a yip of disappointment, but returned to her pillow.

It seemed odd to see folks wandering around the exhibit hall in coats, but one thing the architect hadn't put into the center was a coatroom, since we so seldom wear coats. Some folks carried them over their arms, while others—like me—wore them and sweltered. I saw several women in fur and fake fur. I hoped they wouldn't get confused with the exhibits.

Having seen Trevor's shop, I thought I was prepared for a taxidermy convention, but I had no idea of the incredible things people could do to bring dead animals to life. At first I was put off by all that killing, but one earnest woman assured me, "A large percentage of the animals were killed for meat, and most of the others were struck down by disease or automobiles." I chose to believe her.

The largest space at the community center—the big room we used for things like the Golf Club dance—was filled with entries in various categories of competition: birds, fish, game heads, and complete animals in habitat tableaux. We saw a wolf that looked so real I expected him to leap at me any minute, and a hawk that surely would swoop after a rabbit when the sun went down. Heads of elk, deer, longhorn sheep, and even one African gazelle stared down from the walls. The most amazing exhibit to me was a mother bear with her cub. I heard that both had been found dead in the woods. They would spend the next several decades behind a silk bush, poking around a plastic log after artificial bugs.

Trevor seemed to know everybody there. He was constantly having to stop and greet somebody, answer a question about the conference schedule, or assure them that he'd be repeating his workshop the next morning. Only people who knew him well would know he was subdued.

During one of those conversations, Joe Riddley and I spoke to Selena and Maynard, who were also browsing the exhibits. "Heard from your daddy?" I asked.

Maynard grinned. "Nope, and don't expect to. That old dog!"

We ran into Gusta, too, with Otis at her elbow. When she stepped aside to examine a scene depicting two ducks, I asked him privately, "Any idea yet what you all are going to do?"

"I'm waiting on the Lord, Judge. All I can do is wait on the Lord."

I reminded the Lord that Otis didn't have many earthly years left to wait.

Trevor took his time in leading us around to Robin's fox with the rabbit, and the fawn he'd mounted for Starr, in its glass case. Both sported first-place ribbons. When I commented on that, he jerked his head toward the fish display across the exhibit hall. "Didn't do so well with Farrell's bass, though. I entered the dang thing to get him off my back, but it only took a third. I was a bit off my stride when I painted it."

"You were preoccupied that day with showing me around."

"And other things." He rested his hand on the glass case. "I'm glad I decided to show this, though. I think Starr would have liked for folks to see it. She loved fawns."

I was glad to hear him getting to the place where he could speak her name naturally. That was definite progress.

Now that I thought about it, in the past several weeks, Trevor had seemed more at peace than he had since her death. Maybe Farrell had been right, for once. Maybe entering the competitions had been what Trevor needed to take his mind off his grief.

Entering the competition had not helped Wylie forget his grievance, however. He stormed up as we were looking at Robin's fox and snapped, "They didn't give me a thing on my buck."

Trevor nodded. "I noticed that. One of the judges mentioned that the antlers were a trifle askew."

I looked in the direction where they were both looking—at a buck hanging on an exhibit panel. Its antlers were jaunty, like it'd been out drinking with its buddies all night—or maybe that was Wylie, before he attached them back to the head.

"It's as good as the rest of them," Wylie protested. His eye lit on Robin's fox and its first-place ribbon. "It's certainly as good as that fox. I don't see what's so wonderful about that thing. Looks like something you'd put in a kid's room, doesn't it?"

He was asking me. I personally wouldn't put a stuffed animal in a child's room, but I couldn't think of a tactful way to say so in that crowd.

Joe Riddley rescued me. He clapped Wylie on the back and said, "You've just started, son. Nobody wins a prize their first year in the business. Give yourself time. Next year you may get a first."

"Well, I don't see what all the fuss is over Robin. She's not so all-fired great." But Wylie seemed a bit mollified as he wandered off in search of new ears for his complaints. Joe Riddley has always been good at smoothing folks down.

Trevor watched Wylie go with a frown of disgust. "He could be a fine taxidermist if he'd complain less about Robin's work and concentrate on his own, but he won't take instruction, gets touchy if you criticize a thing he does—he thinks he knows it all."

I'd seen that brand of arrogance before. My mama used to say, "Nobody is as stupid as somebody who won't say 'I don't know.'" I have found it's true in almost every realm of life.

"Where's Bradley this weekend?" Joe Riddley asked Trevor.

"Ridd and Martha offered to keep him for me both nights and tomorrow, so I can socialize a bit, and Robin took him and the girls over to Atlanta today, to see the aquarium. She only agreed to register for the convention and enter her fox if I wouldn't make her come. Crowds spook her."

"From the crowds we were in the only time we went to the aquarium, she's likely to come home more spooked than if she'd come to the convention," I informed him.

He laughed. "Could be."

Somebody else called his name and motioned for him to come over and join them.

"Go ahead," Joe Riddley urged. "If it's all right, we'll look around a little more."

"Stay as long as you like." With a farewell wave, Trevor strode through the crowd. Soon he was in the middle of a group of men who were laughing and carrying on. I was glad to see him joining in.

Joe Riddley wanted to amble around the adjacent room, where the manufacturing exhibitors were. I peered in and saw it was full of knives, animal forms, eyes, and other paraphernalia used by taxidermists in their work. "I think I'll go back and make one last trip around the exhibits," I told him. "Just to be sure I've seen them all."

As I got back to Robin's fox, a couple stood beside it in deep discussion. They looked younger than we were, but more life-worn. She was thin, with a lined face and anxious eyes. He was tall and gaunt, stoop-shouldered and gray, as if he carried a lot of burdens.

The woman's voice was low but hysterical. "Look at the eyes!"

"Now, Mother." The man put his hand on her arm, and she gave a quick, guilty look around the hall.

"Can you see a sign of a seam?" she demanded in a lower voice.

The man bent down to peer at the fox's back. "Nope. It's good work, I'll give you that. But before you get excited, let's see what we can find out."

I stepped up. "May I help you?" It seemed the hospitable thing to say.

"We are wondering about the man who entered this fox, Robin Parker," the man told me. "It's a fine job of taxidermy." He was trying to sound casual, but his voice wobbled. "Do you happen to know if he's from Georgia?"

"Robin is a woman," I informed him. "She lives and works right here in Hopemore."

They exchanged a look that might have spoken volumes if I'd known the language.

"Do you know her?" The woman eyes were fired up like those of a horse that knows it has to wait but is eager to bolt out of a gate. "We sure would like to meet her. She did a fine job on this."

"We'd be interested in buying, if she'd like to sell," the man added.

"I do know her, but she's not here today. That's her boss over there, the tall man with the—" I almost said "brown beard," but quickly amended it to "gray beard. He entered the fawn."

They threw the fawn a quick, polite look, but it was the fox that had their full attention. The woman's hand reached out to stroke it, but pulled back before she touched the fur. She was strung so tight, she almost strummed. The man put a hand on her shoulder. "Let's go talk to him, Mother." They made their way through the crowd.

They had scarcely left when a man stopped by the fox and bent down to get a better look. What I saw best was penny-bright curls. When he stood, he gave me a startled look. I'm sure mine was equally startled. Why was that young soldier still in the area? Was he expecting to find his wife at a taxidermy convention? Or was he genuinely interested in taxidermy? He seemed pretty knowledgeable about the fox. "You know who did this?" he asked forcefully, examining its back and tail.

"A local taxidermist. She's good, isn't she?"

He bent down and examined the fox again. "She sure is. This thing is mighty near perfect. You know where I could find her? I'd like to talk to her about buying it."

"You may have to stand in line. The couple over there"— I nodded toward them—"are asking her boss the same thing this very minute."

"Then I'd better get over there." He threaded his way through the crowd.

I had no idea whether Robin would sell the fox, but she'd never struck me as the sentimental type, and if I were a taxidermist, I'd be glad to sell to folks who got that excited over my work. I didn't know how much something a tableau like the fox and rabbit would bring, either, but if two bids were being offered, the price could go up. I hoped so. A single mom could generally use every penny she could get.

I had seen enough dead animals. I headed to the next room to find Joe Riddley. He was examining with great interest what might have looked like a polar bear if I hadn't known it was simply a bear form. "You thinking of ordering one of those?" I asked, staking my claim to the arm he used to reach for his wallet.

"Thought I'd give it to you for your birthday. We could put it in the front yard to entertain the neighbors."

"As is, or are you planning on getting him covered with brown bear fur?"

"I kinda like him like he is. Besides, it's tricky, getting hold of bear fur without riling the bear."

"Maybe we ought to comparison shop before we make a final decision on my present. We might find something I'd like even better, like diamond earrings or a cruise to Hong Kong."

He shook off my hand and reached for his wallet. "You wanting me to buy this thing right here and now? If not, don't start talking about cruises and diamonds."

"How about if I start talking about supper?" I pulled him toward the door. "We don't want to miss the buffet."

The Hopemore Country Club had a seafood buffet every Friday night, and we made a point of eating light at noon to save room for it. Our son Walker, the club's president that year, swore that a major topic at every board meeting was how much money they lost each week on Joe Riddley's capacity for seafood and my own for dessert. We didn't let him slow us down.

As we headed toward our car, I saw the young soldier hurrying out of the building, his color high and his strides long. Was he trying to beat the couple to Robin, to buy her fox? If so, he'd better hurry. They were already backing out of the parking lot.

⤳ 17 ⤔

Of what happened that dreadful evening, I have no firsthand knowledge. Here is how I reconstruct events from later conversations and the *Hopemore Statesman*:

Robin Parker and the children got back from Atlanta around six thirty, and she dropped Bradley off at Ridd's. She and the girls ate at Hardee's, and she took them home. She found a note on her door that would change her life.

She called her brother and left him a message to come keep her children; then she got the girls ready for bed and told them Uncle Billy would be there soon. She dressed, paying special attention to her clothes, and left sometime after eight.

Trevor Knight had been invited by friends to join them for dinner, but he had an out-of-town appointment late that afternoon. He suggested he drop by his friends' room after he got back and they could go out for drinks. Bridges were icy, so he drove slower than usual. Around nine, he pulled into the motel parking lot.

As he got out of his car, he saw Dan and Kaye Poynter, the couple who had earlier been asking about Robin Parker's fox. "We never expected to see our breath in central Georgia," Kaye said as a greeting.

They moseyed together toward the right-hand motel elevator.

"Every place in town was packed, so we drove out to the Candlelight Inn by the river," Kaye continued. "It's real nice, and the food was delicious."

"It is a nice place," Trevor agreed. "Did you ever find Robin, to ask if she'll sell her fox?"

Dan answered as he took Kaye's elbow to help her up the curb. "No. We went by her house on our way to dinner, but there was nobody home."

"She was probably late getting back from Atlanta, and most likely took the girls out to eat afterwards. She's not much on cooking after a long day."

"We thought we'd go freshen up a bit, and try again." Kaye's voice grew anxious. "You don't think it's too late, do you?"

Trevor checked his watch. "My guess is she's getting the girls to bed around now. Shall I call her and see—and tell her to expect you?" He pulled out his cell phone, but Kaye put out a hand to stop him.

"Don't bother. We'll drive out that way in a few minutes and see if she has any lights on. If not, we'll check again tomorrow."

At the elevator, Trevor stepped back to let them go first. Dan motioned for him to go ahead of them, but Trevor insisted. They were guests in town. Dan pressed the button and the door opened.

Inside, a woman lay on the floor, her head bent at an unnatural angle. She wore a brown mink coat. A mass of curls covered her face.

Dan and Trevor both stepped forward, but Dan reached her first. He dropped to his knees to check for a pulse. "He works with our local emergency management team," Kaye said, her eyes anxious. "He knows CPR."

The woman's coat hung open, revealing a red dress and a stunning figure. Trevor did not recognize her, but he could not see her face.

Dan looked up at the others. "She's dead." He climbed unsteadily to his feet and stepped back, his face pale.

Kaye darted into the elevator and brushed the hair back from the woman's face and neck. Blue eyes stared unseeing at the elevator ceiling. Before Trevor could remonstrate that they must not touch anything, she had flung herself across the soft fur coat. "It's Bobbie! Oh, Dan, it's Bobbie! Look at her neck! And that's the coat . . ."

Dan gave a moan, clutched at his chest, and crumpled to the pavement. Kaye fainted across the dead woman's torso.

Trevor, afraid someone would summon the elevator from above, stepped awkwardly over Dan and went far enough inside to rest his back against the door to keep it from closing while he punched in 911. It was while he waited for the operator to answer that he got his first good look at the dead woman's face. The light was dim and the face was bright with cosmetics, but she seemed familiar. He bent closer to get a better look.

It was Robin Parker.

An ambulance arrived and whisked Dan and Kaye both to the hospital. The sheriff came with flashing lights. The parking lot filled with motel guests and curiosity seekers. The only person Trevor remembered later was Wylie Quarles, standing over at one edge of the crowd.

Trevor felt queasy, but he stayed to answer questions as best as he could. After a while, he told the sheriff, "Look, I'm worried about Bradley. He's gone to Cricket Yarbrough's to spend the night and I want to be the one to tell him what's happened. He liked Robin, and after losing his mother, I don't want him to hear this from anybody but me."

The sheriff suspected Trevor needed Bradley more than Bradley needed his grandfather, but he nodded. "I think we've got all we need from you. I'm terribly sorry you had to find her."

Trevor's chest heaved with a sigh that made his beard tremble. "Me, too." He stumbled off toward his car.

The sheriff, not being a family man, didn't think about Robin's girls until past eleven, after he'd set in motion interviews with motel guests and staff, interviews with the Poynters at the hospital, and a detailed investigation of the crime scene. Only when one of his deputies asked, "Does she have any family we ought to notify?" did Sheriff Gibbons remember those girls.

He was in the process of going through her purse at the time, so he took her keys and asked a deputy to accompany him.

"That oversight will haunt me all my life," he would tell me later.

Trevor, too, would be sorry he hadn't given the two little girls a thought.

Robin lived in a small ranch house not far from Trevor's, far back from the road and built on a hill that sloped from front to back. The lot was surrounded on three sides by woods, and the nearest neighbors were quite some distance away. "Isolated for a single woman," the deputy remarked.

"But probably cheap," the sheriff pointed out.

The blinds were all down, but the house glowed with lights in several rooms. They went to the door and knocked loudly. Nobody came.

"It's the sheriff. Open up!"

The only sounds were a barking dog in the distance and the sound of an animal—perhaps a possum or a deer—working its way through the woods behind the house.

Buster knocked and called again. He hoped Robin had left so many lights on because she knew she'd be coming home late, and had taken her children to stay with a friend as Trevor had—although that would mean more work to locate them.

He was sticking Robin's key in her lock when he heard

a high little voice. "How do we know you're really the sheriff?"

"Look out the window. You'll see I have on my uniform."

He heard a scraping sound inside. The porch light came on. A thin white face peered through a gap in the venetian blinds. "It's him," she said. They heard a lock turn, then the knob. The door opened a crack.

The smaller sister stood inside the door, peering out at them. "Can I go home with you?" she asked Buster.

"Anna Emily, you know you are not supposed to ask that!" Exasperation oozed from every word as the older sister jerked the door wide open.

The two girls looked up at the sheriff and his deputy. Their hair was tousled and they wore flannel nightgowns. Both had tear tracks down their cheeks.

"Can you tell me your names?" the sheriff asked.

The big one took a breath of self-importance. "I am Natalie and this is Anna Emily. I am five and she is three."

"Who is here with you?" He squatted down to their eye level to ease their necks.

Anna Emily snuffled and reached for his hand. "Uncle Billy was supposed to come, but he never did. Can I go home with you?"

Natalie pushed her away and took charge of the explaining. "Uncle Billy probably got lost. Mama said he'd be here right after she left, but he didn't come. But Daddy angel protected us and we slept in Mama's bed."

"Maybe Mama's in my bed." Anna Emily turned toward the hall.

Buster reached out to stop her. "Your mother has had an accident." He spoke as gently as he knew how.

"Is she hurted?" Anna Emily demanded.

"Is she dead?" asked Natalie, her blue eyes anxious.

Buster nodded at Natalie. "I'm afraid so, honey."

Natalie's lower lip began to quiver. Tears filled her eyes. "She's not ever coming back? Just like Bradley's mommy?"

"I'm afraid so."

"Are we norphans?"

Anna Emily stepped up and repeated, "Can I go home with you?"

The older sister huffed. "Anna Emily, you know Mama said . . ." She stopped and looked at the sheriff with five-year-old shrewdness. "Are you funning us? 'Cause if you aren't, you better find Uncle Billy and find him quick. He's the only living kin we got. That's what Mama says."

"Do you know his last name?"

She put one hand on her hip. "I told you: Billy. His first name is Uncle and his last name is Billy."

"Is he Billy Parker?"

She looked uncertain, then shrugged.

The deputy spoke behind Buster. "Maybe she'll have his name written down somewhere."

The sheriff nodded, and addressed the children again. "We're going to look around here, trying to find your Uncle Billy's phone number. Do you know where your mother might have written it down?"

They shook their heads in unison.

Buster called the Division of Family and Children Services and asked them to pick the girls up. While they waited, he and the deputy searched the house. They found no address book, no telephone lists, and no numbers written inside the phone book. In fact, except for a few recent bills, Robin had no papers at all—no correspondence, no journals or diaries, not even a grocery list. She seemed to pay her bills in cash, for they did not find a checkbook. But they found no money, either. Finding Billy seemed impossible without a last name.

A DFCS worker arrived and took the girls to Ridd and Martha, who had agreed to take in foster kids that late at night. Buster went back to the scene of the crime.

The deputy to whom he had handed Robin's purse had news for him. "We found this." It was a scrawled note on the back of an envelope addressed to Captain Grady Handley in Augusta.

Robin?
Saw a fox today that I'd like to talk about. Staying in
room 307 at the motel. Give me a call. I'll be there
after supper.
Grady Handley

"Have you checked out his room?"

"Yessir. He registered for the whole weekend, but he's not there now and his bed has not been slept in."

The sheriff frowned down at the note. "Then maybe we'd better find out who and where he is."

⋟ 18 ⋞

Joe Riddley and I heard nothing about the murder until Saturday morning. We'd scarcely opened up when the sheriff dropped by the office. We were in the middle of a friendly but heated bicker about how much we ought to invest in perennials for the spring market, so I was glad to stop and welcome him. That would give Joe Riddley time to decide I was right.

Sheriff Gibbons sank wearily into our wing chair, dropped his hat on the floor, and rubbed his hands to warm them. "Not much warmer today than yesterday."

Lulu scooted across the floor on her belly so he could scratch behind her ears.

Bo flew down from the curtain rod and perched on his shoulder to give his ear a friendly nip. The sheriff flapped one hand. "Go away, bird."

"Not to worry." Bo flew once around the office and resumed his perch.

We swiveled our chairs to face the wing chair.

"You didn't come over here to discuss the weather," I remarked.

"And you look like something the cat dragged in and took back out," Joe Riddley added with what passes for tact between men who have been friends for sixty years. "Didn't you sleep good last night?"

"Didn't sleep at all, but it's on my to-do list." The sheriff let out a deep breath that he seemed to have been holding for a very long time. "You got any coffee?"

I fetched his usual mug—one with dancing penguins on it that Walker had brought back from Las Vegas—and while I was at it, poured out two more. Fighting with Joe Riddley uses up a lot of energy.

I waited until the sheriff had taken a restorative sip before I asked, "Why were you up all night?"

Joe Riddley spoke before he could answer. "Was it about whatever was going on over at the motel? I saw your lights in the parking lot on our way home from dinner. Little Bit was dozing, having consumed half the dessert buffet, but I saw you had every cruiser in the county there. Later, I had to pull over to let an ambulance pass."

I could have smacked him. "You never said a word to me about seeing the sheriff at the motel or pulling over for an ambulance."

The sheriff took another fortifying sip before he enlightened us. "Robin Parker got murdered. Somebody broke her neck. Trevor and two of the folks from the taxidermists' convention found her, around nine."

"Poor Trevor!"

That popped out before I thought. I was also sorry for Robin and her girls, of course, but Trevor was the one I knew best. "He's only begun to deal with Starr's death, and now this. It's enough to get his guardian angel fired." I took a gulp of coffee and scalded my tongue. "Ow!"

The sheriff grunted. "Trevor finding her was only one bad part of a terrible situation."

"What happened to the children?" Joe Riddley inquired.

"That was another bad part."

I suspected what he wasn't saying. "Were you the one who had to tell them?"

"Yeah."

"That must have been rough."

"About the roughest thing I ever had to face. I don't like bringing that kind of news to anybody, but to two girls! Then I had to call social services to come get them. They were home all by themselves. Can you believe it?"

"Not hardly. Robin was always very protective of those kids. I can't imagine her going off and leaving them alone."

"Well, they were. Said they were sleeping in their mother's bed. I think they had cried themselves to sleep. The older one, who can talk the ear off corn, said their uncle was supposed to come, but he never showed up."

We shared a few moments of silence while we contemplated children being left alone in a house at night. I still had a hard time believing Robin would have done that.

The sheriff spoke first. "I wish I could have found a name and address for the uncle, so they could have gone to him. I hate to think of those kids stuck in a foster home. But they didn't know his last name."

"We met him over at Trevor's after Starr was killed. What was his name?" I searched my mental Rolodex, but came up blank. "Do you remember, Joe Riddley? Robin introduced us."

"I don't remember that. Are you sure?"

Buster and I exchanged a look. Joe Riddley's memory had been erratic ever since he got shot. I hurried to take our minds off that. "Robin was in the store one day and mentioned to Evelyn that her brother lived down near Tennille. Maybe Trevor would know."

The sheriff shook his head. "Trevor claims he never heard of the man. Says Robin didn't list a next of kin on her employment forms, and told him she was an orphan with no living relatives. That's partly why he hired her, because he felt sorry for her."

"Besides the fact that she's a darned good taxidermist," I added, "but it's weird she didn't mention her brother."

"I'd sure like to locate him, for the kids' sake."

We seemed to have exhausted that subject, so I asked, "Do you know what she was doing at the motel?"

"Meeting somebody, we presume. We found a note in her pocketbook from a man saying he was staying in room three-oh-seven and wanted to talk with her about a fox. We're still looking for him. His bed wasn't slept in last night."

"Was she killed in his room?"

"No, she was killed where she was found, in the elevator. Like I said, Trevor and a couple from the convention discovered her. The couple had to be taken to emergency. He was the one who reached Robin first, and when he found out she was dead, he had a mild heart attack." The sheriff shifted in his chair in a way that made me suspect he wasn't telling us everything he knew about the man. "When he crumpled, his wife fainted, so Trevor called for help. He stayed to talk with us after they were taken to the hospital, but he was pretty shaken up, too."

"I can imagine. I think Robin was becoming like a daughter to him." I took another exploratory sip of coffee and found it was finally cool enough to drink.

Joe Riddley gave a derisive snort. "Daughter, my foot. She was a beautiful woman."

I stared at him. "Beautiful? She was plainer than dishwater."

"She had good bones and a good figure under those loose clothes she wore. She'd have been a looker if she'd fixed herself up a little."

You live with a man for over forty years and know him for nearly sixty, so you think you know exactly how he thinks. Then he comes out with something like that.

Buster chuckled at the look on my face. "She was a looker, last night. She was all dolled up in a mink coat—"

"Mink?" I was flabbergasted. Surely he had that wrong.

"The real McCoy, or so I understand. Under it she had on a sexy red dress, high heels, makeup, the whole shebang. I think somebody mentioned she had even curled her hair.

And you're right, old buddy, she was something else. Even Trevor didn't recognize her at first."

I cradled my mug to my chest. Except for my tingling tongue, I felt chilled. "That's weird. I don't recall ever seeing Robin in anything except jeans or a denim skirt. And that's not how a woman would dress to go discuss the sale of a fox."

Seeing their faces, I explained about the man at the taxidermy convention.

"Well, that's what she had on," Buster insisted. "We searched the place looking for her brother's contact information and hoping to find some clue to what had happened, and you're right that what she mostly had in her bedroom were jeans and T-shirts, but she had several fancy outfits, too. Her bedroom looked like a tornado had hit, or like she had tried on everything in her closet getting ready for a hot date. My hunch is that whoever he was got drunk and tried to get fresh, she pushed him away, and he reacted more violently than he intended. Maybe somebody will come in later today and confess."

I was still baffled. "A hot date isn't what I'd expect of Robin—any more than leaving her children alone. Are you positive it was her?"

Joe Riddley leaned over and grabbed my wrist. "Stay out of this. You hear me?"

Buster picked up his hat and stood. "You two can fight that out in private. I gotta get back to the office and fill out some paperwork. I just wanted to put you in the loop—and get some coffee. Sometime when you're down at the detention center, Judge, teach them how to make it, will you?"

He knew that would get my goat. I glared. "Not in your lifetime. I have the dignity of my office to preserve. Now, would you tell this old codger to let go of me?"

Joe Riddley dropped my wrist, but warned, "If you get Little Bit het up about this case, Sheriff, I'm gonna give her to you on permanent loan."

The sheriff settled his hat on his head. "Let's not get carried away now."

Joe Riddley reached for his cap as well. "I need to run down to the nursery. I'll walk you out."

At the door, the sheriff turned and gave me the look that always reminded me of a mournful bloodhound. "That littlest girl nearly broke my heart. She begged to go home with me. Can you believe that? Scared the socks off me. I thought I was gonna have me a daughter for a minute there."

"She'd beg to go home with anybody. Don't take it personally."

"Oh, shucks. I thought she found me cute."

19

For years it had been our custom to eat with Ridd's family on Saturday nights. When we lived in the big house, they came to us. We'd eat supper and swim in the summer, and we'd play dominoes or a board game during cooler months. Walker's family was invited, but seldom availed themselves of the invitation. Once Martha and Ridd moved to the big house and we moved into town, we reversed the process and Joe Riddley and I went down to eat with them. It wasn't fancy—hamburgers on the grill or a big pot of soup with sandwiches—but it kept us in touch, as busy as we all usually were.

That Saturday night it was too cold for Cricket to be playing outside like he often was when we arrived. Instead he was entertaining Bradley Knight and Robin's two girls in the kitchen. Natalie was paler than usual, her thin face pinched. Anna Emily walked around behind Martha holding on to the tail of her apron. As soon as she saw me, she let go of Martha and came over to cling to my pants. She peered up at me with those big chocolate eyes and asked the predictable question: "Can I come live with you?"

Natalie spoke sharply to her. "We have to live with Cricket now, because our mama has gone to heaven." She turned to me, her lower lip quivering. "I told them and told them to call Uncle Billy, but they don't know where he is, and I don't know how to find him, so we're gonna stay here until they can, but as soon as he comes, we'll go stay with him." She managed to say all that without pausing for breath. She took one quick gasp, as if afraid somebody else might get a word in, and added, "We were by ourselves, but Daddy angel kept us safe."

Martha made a shooing motion with her hands. "Cricket, take Bradley and the girls up to your room and let Me-Mama and me cook. We'll call you when supper's ready."

The smell of vegetable soup wafting across the big kitchen from a stockpot on the stove made my stomach rumble. Makings for grilled cheese sandwiches stood ready for assembly. I headed to the counter to begin putting the sandwiches together, for Martha and I had cooked together so often we didn't need to discuss what had to be done.

As soon as the children's feet could be heard in the upstairs hall, I said, "Buster told me DFCS had taken them to an emergency shelter, but I didn't know they came to you."

She gave a short, not-funny laugh. "Poor Ridd has had the weekend from hell. I had offered to keep Bradley all weekend so Trevor could attend the convention and go out with his buddies during the evenings, but the supervisor at the hospital who was supposed to fly in yesterday and be on duty last night got stuck in the Philadelphia airport because of that snowstorm up north, so I had to go in at seven. Robin was supposed to bring Bradley by six, but they didn't get back from Atlanta until I'd already had to leave, so Ridd had to feed both boys. They watched a video and he put them to bed, thinking he was done for the night. Instead, Trevor showed up at ten thirty wanting Bradley. Ridd said Trevor was shaking so badly he could hardly talk, and his voice woke Bradley, who heard him telling Ridd that Robin was dead. Bradley had hysterics in the upstairs hall, which woke Cricket. Trevor took Bradley home and Ridd spent nearly an hour trying to calm Cricket down. He finally rocked him until he fell asleep. All these mothers getting killed is really getting to Crick. He has scarcely let me out of his sight since I woke up this afternoon."

Martha shoved back her hair with both hands, then automatically moved to wash her hands with soap—the "nurse's reflex."

"Ridd finally got Cricket to bed about twelve, and at two o'clock the social worker called to ask if we could take the girls. Poor Ridd had to get up and dress to welcome two sad girls in their nightgowns. Since they are terrified of dogs, he had to put Cricket Dog in the pen with the yard dogs, which didn't thrill *him*, as you can imagine. He barked all night long—an accompaniment to Natalie, who cried all night."

"Oh, dear. We brought Lulu, so I guess she'll have to go in the pen, too. Good thing you don't have any close neighbors. We're likely to have an evening serenade."

Martha heaved an enormous sigh. "They assure us this is only a temporary placement, but I'm not sure I can stand listening to dogs barking and Natalie talking for another twenty-four hours. She goes on and on without stopping. Meanwhile, Anna Emily informs me at least five times an hour that she wants to live with us forever and ever, but you heard her when you came in. She'd go with anybody."

"I know. She even asked Buster if she could go live with him. Flustered him to death. So when did you get Bradley back?"

"Trevor brought him this morning on his way to the convention. I asked if he felt like going and he said he didn't, but he was supposed to lead a workshop and hated to let them down. Poor guy. Bradley said he heard his T-daddy crying all night long."

"You reckon he was falling in love with Robin?"

"Could be. But even if he just liked her as a friend, I don't know how he'll stand to lose her so soon after Starr."

I moved closer and spoke softly. "Do you know anything about the murder that I don't?"

"What do you already know?"

"Not much. Joe Riddley's got me on a leash so short I'm

about to strangle. If he wasn't interested in Ridd's new pig, he'd probably be standing at my shoulder right this minute. Quick, tell all. I know the couple who found her came to the emergency room."

"Let's sit down a minute. I don't want to talk too loud, in case little pitchers with big ears are hovering in the upstairs hall." She fetched two glasses of tea and we pulled up adjoining chairs to the big round table that had served generations of Yarbroughs.

"Remind me of the couple's names," I said to prime her pump.

"Dan and Kaye Poynter, from Virginia. He had to be admitted, and I got the story from Kaye while we were waiting to find him a room. She claims that Robin is their daughter."

Martha stopped to enjoy my reaction. She had sure let the steam out of my engine. I couldn't say a word.

"Kaye said they both recognized her, although they haven't seen her for seven years. Dan is a taxidermist in Virginia, and Robin—or Bobbie, as her mother calls her, because her real name was Roberta—used to work with her dad. Won blue ribbons from the time she was fourteen, her mother claims." Martha sighed. "That woman can talk your ear off—just like Natalie."

"Maybe it's hereditary."

"That's as good an explanation as any. Come to think of it, if they can prove they are related to Robin, they'll be her next of kin and the ones who ought to have the girls. But they're both so fragile, I don't see how they could handle those two. They're a handful." Her forehead creased with worry.

"You were telling me about Robin leaving home," I reminded her.

"Oh, yeah. Kaye said Robin had never had much in the way of emotions. She was cold to her parents all her life, and real headstrong. If they told her no, she'd keep arguing until she wore them down. If she couldn't wear them down, she'd sneak. Her senior year, she started going around with a man her parents despised. He was four or five years older than Robin and 'smarmy,' according to Kaye. Dan suspected he was dealing drugs, so they put their united foot down and told her to stop seeing him or they wouldn't send her to college. That week, Robin forged a check on her parents' money market account while they were at a church retreat. She emptied the account—which was supposed to be her college fund—and ran off with the man. She wrote a note so they wouldn't think she'd been abducted, but she stole her mother's mink coat and a lot of her daddy's taxidermy equipment, presumably so she'd have a way to support herself and her boyfriend. Dan called the police, but since the girl was eighteen, the police said she had a right to leave home. Unless they pressed charges for the coat, the tools, and the money, the police couldn't do anything. Dan refused, because he hoped Bobbie would contact them soon and he didn't want to utterly estrange her. However, they never heard from her again."

"And they just happened to run into her on the day she died?" That stretched the web of coincidence pretty thin.

"No, they've been looking for her ever since she disappeared. Because she took the tools, they figured she'd do taxidermy somewhere, so they have spent the past seven years visiting taxidermy conventions, hoping to find her or her work. Isn't that sad?"

"Very, but it doesn't prove Robin was their daughter. People change a lot in seven years. Maybe Robin simply resembled their daughter and they wanted to find their daughter so badly that they concluded Robin was her."

"No, they said she was wearing Kaye's mink coat. Dan had prepared the hides himself and ordered it made, so it's very distinctive. Besides, Robin—Bobbie—had a pattern of moles on her neck that formed a C. Kaye recognized it. They had already spotted a fox yesterday afternoon that they were sure she had done. Something about the expression on its face and a seam she'd sewn—I didn't understand all that. But they were absolutely positive it was her work."

"I met them! I sent them to talk to Trevor." The anxious woman and the gaunt, gray man.

"How odd. They said they'd already met him, which is why they recognized each other in the motel parking lot and walked in together. They didn't tell him why they wanted to talk to her, though. They merely told him they were interested in buying the fox and would like to talk to the person who had—what? Stuffed it? Mounted it?"

"Whatever. But they hadn't talked to Robin?"

"Kaye said Trevor gave them her address and her phone number, and they went by her house and called her a couple of times, but she never answered and her car wasn't there. They didn't like to leave a note, in case she ran away again, so they decided they'd go to dinner, run by the motel to brush their teeth, and try once more, hoping she'd be home by then. When they got to the motel parking lot, Trevor was getting out of his car, so they walked to the elevator with him. He stepped back to let them enter—'Such a gentleman,' Kaye said—so they saw Robin first. According to Kaye"—Martha sketched quotes with her fingers—" 'she was lying on the floor looking like she was asleep, with her hair curling all over her face.' "

"Can you believe Robin had curled her hair? Buster said she had on a lot of makeup, too, and a sexy red dress and heels. I find that hard to believe."

"Me, too. She usually looked like plain Jane personified."

"You reckon that was her disguise?"

"Must have been. Anyway, Kaye said Dan has had some Red Cross training, so he knelt down to see if the woman was okay. He figured out she was dead, and was just wondering why that coat looked so familiar when Kaye, claiming a mother's instinct, bent down and pushed the hair off her face and neck. When she saw the moles on the side of her throat, she knew it was their daughter. She told Dan, he had a mild myocardial infarction, and she fainted."

"Even if Robin was their daughter, doesn't a heart attack seem like a drastic reaction?"

"He's got a bad heart. He was fortunate the attack wasn't worse. Kaye wasn't much better, though. When they came in, she was so hysterical that we had to sedate her. Thank goodness Trevor was with them when they found her. As hard on him as it must have been, he was able to call EMS and the police, and he stuck around to talk to the sheriff while the Poynters were brought in to us."

I rested my chin on one palm. "I cannot imagine locating your daughter after all those years and finding her dead. Can you?"

"I can imagine it, but I hope I'll never have to experience it." Martha shoved back her chair and went to stir the soup. Her back was to me, but I had seen tears fill her eyes.

My own were stinging, even though Bethany had never given us a speck of trouble and was unlikely to turn up dead in an elevator wearing a red cocktail dress. I got up and started buttering more bread for the sandwiches.

Martha cleared her throat. "There's one good thing about having the girls here. Ridd hasn't mentioned Bethany all day. Anna Emily and Natalie seem to adore him, and he really is an old softie where little girls are concerned."

She reached for a tissue and dabbed her eyes. "I feel so sorry for Kaye and Dan, and sorry for Trevor, but Ridd and I are both worried about those girls. I don't think Kaye, Dan, or Trevor could raise them. Trevor's got his plate full with Bradley, and Kaye and Dan aren't strong enough. Those girls need lots of attention and security. Anna Emily could be seriously troubled."

"Maybe their uncle will come get them."

"Kaye said they had only one child."

"But I met their uncle at Trevor's the night we went over after Starr's death!"

Martha shook her head. "Whoever he was, he wasn't Robin's brother."

We reached the obvious conclusion at the same time.

Martha voiced it. "Do you suppose he's the boyfriend Robin ran away with?"

"That could explain why Natalie looks so much like him. But Anna Emily doesn't look like either one of them."

Martha had seen so much, she immediately jumped to the darkest conclusion. "You don't reckon they kidnapped her, do you? Or inherited her from a friend who was doing drugs and went to prison?"

"That could explain why she never bonded with Robin."

"But why weren't Robin and Billy living together? Why lie about their relationship?"

"Heaven knows—but I don't. Maybe he's got a wife somewhere else. I think we ought to tell Buster what we suspect, don't you?"

The sheriff didn't go so far as to congratulate us when I phoned him, but he admitted we could be right where Billy was concerned. "I'll see if the Poynters can recall the name of the man she ran away with."

"If she really was their daughter," I added.

"There's no doubt of that. We've sent for her high school dental records to confirm it, but the Poynters had her high school graduation picture, and it looked very like Robin as we found her."

"You knew that when you were talking to us this morning, didn't you? Why didn't you tell us?"

He chuckled. "Have to keep some things to myself. Thanks for the tip. I'll talk to the Poynters again tomorrow."

"Do you have any leads to the killer?"

"Not yet, except it was somebody strong. Whoever killed her broke her neck with his bare hands. We ought to be able to get prints from her skin, unless he wore gloves."

"Which almost everybody has been doing this weekend. Do you reckon—"

"No more questions. Joe Riddley made it very clear this morning that you are not to get involved with this case."

"All I was going to ask—"

Before I could finish, Martha spoke at my shoulder. "Let me talk to him a minute."

I handed over the receiver and stood there fuming. So help me, I was going to think of something dreadful to do to Joe Riddley in the next few days. He talked about me meddling, when all he seemed to do anymore was meddle in my life. I scarcely listened as Martha asked, "Is there any way I could go to the Parker house and get these girls some clothes? They arrived in nothing but their nightgowns. I've scrounged up some pants and sweatshirts of Cricket's for today, but they need something to wear to church tomorrow, and the social worker didn't bring any underwear."

She listened while he talked, then said, "Great, but I'll probably bring Mac instead. Ridd and Pop like their Saturday-night television. Thanks."

She was about to hang up when one of those flukes of memory occurred. I grabbed the phone. "Baxter. Robin introduced her brother as Billy Baxter. See if you can find him somewhere down near Tennille."

❧ 20 ❧

After supper, Cricket insisted that we all play a game of Go Fish, which was his current passion, and it was nearly eight when we finished. I offered to take the kids upstairs and put them to bed while Martha loaded the dishwasher. The men offered to retire to the den to watch television.

I supervised while the children put on pajamas (the boys) and nightgowns (the girls) and brushed their teeth; then we all gathered in Cricket's room—which had been his daddy's, when Ridd was small—for a story and prayers. The four of them perched on Cricket's bed and I sat on a chair beside the bed. I told the story of the three little pigs, which was all I could think of at the moment, and Bradley and Cricket said prayers. Natalie and Anna Emily seemed baffled by that process.

Cricket concluded his, "And dear God, let Me-Mama find the bad man who killed Natalie and Anna Emily's mama. Amen."

He opened his eyes and cut them my way. "You are looking for him, aren't you?"

I shook my head. "Not this time, honey. Pop has told me not to do that anymore."

"You have to! I promised you'd find him. I told them

you're the best detective in the whole world, and that you find bad guys fast."

"The man who killed my mommy was real bad," Natalie assured me.

"Just like the one who killed my mommy," Bradley said soberly.

Cricket bounced on the bed for emphasis. "There's lots and lots of bad guys. They could huff and puff and blow this house down and kill us all!"

The four of them huddled together. Four sets of eyes regarded me with terror and expectation.

"You could look a little," Cricket wheedled. "Before *everybody's* mama gets killed."

What grandmother could deny that plea?

"I'll look a little," I agreed. "But don't you tell Pop, or he'll skin me alive."

"If he does, T-daddy will mount you so Cricket can keep you," Bradley promised.

On that cheerful note I kissed them all, tucked Cricket and Bradley into the bunk beds in Cricket's room, and accompanied the two girls to the guest room across the hall. When I had tucked them into the big double bed, Natalie held one finger to her lips. "Shhh. Do you hear that?"

I listened, but didn't hear anything unusual. "What?"

"Those dogs. If they get out, they could come in this house and eat us." She burrowed down in the covers and pulled them over her head.

I pulled the covers back and stroked her wispy hair. "Those dogs are my friends, and they don't eat people. They eat dog food. Besides, they live in that pen. They don't want to come in the house. They are singing you a lullaby. Hear them? The one with the real high voice is my dog, Lulu, and the one that goes *ooooh* is Cricket Dog. They'll sing you to sleep if you'll let them." I hoped that was so.

Anna Emily held out her arms and squeezed me tight around the neck. "I want to go home with you," she whispered.

"Not tonight, honey. Go to sleep."

I tiptoed down the stairs, hoping Martha and Ridd would get some rest. Barking dogs and grieving children can be hard on a good night's sleep.

When I got to the kitchen, I asked, "You got any more of that tea?"

Martha looked at the clock. "We don't have time. Buster said he'd meet us at Robin's house at eight thirty. Do you have your car? Mine's out of gas and I was too tired this morning to fill it up on my way home."

The air was still crisp and frosty, the sky full of a billion stars. The sheriff was sitting in the drive when we arrived, sipping a drink and eating a hamburger. "Have you been home to bed yet?" I greeted him.

"No, but I'm working up to it. Just had to wait for two women to come by the house, but you know how women are. Always late."

His breath rose like smoke as he climbed out of the cruiser, ambled up the steps to the door, and let us in with a key. "Don't take anything except the kids' clothes," he warned.

"Stuffed animals, books, and toys?" I bargained. "To make them feel more at home?"

"Okay, but nothing except their possessions."

He propped himself against the doorjamb, looking dead on his feet.

"Go on home," I commanded. "You can trust Martha, if you don't trust me. And this door can be locked from the inside. We'll lock up when we leave. We won't be long."

I could see he was tempted.

"Go!" I gave him a shove and he let himself be persuaded.

Inside, the heat was so low that we left our coats on. Martha headed toward the bedrooms at the back of the house. "Could you get me something to put these clothes in?" she called. "I forgot to bring a suitcase."

I almost didn't hear her. I was staring at the living room

and dining room in astonishment. They were full of antiques. Not the kind of antiques we have, bought several generations ago for durability and not yet worn out. These were the gorgeous kind—the sort that Maynard sells—which I would never trust around children.

Come to think of it, the rooms didn't look like they had been lived in by children—or by anybody else. I did not see one book or magazine, one toy, or one photograph. The pictures on the walls were oil paintings in wide gold frames that looked like they ought to be in a museum. Two even had lights above them, although their cords dangled down the wall unplugged.

The floor creaked beneath my feet as I moseyed to the kitchen to look for grocery bags. The place felt creepy even with Martha opening drawers and rattling hangers in the girls' room.

I couldn't find the kitchen light switch at first, but in light reflected from the dining room I finally saw a double switch across the kitchen beside the back door. The place must have been wired by the man who did our new house, because none of these switches were where they'd be most convenient, either. When I flipped what would logically be the kitchen switch, a light came on outside, illuminating a back patio. Something that looked like an antique quilt lay folded on a chaise out there. It would be ruined if it stayed out in the frost and sun very long, not to mention what squirrels and birds would do to it. Since there was no crime tape on the patio, I opened the back door, retrieved the quilt, and set it on a dining room chair.

"Are you bringing me bags?" Martha called.

I shut the back door, pulled my coat tighter around me, and found four paper bags folded and stacked in a paper box beside the refrigerator. I also found three plastic bags stuffed into another plastic bag hanging on the inside of the pantry door. If I'd hung our plastic bags inside my pantry door, their bulk plus the food on the shelves would have kept the door from closing. Robin had one single shelf of food, containing only a box of Cheerios, a jar of peanut butter, a loaf of bread, an unopened jar of applesauce, and a couple of cans of peaches. It looked like Anna Emily had been right: The girls had been raised on peanut butter and apple-sauce. Had that woman spent her money on antiques instead?

I went to take Martha the bags and met her in the living room, coming to see what was taking me so long. While she headed off to fill the bags, I peered around the living room. There was something I had forgotten in there, something about Buster. What was it? I couldn't remember. Memory is a funny thing. You can remember you have forgotten something, even remember what the thing was about, and still not remember what it was.

I moseyed into the dining room and inspected the china cabinet, which held two sets of china. Feeling a bit furtive, I opened the doors and took a quick look at the bottoms of plates. Robin had a set of Lenox for twelve and a set of Royal Doulton for ten. She must have done either a lot of entertaining I hadn't heard about or have preferred to invest her money in valuables rather than trusting a bank.

I was still bothered that I had forgotten something.

While I tried to remember, I decided to explore Robin's cabinets. You can tell a lot about a woman by her kitchen. Martha, for instance, has practical, childproof dishes and is a saver. I think she's got every plastic container she ever carried home from the grocery store. She uses them to store leftovers and for freezing fruits and vegetables each summer. Walker's wife, Cindy, is a thoroughbred who has china everyday dishes and stores leftovers in fancy containers she bought at a gourmet party. And me? That's my business.

Robin's cupboards astonished me so much that I called, "Martha, come here a minute. I want you to look at something."

Martha arrived with a small shirt in her hands.

"Stand there and tell me what you think." One by one I opened the cupboard doors.

The shelves were full of gray flannel lumps. I touched several lumps on the bottom shelf and described their contents, one by one. "A Paul Revere sterling silver bowl. A sterling silver vase. A silver coffee service: coffeepot, teapot, sugar bowl, creamer, and slop bowl. Over here"—I opened another cabinet where the contents were self-evident; I named them anyway—"a set of Waterford crystal for twelve."

I pointed toward the china cabinet behind her in the dining room. "One set of Lenox china and one set of Royal Doulton." I moved to the pantry. "Here you'd expect to find food, right? You would find very little." I opened the door and pointed to the solitary shelf containing foodstuffs. "But that mahogany box on the top shelf? That's a Gorham silver flatware service for twelve. I climbed on a chair to look. And that"—I pointed to a large flat object wrapped in gray flannel, standing on the floor beneath the shelves—"is the tray to the silver service. There's not a single dish in the place that children could eat on, except the stack of paper plates on the counter and a few plastic forks and spoons in one drawer. There is milk and a half-empty jar of applesauce in the fridge"—I opened the door to demonstrate—"and a good supply of frozen dinners." I closed the lower door and opened the upper one. Most of the freezer space was taken up with dinners, but the compartment also held ten medium cans of frozen juice.

"Now look at this." I took out one of the cans and pried up the lid with my fingernails. "Voilà!" I pulled out a wad of paper towels and carefully unfolded them on the counter. Diamonds sent sparks all over the kitchen as I dangled a necklace in the air.

Martha's eyes were wider than salad plates. "Do you reckon Buster saw all this?"

"Not the jewelry. If he'd seen the silver and dishes, he'd most likely have said to himself, 'The woman had some nice things.' I doubt he'd wonder where the dishes were for her children, or think to take the tops off her frozen grape juice cans."

"Why did you?"

"I'm short. I was trying to see if she had any meat in the freezer, and I had to move this can to see what was behind it. It didn't feel like solid juice, so I wondered if the freezer was thawing and I lifted the can to shake it. That's when I noticed that the white strip that connects the top to the can was gone."

Martha came over and lifted another can. "This one isn't juice, either. I think we ought to call Buster."

"I think you ought to put that right back where you found it and get out of here," said a male voice.

The young man I'd seen around town back in the fall and again more recently, searching for his wife, came through the back door. I'd forgotten to lock it in my haste to find Martha some bags.

He wore a brown leather bomber jacket and gloves. His red hair gleamed in the kitchen light.

I remembered the other things I had forgotten, too—to lock the front door behind Buster. How stupid could I get, leaving two doors unlocked when we were prowling around the home of a recent murder victim? I shot Martha a look to say, "I'm sorry," but her attention was on the young man.

"That stuff is mine," he told us, stepping into the kitchen. "All the jewelry, silver, dishes, and furniture. Bertie took it when she left." Our skeptical looks must have registered, because he nodded toward the cabinet shelf. "Take down one of those bags and look on the bottom of what's in it. Go ahead. Look."

I pulled out the Paul Revere bowl and turned it over.

He didn't come near enough to read it. "IWH 173475910. Right?"

I nodded.

"My mother was Iris Wilson Handley, and the numbers are our family's birthdays. You'll find that engraved on brass plates attached to all the furniture and etched onto all the silver, except the coffee set. That has SSW 122345. Sara Shelton Wilson was my grandmother and she got married on December 23, 1945. The jewelry isn't marked, but I have pictures of it on file with my lawyer. I did that before I went overseas, while I was updating my will."

He started across the room with his gloved hand out for the necklace. I put it behind me. Martha was eyeing the wall telephone beside the fridge, but it was too far away for either of us to reach it first.

"Look, I don't want to hurt you. I just want my stuff." As he moved, something bulged in his pocket. It looked like a gun.

I reminded myself that he hadn't threatened us—yet. Besides, he had eaten a meal on my tab at Myrtle's. He had no reason to hurt me, or so I hoped. "You gave me your card, but I've forgotten your name," I told him.

"Grady Handley, ma'am. Formerly Captain Grady Handley, of the U.S. Army."

"And you think Robin Parker was your wife?"

"I don't *think* she was my wife. She *was* my wife."

"But you called her Bertie."

"Her name was Roberta. At least, that's what she told me. After all the other lies, I don't know what's true anymore."

"The children are yours?"

He gave a short, not-funny laugh. "That's one of the things I don't know. The little one must be, but I never knew a thing about her. It gave me a real shock to see her on the sidewalk that day, asking if she could go home with me. It was like looking at my own picture at that age. I guess Bertie was pregnant when I left to go overseas, but she never mentioned it. Never said the kid had been born, either—just like she never mentioned she was pregnant when she married me. For years I actually believed Natalie was mine and born early, even though she never looked a thing like either one of us. Can you believe I was that dumb?" Again he barked that sarcastic laugh. "You'll believe anything when you're bewitched."

"Her name is Anna Emily," I told him. "The little girl."

"No kidding? That's weird. Anna was my sister's name. She died last year."

"Did your wife like her? Were they close?"

"No, on both counts. Anna did everything she could to convince me not to marry Bertie, saying that she was only after my money. I wouldn't listen." For the first time I saw his smile. It was lopsided and could have been endearing in other circumstances. "She's probably leaning over the edge of heaven right now calling, 'Told you so, Bro.'"

"What happened to her—your sister, I mean?"

His expression darkened. "That was the other mess I came home to. While I was in Afghanistan, they found her body in a hotel room in Charlotte. The official report says she died of a drug overdose, but that's a lot of hooey. Anna never used drugs."

"What did your parents think?"

"They were killed in a car accident while Anna was in grad school at Carolina. That's why I had all the family stuff. Anna didn't have any storage space, so I stored the furniture and put the jewelry in a bank safe-deposit box until Anna and I could both get settled and decide who wanted what. I figured when I got out of the army, Bertie and I would build a house worthy of some of it." His lip curled. "I guess Bertie couldn't wait. While I was overseas, she took the furniture out of storage, cleaned out the safe-deposit box, and emptied the bank account. Then she disappeared."

Martha and I exchanged a look. His story echoed that of Kaye Poynter. What we had not known about Robin Parker would fill a flash drive.

Still, a houseful of antiques, silver, and jewelry made an awfully good motive for murder. I wanted to get out of there and call Buster, even if I woke him up.

I rewrapped the necklace in the paper towel and dropped it back in the juice can. "Well, Captain Handley, I'm afraid this is currently a murder scene and nothing can be removed from it. We were given permission to get clothes for Robin's children. Unfortunately, she was murdered last night."

I expected him to be shocked or at least to pretend to be. Instead he nodded. "I know. I'd been staying over at the motel, and I got back around midnight and found the elevator draped with crime scene tape and the parking lot full of law enforcement types. I asked some dude who looked like a newspaper reporter what was going on, and he said a woman named Robin Parker had been killed in the elevator. I already knew Bertie was using that name, so I decided to hightail it out of there and lay low. I didn't want anybody to know I was connected to her. I went back over to the taxidermy convention around noon today to see if there was any more news, and folks were saying Bertie had been going to meet some man on the third floor. I knew then that they must have found a note I'd taped to her front door yesterday afternoon telling her we needed to talk. I thought about going to the sheriff, but I don't have an alibi for last evening, so I decided I'd stake out the house to be sure nobody took out my stuff, and wait to see if they came up with another suspect before I talked to the sheriff. When I saw you find the jewelry, though, and recognized you as the woman who offered me a free meal, I figured I ought to step up and stake my claim."

He sounded credible, but I've known a lot of credible criminals. "Go down to the sheriff's detention center and tell them your story. They can come over with you and release the stuff. We only have permission to take the children's clothes and toys."

To emphasize my point, I put the can back in the freezer and shut the door. "Martha, let's take the clothes and let's *all* get out of here."

Grady Handley didn't budge.

"If you have a connection to Robin's stuff, go down and tell the sheriff about it," I urged.

When he still didn't move, I added, "I'm a judge, remember. I cannot let you remove anything from this house without the sheriff's permission."

His eyes flickered. "You don't believe me, do you?"

"I'd like to, but I hear all kinds of believable stories, and not all of them are true. And when a young woman gets all gussied up for a date with her ex-husband—"

"As far as I know, I'm not her ex. She never filed for divorce."

"That's worse. When she's heading for a date with her estranged husband, whom she's done wrong, and she gets killed on the way to that date—and when nobody else in the area is known to have any reason whatsoever to do her harm—you have to admit there are grounds for skepticism."

"I'm not admitting a thing, except I want my stuff and to find out about the girls."

"So go talk to the sheriff."

"That won't be necessary." Buster stepped into the kitchen and blocked the door. "Grady Handley? I want you to come down to my office and discuss the death of your wife, Roberta."

Grady had gone white to the gills.

"You'd better hold him up," I warned. "He looks likely to faint."

Buster stepped forward, but Grady was faster than any of us expected. He crossed the kitchen in two strides, flung open the back door, and dashed into the woods.

Buster ran to the door and looked after him, but there were no lights back there. "I remembered when I was halfway home that we didn't lock the front door," he said. "Thought I ought to come back to be sure you all were okay."

"We were okay. That young man claims all the furniture and stuff in the cabinets is his, that Robin was his wife and cleaned him out while he was in Afghanistan, but he swears he didn't kill her."

Buster scratched his ear, a sign that he was thinking. "It's as good a motive as any. His fingerprints were on a note in

Robin's purse and on two elevator buttons, the one to hold the door open and the one for the first floor. He seems to have been the last person to use it before she was found. Get what you need and come on out. I'll be calling for backup."

"You'd better post a guard out here, too. Robin had some really valuable stuff, and whoever owns it now, you don't want it disappearing on your watch."

Martha carried out several bags of clothes from the girls' room. "I can't find any books, toys, or stuffed animals," she reported. "The only thing in their room besides clothes is a television."

I took that load to the car while she went back for another. My cell phone rang as I stuffed the bags into my trunk. It was Joe Riddley.

"You all need to get back over here. Anna Emily has gone missing."

⤜ 21 ⤛

"What happened?" I had to hold on to the door of the car, I felt so weak.

"Ridd went up to check on the kids, and she was gone. We've searched the house, but she's not here, and the front door was cracked. He's searching the barn and the yard right now. We need you to come home and help us look."

I drew a sharp breath. "We're loading the car. We'll be right there."

Neither of us mentioned what we were both thinking: Ridd's place was surrounded by acres of cotton fields, a small pine forest, and Hubert Spence's cattle pond.

While I waited for Martha to bring out her load, I hurried to the sheriff's cruiser. "That was Joe Riddley. Anna Emily has wandered off."

Fields, woods, and the cattle pond were mirrored in Buster's eyes. He heaved a mighty sigh. "I'll see if I can send some folks out to help you look."

"No, your plate is already more than full. We'll find her." I nodded toward the woods. "I think that young man who escaped might be her daddy."

"If so, she may be about to lose both her parents in one fell swoop."

As soon as Martha returned, we threw the things in the

backseat and I scratched off. Normally I love driving fast. That night I only wanted to arrive.

We were passing Hubert's watermelon patch when Martha screamed, "Stop!"

Ahead of us, Anna Emily sat smack in the middle of the road, wearing only her flannel gown.

I slammed on the brakes. We fishtailed on the gravel. I fought the wheel and managed to roll into a pine tree instead of the child. I was shaking too hard to move.

Martha scrambled out. "What are you doing out here, young lady?"

Anna Emily held up her arms. "Can I go home with you?"

"You certainly can. What do you mean by going out of the house in the middle of the night? Without even a coat!" She picked up the child and wrapped her inside her own coat so tightly that she squealed. Martha brought her back to the car and held her in her lap while I backed away from the tree, hoping I'd done no more damage than bend the fender, and headed toward the house. I didn't say a word about seat belts. We were so close we could see the lights.

When we turned in, Ridd came up from the barn and Joe Riddley came out onto the back porch. Three small people clung to his pants.

When I climbed shakily out, Natalie let go of Joe Riddley and more flew than ran down the steps. "Me-Mama! Anna Emily is lost! Nobody can find her. She's not in the house—" She jumped into my arms and flung her arms around my neck. Accustomed to Cricket's weight, I felt like I was holding air.

"It's okay. We found her."

Her head whipped around and she saw Martha climbing out with her sister. "Anna Emily," she warned, "you are gonna get a whipping. You know you're not supposed to run off like that."

Anna Emily buried her face in Martha's neck and didn't say a word.

*   *   *

The sheriff called out the bloodhounds, and they literally treed Grady Handley in two hours. "Got him up in the branches of a pine hardly big enough to hold his weight," the sheriff told me when he woke me up at one thirty and asked if I'd come down and hold a hearing.

"You charging him with murder?" I asked when I got there. "You better have some real good evidence."

"At the moment I'm charging him with trespassing and interfering with a crime scene, but I'm urging you to deny bond until we can investigate the murder charge. I want him where I can get to him for questioning."

Grady was not at his best for the hearing. His pants were torn and his shirt filthy, and he still had leaf scraps in his hair. He also looked plumb exhausted. The only time he roused from a stupor was when I asked, "How do you plead?"

"Not guilty!" His face was white, his skin taut over his skull. "I never killed her. I was mad, sure, but I never killed her!"

"You aren't being charged with murder, son. Sheriff, repeat the charges."

When they were read, he shrugged. "I was there. You both saw me. I guess I can sleep in jail as well as anywhere else tonight."

When it was over, I told him what I would have said to my own sons. "Go get some rest. Things ought to look better in the morning."

I hoped it was true.

Martha called early the next morning. "I just overheard the oddest conversation between the girls. It sounds like they're worried about a dog. Anna Emily said, 'Daddy angel will feed him,' and Natalie said, in that exasperated tone she gets with her sister, 'Daddy angel doesn't even know he's there. He's Uncle Billy's dog. He's gonna starve.' Then Anna Emily said, 'Good. He can't eat us up.' I went in and asked what was the matter, but Natalie said, 'Nothing' at the same time Anna Emily said, 'Mama said not to tell.' I didn't see or hear a dog, did you?"

"No. Go and ask them what kind of dog they have and if we need to feed it. Maybe a direct question will work."

Martha came back in a minute. "They didn't want to tell me, but I got the information. He's big and black, according to Anna Emily, and Natalie says he lives in the basement and only barks if somebody tries to go down there. Then he eats them up."

"No wonder they're terrified of Lulu and Cricket Dog, if that's what they're used to. The place is pretty isolated, so Robin may have felt she needed a guard dog. It's odd that he didn't bark last night, though, don't you think?"

"And I didn't know the house had a basement."

"Come to think of it, the floor creaked under me last night, which means it's not on a slab. I'd have guessed a crawl space, but if there is a basement, there could well be a dog in it."

"Ridd and I have to teach Sunday school this morning," Martha said. "Could you and Pop go over and check? If Buster has a deputy stationed there, he could let you in. You might want him to go down with you, in case the dog is as fierce as the girls say he is."

I was all for calling the deputy and asking him or her to feed the dog. Hungry dogs can be mean, and big black dogs have never been on my favorite-creatures list since one took a chunk out of my arm when I was eight. However, when I called, the sheriff was home getting some well-deserved rest and the department was short-staffed and short-tempered after their long weekend. A grumpy deputy informed me that feeding dogs wasn't in their job description. He would instruct the person assigned to watch the house to let us in, but that was all they could do for us that morning.

I promised myself to remember his cooperation the next time he wanted me to come down to the detention center in the middle of the night.

The only dog food we had was for Lulu, since Joe Riddley had left his yard dogs down at Ridd's when we moved. As I carried the bag to the car, along with a bowl for the food and another for water, Lulu uttered sharp objections to her food going somewhere she wasn't invited.

Joe Riddley started back to the house. "Be back in a minute. Wait here."

It was nearly five minutes before he came out carrying a plastic sack. "Sorry. I had to microwave it."

"Microwave what?"

"A treat I brought."

"You think he's going to object to a diet designed for a small, elderly beagle?"

Joe Riddley grunted. "If he hasn't eaten since Friday, he may settle for a diet of small, elderly judge."

"I am not elderly."

"You're not thirty any longer. I mean it, Little Bit. I want you to stop getting involved in these investigations. It's hard on you and equally hard on me. I'd like to have some years when I didn't have to worry myself sick about what you were going to do next."

"I'd like some years when I knew we were going somewhere fun. I'm not asking for six-month cruises around the world, although I wouldn't object to one. But how many good years do you think we've got left to travel overseas? How long will our stamina hold out—and our health? Not to mention our stomachs. Besides, I heard somewhere that once you are seventy-two, you aren't allowed to drive in foreign countries."

"I've never hankered to drive in foreign countries."

"I have. I'll make you a deal. I'll stop looking into murders if you'll promise to take me somewhere special each year. How's that?"

"I'll have to think about it. Meanwhile, when I walked Buster to the car yesterday morning, I borrowed some cuffs again. Don't forget I know how to use them."

What I had forgotten was my promise to Cricket.

All right, I vowed when I remembered it. *As soon as this murder is solved, I'll stop for a while.*

Marriage, I have discovered, is a process of shaping each other by decisions you make. You can't set out to change your husband, but if you change yourself, he changes, too. Who knew? Maybe Joe Riddley would change into a world traveler.

He pulled into Robin's yard. The way the deputy sat up straighter when we drove up beside him, I suspected he'd been napping, but he was parked so he blocked the drive for anybody coming in. He recognized us and lowered his window.

"Have you heard a dog barking?" Joe Riddley asked.

"Haven't heard a thing, but it's been freezing here all night, so I had the windows up. Only action I've had was a car that turned in around two a.m., got me in its lights, and backed out. Another—or the same one, I couldn't tell— came around six, saw I was here, and disappeared. Here's the front-door key. Be sure to lock yourselves in. Since you're here, I'm gonna go get some breakfast. I hope you won't leave before I get back, but if you do, be sure to pull the door shut behind you and lock it."

"No problem. We'll wait until you get back." Joe Riddley was already climbing out. He reached into the backseat for his plastic bag.

We went in through the front door and I pointed out the antiques in the two front rooms.

"We aren't here to admire the furniture, Little Bit."

"No, but while we're here, I want to look at the bedrooms. I didn't get to see them last night."

After I had, I wished I hadn't. One contained a lovely walnut bedroom suite that could have been two hundred years old. As Buster had said, though, the room was a mess. Obviously Robin—Roberta, I corrected myself—had tried on several outfits before she found one she liked. The pillows still bore the imprints of two small heads.

The girls' bedroom was a dump: stained carpet, a double

mattress on the floor, a battered chest of drawers, and a television. No toy chest, no bookshelf, no stuffed animals. I was beginning to revise my opinion of Robin/Roberta as a devoted mother. She wasn't destitute, for heaven's sake. She'd surely had enough left over after paying bills to buy her girls a few toys and books, even if she got them at a thrift store.

"So where's this basement door?" Joe Riddley interrupted my ruminations.

"I have no idea. Maybe in the kitchen?"

It had only the door to the backyard and the one to the pantry.

Joe Riddley went out the back door and walked around the house. "Looks like there could be a basement. The foundation is over four feet high where the hill slopes down in the back. I saw places where it looks like windows were bricked up, too, and a couple of things that look like air vents. There's no door, though. It has to be inside."

Doors in the small hall served the two bedrooms, a linen closet, a coat closet, and the bathroom. Joe Riddley leaned into the linen closet and the coat closet and rapped on the back wall. Neither sounded hollow.

"You could try the pantry, but it looked solid to me."

Joe Riddley saw something I had missed. "These shelves lift right out, and the floor looks like it was put down before the pantry was built. I think the pantry was built at the end of the cabinets after the house was finished."

He lifted out the lower shelves and uncovered a recessed handle hidden behind the shelf where the food had been. When he lifted down the silver and removed the top shelf, we saw the line of a door that had been concealed by the line of the shelf. He pulled the handle. The door didn't open, but something threw itself against the door and gave a low, menacing growl.

"You've found the dog." I shoved him out of the way and slammed the pantry door. "What are you going to do now?"

"The door must open inward." He worked out the problem aloud. "The dog keeps it from opening as long as he's there, unless he recognizes an order from his master or mistress."

"Who aren't around," I pointed out. "But why keep a dog in a dark basement?"

"We don't know that it's dark, but he will be needing food if he's been there more than twenty-four hours without attention. You get up on the counter there." He jerked his head toward the counter next to the sink.

"How am I supposed to do that?"

"Climb on a chair. Oh, heck. Here." With one motion he lifted me at the waist and sat me on the counter. "Pick up your feet now."

I saw what he was after. "If you think I'll be safe from a big dog up here, you can think again. Any dog that size could stand on its hind legs, reach the counter, and make me his dinner."

He frowned. "I need an observer to watch the animal."

I wasn't sure I was keen on being that observer, but I didn't want him doing it, either. However, if I had to observe, I wanted to do so from as close to the ceiling as possible. "Maybe I could climb on top of the fridge. Let me try."

I hoisted my legs onto the counter, climbed onto my knees, and worked my way to my feet. There are times when being short has its advantages. I scarcely had to stoop to stand erect.

Feeling like a tightrope walker, I inched along the countertop to the fridge and considered the problem. "It will be a tight fit. Will you get me down if I get up there?"

"If I'm still around. You have your cell phone? Let me have it." He handed me my pocketbook, and I gave him the phone. He slipped it in his pocket.

Next he filled one bowl with Lulu's food and another with water and set them far across the kitchen next to the dining room door.

I was liking the looks of this less and less. "Where are you going to be?"

"Hopefully outside calling animal control."

"Why don't we call them before you let the dog out?"

"Good idea." He punched in the number. "We've got an abandoned dog down on Lower Creek Road. What's the number here, Little Bit? Never mind, I'll go look." He ambled across the living room and read the number off the front of the house. I heard him say, "Yes, in a basement. You'll be right out? Thanks."

He came back to the kitchen. "They're on their way. You ready?"

"Why aren't we waiting for animal control?"

"Because the animal is starving. I'd rather we fed him before they arrived. Mind your feet."

I pulled my feet up and sat cross-legged on the refrigerator, my back hunched to avoid the ceiling. "I'm gaining a new appreciation for what babies go through in the womb, but I'm as ready as I'm ever going to be."

He went over and opened the back door wide, then reached into his bag and pulled out ground meat, dripping red. "Watch the floor," I rebuked him.

Instead, he deliberately squeezed the meat and dribbled red blots up and down the floor from the pantry door to the food and water bowls. Still carrying the glob of meat, he opened the pantry door, stepped inside, and leaned his shoulder against the basement door. It moved a few inches and I saw that the basement was bright with light. At least the dog wasn't living in the dark. It wasn't a happy beast, though. It hurled itself against the door with a snarl.

Joe Riddley leaned against the door again and pitched a small ball of meat through the crack down the stairs, then he shoved hard against the door. I heard the dog scrabbling for footing as he fell, and then I heard him snuffling up the meat. Joe Riddley flung the basement door wide open, heaved the glob of dripping meat in the direction of the two bowls, and hightailed it to the kitchen door. A black and brown streak snarled through the pantry after him.

"Run!" I screamed unnecessarily. Joe Riddley pulled the

back door shut behind him a second before the dog reached it. My stomach ached at how close he had come to being grabbed by those powerful jaws.

The dog propped its front legs on the door and barked furiously. He was the biggest, meanest Rottweiler I had ever seen. His coat was sleek black and tan, his shoulders muscled and strong.

At last either he tired of fruitless barking or he scented blood, for he dropped to the ground and started licking up the drops, snuffling his way across the floor. He approached the meat warily, sniffed it, and gobbled it down. When he'd finished the meat, he ate Lulu's food and slurped up all the water in the bowl. I had to feel sorry for the creature, hungry and alone for two days.

"Is it eating yet?" Joe Riddley called from outside the door.

"Just finishing," I called back.

That was a mistake.

The dog's big head whirled, his eyes red and malevolent, seeking the source of the voice. When he spotted me, he hurled himself toward my perch with a bay of fury. Saliva dripped from his jaws. His bared incisors were yellow and long.

Clear as anything, I heard my mama tell me, "Don't ever let a vicious dog know you are afraid. Speak in a voice of authority."

"Down!" I shouted. "Down, boy."

He hesitated, but ultimately that had the same effect as shaking a warning finger at an approaching locomotive.

Again and again he leaped, trying to reach me. My world was reduced to his determined bays and the snap of his jaws. Every muscle in my body ached from terror. I drew myself into as small a space as possible, leaving no loose ends dangling in his reach.

It was worse when he stopped leaping. He gave me a calculating look and backed crookedly across the room, eyeing the countertop. His intentions were clear.

"Please, God, please, God," I whispered. If he was able to reach the counter, I was finished.

He gathered his muscles in a crouch, ready to spring. Then, without warning, he keeled over and fell with a thud.

"Is he out?" Joe Riddley called through the door. "I can't hear him. Is he out?"

I was shaking too hard to reply.

"Is he out, Little Bit? Are you okay?" I heard his hand on the knob.

I didn't want him coming within range of the beast, so I rallied what energy I had left. "He's snoring."

While speaking, I eyed the dog warily. I expected him to rouse, shake himself, and stand for a second onslaught.

He did not move.

"Good." Joe Riddley sounded like he was congratulating me on a job well done.

"You'd better call the fire department and tell them to bring the Jaws of Life. I'm not sure I'll be able to get down from here without them."

He cautiously opened the door. "You think it's safe for me to come in there?"

"I wouldn't trust it. If the dog doesn't kill you, I might. Do you know how close that animal was to leaping up to the countertop and finishing me off?"

"I hoped he'd go out faster than that." He tiptoed over and looked down. At the moment the Rottweiler looked like a wimp.

"What was in that meat?" I flexed my muscles, but they would not relax.

"The rest of those tranquilizers they gave you the last time you were in the hospital."

"Those things may have expired by now."

"Nope, the bottle said they were good for another month. They used to put you out for hours."

"But you had no idea how well they'd work on a dog."

"No, but he looks like he's out cold."

The dog twitched and moved a paw.

My muscles contracted again. "I'd feel better if you went outside to watch for animal control. I'll keep watch here."

I sounded brave, but when he left, even though the dog continued to snore and snuffle, I didn't budge from my throne. I couldn't have. My limbs were shaking like a paint-stirring machine.

I had never considered kissing animal control officers before, but if the two who came for the dog had been close enough, I'd have given them each a buss to remember. The beast was sleeping so deeply that he didn't stir as they lifted him into a cage and carried him out.

The deputy sauntered in as they left. "What's been going on?"

"We've been feeding a dog." Joe Riddley was rinsing out the food and water bowls.

"You've forgotten something," I informed him with as much dignity as I could muster.

"What's that?" He grinned up at me.

"Get me down from here!"

I wish I could say I descended with grace, but by then I was so stiff that it took Joe Riddley and the deputy together to pull me off that fridge. I tumbled down on top of them, nearly taking them to the ground with me. Since I could not stand, Joe Riddley picked me up and carried me to the living room, where he deposited me on an antique sofa designed more for looks than comfort.

Gradually, feeling crept back into my feet, legs, and shoulders. Once the initial needles wore off, I was racked again by shakes. I kept seeing the beast leaping, leaping, toward me. I shook so hard that the couch shook with me.

Joe Riddley gathered me into his arms and held me until my body stilled. "You were very brave, Little Bit," he whispered.

"I'm gonna be sore tomorrow—not only from being all curled up, but from getting so tense while the dog was attacking. That booger nearly got me, you know."

"He was bigger and meaner than I expected. Do you feel up to going to church?"

"An hour in church is exactly what I need, but we're gonna have to go home and change first. The top of that refrigerator was filthy, and you've got hamburger blood down your leg."

"Hey!" the deputy called, his voice sounding far away. "Come see what I've found!"

Joe Riddley hurried toward the kitchen. I tottered after him and arrived in time to see him disappearing down the stairs.

I decided I'd might as well go for the whole nine yards. I descended on trembling legs.

The basement did not extend under the entire house, but only under the back half. The room was painted white and lit by long fluorescent bulbs hanging from the rafters. It contained a hot-water heater, a long table with cupboards hanging over it, an upright freezer, and a stove.

"Another kitchen?" I asked, bewildered. "Why would a house this size need two kitchens?"

The officer was looking inside the cupboards, using a handkerchief to protect the doors from his prints. "By golly!" he kept saying over and over. "By golly!"

"What?" I felt ignorant, which always annoys me.

I staggered over and looked. I saw some muriatic acid like we used in the pool. I saw Red Devil Lye like Daddy used to put in Coke bottles with water—then he'd shake them and use the gas that was produced to inflate balloons for us kids to shoot with a .22 rifle. I saw gallons of distilled water and some engine starter fluid. "Looks like that stuff ought to be out in the garage, not in a kitchen. And what are those inhalers doing down here? They should be in the medicine cabinet."

The deputy moved to the next cupboard. At least its contents were more appropriate for a kitchen: small glass bottles, Pyrex meat loaf dishes, quart jars, a box of coffee filters, another of rubber gloves.

"I still think it's odd to have a second kitchen." I started over toward a tall metal cabinet, but Joe Riddley put a hand on my shoulder to stop me.

"It's not a second kitchen, Little Bit. It's a lab where they make methamphetamine. Don't put your prints on those doors. That cabinet may have drugs in it, and I don't want you spending your old age in federal prison. Let's get out of here so we don't mess up evidence."

"Woo-ee!" The deputy had just opened the freezer and found it filled with stacks of bills, fastened with rubber bands. "Looks like somebody made more money than they wanted to deposit in the bank."

He clattered up the stairs after us, as excited as if he'd won the lottery. "We've been looking for this place all over the county, and here it was, literally under the sheriff's nose when he was searching the house Friday night." He pulled out his phone.

I mulled things over as we headed back to the car. Natalie had told me, plain as day, that Robin and Billy cooked together at night after the girls were asleep. No wonder Robin kept such an eagle eye on her kids. It hadn't been overprotection. It was self-preservation.

❧ 22 ❧

Monday I felt like I was on a seesaw going up and down, except sometimes while I was up, the person on the other end got off.

We arrived at the store that morning to find Evelyn fitting the cash drawer into the register. Joe Riddley took Bo and Lulu back to the office and left me to ask questions.

"What are you doing here? Mardi Gras isn't until tomorrow."

"I decided to come home early." Her tone didn't invite curiosity.

I tried the oblique approach. "I've heard Mardi Gras is pretty wild down there."

She fiddled with stuff on the counter, acting like I wasn't present. Normally I would have gone on back to the office. Like I said earlier, Evelyn and I didn't talk much about our personal lives. In past years we had been too busy, and relating like that gets to be a habit. But something about the way she was standing made me ask, "Honey, is there something wrong?"

Like a stream dammed by twigs and branches until a spring flood comes downhill, Evelyn gave way and told all.

"Mardi Gras wasn't half as wild as Hubert's ideas were. The deal was, we each bought our own plane ticket, I was to pay for our meals, and he was to reserve and pay for our lodging. We would split entertainment costs."

"He wasn't paying for everything?" I was disgusted. Hubert had a lot more money than Evelyn.

"No, I insisted that I pay my share. That's what women do nowadays, you know?"

I'd been a girl in the days when a smile and fluttering lashes were enough to get you a good dinner and a movie. However, having raised sons who'd sweated prom costs, I could approve the fairness of sharing if the partners had roughly the same amount to spend. In this case, it sounded to me like cheap old Hubert had gotten a good deal.

"So did he eat you out of house and home? Did you run out of money and have to come home early? Will you have to take out a loan to pay your credit card bills?"

I hoped for a smile.

She glowered.

"No, because we didn't eat but one meal before we got to the hotel. I was excited, it was so fancy, but do you know what he did? Reserved only one room. Can you believe it? He said it had two beds, it would save money, and we are both grown-ups."

That sounded exactly like the Hubert I knew. He pinched pennies until they squealed. Had Evelyn imagined she had been abducted by a Lothario? Apparently so.

"I knew what he was after, and I wasn't having any. I told him if that was the kind of woman he wanted around, he could find one out on the street."

"What did he say to that?"

"He got all red in the face and said he could be trusted, that—that"—her voice wobbled—"that he didn't think of me that way!"

She tried to smile, but pain was sharp in her eyes. I could have gladly slugged Hubert at that moment.

She cleared her throat, and I knew it was to get rid of a lump. "So I asked, 'If you don't think of me that way, why did you invite me to New Orleans?' And he looked like he didn't have a clue what I was talking about. Can you believe it? I bought all those clothes, got my hair cut, even got a manicure. . . ." She spread her hands and looked at her nails, which were beginning to chip.

Her disappointment was so keen, I would have hugged her if we'd been hugging friends. "So what did you do?"

"I picked up my suitcase and walked out—and slammed the door behind me. It felt good, but it was really dumb. New Orleans was crammed with people. The only vacant room the hotel had was a suite. I tried to find another place, but there weren't any vacancies in nearby hotels and I didn't know the city, so I didn't know where else to try. Finally I plunked down what I'd planned to spend on food all week and spent one night in the suite. It was snazzy—I had a Jacuzzi in my room, and I ate breakfast on my balcony, not wanting to run into Hubert downstairs—but I couldn't afford to stay any longer. Friday morning I tried to find another place, but everybody was full and the streets were clogged. I got so tired of dragging my suitcase around—I know, I could have left it at the hotel, but like I said, I didn't want to run into Hubert, so I took it with me. I finally got so exhausted that I hailed a cab and said, 'Take me to the airport.' I figured I'd pay the premium and fly home."

"You've been back since Friday?" I wondered if she'd been holed up at home all that time, licking her wounds and replaying "What Might Have Been."

"Don't I wish. A big storm up north was grounding flights all over the country, so nothing went out the whole day."

Where had I heard about that storm before? Oh, yes. Martha had to work Friday night because the other supervisor got stranded in Philadelphia. It was tendrils of that storm that had given middle Georgia such a chill for the weekend.

"Then you didn't get out until Saturday?"

"Not even then. Once planes started going out, they were full. For two solid days, I lived and slept at that airport, hoping to get on the next flight to Atlanta. Eventually, I flew via Dallas and Cincinnati—anything to get home. And then, since we had taken Hubert's car to the Atlanta airport, I had to take a bus to Hopemore. Don't ask how my vacation was. Okay?"

"Sounds pretty grim."

"It was. Anything happen around here while I was gone?"

"We've had some grim times, too." I fetched coffee for us both and filled her in on the weekend.

It wasn't the murder she found most shocking. "Robin was making drugs in her basement? With those two girls right there?"

"Upstairs asleep, presumably. But yes."

"What on earth was she thinking?"

Evelyn has always loved children. If her life had turned out differently, she'd have been a great mother. I wasn't surprised it was Natalie and Anna Emily she thought of first—and last. "What will the girls do now?"

"The sheriff is looking for relatives." I didn't think I ought to mention Grady, or that he could be their father. Where small children are concerned, a father in jail isn't much better than no father at all.

"The sheriff is sure Robin was murdered?"

"What do you think? She was found with a broken neck in the motel elevator, wearing a red cocktail dress, red high-heel sandals, and a mink coat."

"Mink? Real mink?"

Mink coats weren't thick on the ground around Hope-more. Winters were too mild for anybody to invest in one of those unless they had money to burn, traveled up north a lot, and specialized in ostentation. Even Gusta hadn't worn one since her brother left the Senate.

"That's what the sheriff said. And speaking of the devil . . ."

The sheriff strode in.

*   *   *

Wouldn't you have expected him to be overjoyed to see me? After all, we had found that lab he'd been looking for. I didn't want a medal, but gratitude was certainly in order.

Instead, his face looked like he had breakfasted on fire and brimstone. He grabbed me by one elbow and said between clenched teeth, "I want to talk to you and that dang fool husband of yours." He more dragged than led me back to the office.

At my last glimpse of Evelyn, she looked like she was watching something better than a Mardi Gras parade.

Joe Riddley was sitting with his feet propped on his desk, cleaning his nails with his letter opener. Buster slammed the door behind us and glowered down at him.

"Of all the stupid things to do. You're the one always complaining that Little Bit here"—he shook my arm so hard it nearly fell off—"gets herself in trouble, then you go and take her to feed a vicious dog and leave her in there with him while you skedaddle. I cannot believe you could be so infernally pea-brained—or that my deputy would let you. He won't again, I can promise you that. She could have been torn apart! Did you even think of that?"

"Back off! Give me space!" yelled Bo from the curtain rod. Lulu, unused to her friend the sheriff yelling at us, began to whine. Buster, who adored animals, ignored them both.

Joe Riddley lowered his feet and looked wary. The sheriff was generally an even-tempered man. "She didn't get hurt. She was way up on top of the refrigerator. I wish you could have seen her, all curled in a ball. I could never have fit. It had to be her."

"It did not have to be her. That dog is a trained killer."

"You've seen him?"

"No, but animal control said it was the meanest beast they ever took in. Yet you left Little Bit in there with that animal while you ran away!"

The last time I'd seen Buster so het up, I was in fourth grade and they were in sixth. We three had been assigned to pick peaches for a cobbler, and instead of using a ladder, Joe Riddley suggested I shinny up and pick them, since I was lighter. I went too high, fell out, and broke my arm. Buster had been furious with Joe Riddley. Right in front of my daddy he stormed at his best friend, "How could you make her do a stupid, dang fool thing like that?"

I had been shocked. Around our house, words like "dang fool" got our mouths washed out with soap. To my confusion, Daddy—who had gotten the whole story from me—put his arm around Buster's shoulder and said in a mild voice, "I agree with you, son, but she agreed to climb that tree, and she's not mortally wounded. She'll survive."

What almost didn't survive was the friendship between the two boys. The next day Joe Riddley came to my house with a split lip and a black eye.

"What happened?" I asked.

He looked sheepish and embarrassed. "Buster and me had a fight. It's okay, now, though. I'm sorry I told you to climb that tree. Will you be my girlfriend?"

When I saw Buster a day later, he had a knot on his forehead and a bruise on his cheek. He didn't meet my eyes as he stood a couple of steps behind Joe Riddley, who asked if I'd like to go to the movies with the two of them. That was our official first date. During the movie, Joe Riddley held my hand in his sweaty one. Buster pretended not to notice. That pretty much set the tone for the rest of our lives.

Until now.

Buster stood glaring down at Joe Riddley like any second he might grab him by the collar, jerk him up from his chair, and pound the tar out of him.

Joe Riddley looked edgy, like he expected the same.

Since Daddy wasn't around to cool things down, I did what I could. "I didn't get hurt," I pointed out, "and maybe we've solved the murder. If Billy was making methamphetamine with Robin, isn't it likely they had a falling-out and he killed her? Why don't we let Grady out on bond? And why don't you let go of my arm?"

I tugged, and he relaxed his grip. I slumped into my own chair, but he wasn't in a sitting mood. He bent over me and pontificated.

"Because it's equally likely that her ex-husband found out what she was up to with his kids in the house, and he killed her. Or, like I thought before, that he got drunk, was mad because she'd run out on him, started to shake her, and ended up by throttling her, like he was taught in the army. The main point here is, that dog could have killed you by jumping as high as the fridge."

"What does Grady say?"

"That's none of your business, if you'll pardon my French. I came about the dog."

"Come on, Sheriff. You owe us that much. We did find the lab, after all."

He still glowered, but my use of his title may have reminded him we were colleagues as well as friends. "Grady doesn't say a dad-blamed thing. Not about where he was between seven thirty, when he left a restaurant up at the I-20 exit, and midnight. He admits to coming by the motel then, seeing us there, and taking off again."

"But he won't say where he was?"

"Says he doesn't have an alibi we could check out. He does insist that he did not kill his wife, but without an alibi he can't prove it."

I figured that wasn't the time to argue Grady's case.

You may have noticed that Joe Riddley was laying low and letting me carry the conversational ball. I looked his way, giving him a chance to speak, but he was again cleaning his nails.

"Any word on the dog this morning?" I asked. "Has his owner come to claim him?"

That was a mistake. It stoked Buster's fires again. He took a breath so hard and angry I was surprised it didn't split his windpipe. "If that deputy I had on duty out at the house had had a lick of sense, he'd have called animal control as soon as he found that meth lab in the basement and he'd have told them to hold anybody who came asking for the dog. Instead, he got so excited about what you all had found, he got my whole weekend crew down there working on it. The dog's owner showed up at animal control yesterday afternoon. I figure he cruised by the house to scout out the situation, saw my folks carrying out the evidence, and went looking for his dog. He called first—asked if they had seen a Rottweiler that his sister had locked in her basement, keeping the animal for him, said it had gotten out by accident. When they said yes, he came in so fast they figure he called from the parking lot. He identified the dog. It responded to its name and obeyed his commands, so the weekend worker let him pay the fine, sign the papers, and go. "

"At least they got his name and address, right?"

"Right, except the name was an illegible scrawl and the address doesn't exist."

"You poor dear!"

I merely said what I was thinking, but it did the trick. He exhaled, and I could see the anger leaving him. He spoke for the first time that morning in a reasonable voice. "What frustrates me most is that if you all had called my office to deal with the dog in the first place, we could have staked out the house and maybe caught the owner. Instead, by barging in to . . ."

He stopped like he couldn't think of a way to describe what we'd done.

"To do a good deed?" I suggested. "To save a starving animal and keep two children from worrying? We did call your office first, by the way. Your folks were stretched real thin by the earlier events of the weekend, and very willing to let us take on responsibility for the dog." I saw no reason to mention Grumpy. I would deal with him later, on my own.

I went on in what I hoped was a reasonable tone. "None of us knew what that animal was guarding. Or that he was such a vicious beast. Now sit down like a sensible person, stop puffing smoke from your nostrils, and let's think if there's any other way to trap that fellow."

He slapped his hat against his thigh again and exhaled more frustration. "I can't stay. I've got more stuff to do today than I'll get done all week. But would you all please stay out of this? Judge, you run the store. Joe Riddley, take care of Little Bit. That's your job."

I saw my husband flinch.

"Sorry. It won't happen again. You do your job, I'll do mine."

Buster squeezed his shoulder and left without looking at me.

I waited until I saw the cruiser pull out of our parking lot, then demanded, "What was that about it being your 'job' to take care of me?"

"Nothing. Just a deal we made years ago."

"What kind of a deal?"

"A men-only deal." He swiveled his chair to face mine. "I didn't hear you voicing your promise to stay out of Buster's case."

I was afraid he had noticed, but how could I? I'd made an earlier promise to four children. To distract him, I asked, "You want to know what happened to Evelyn?"

He laid his letter opener on the desk, propped his feet up again, and folded his hands across his stomach. "Sure. But we aren't finished with my prior question."

"We aren't finished with my prior question, either. But let me fill you in." I told him the whole thing, ending with, "She ought to have shoved Hubert out the door and let *him* find another room."

"Don't bad-mouth poor old Hubert. He's not real wise when it comes to women."

"You'd think he'd be wise enough not to invite a woman to Mardi Gras unless he was interested in her. I mean, you wouldn't ask somebody of the other sex to go along as your buddy—would you?"

"I wouldn't ask somebody of the other sex to go, period. You'd be sitting right behind us on the plane. However, we are talking about Hubert. He never has known how to treat a woman. Remember him in high school? Or maybe, being two grades behind us, you didn't notice."

"What was there to notice? He was smart and short."

"And shy."

"Hubert? Mr. Glad-hand? He's never been shy. Wasn't he elected Most Congenial? And look at how he was shaking hands all over town last fall, running for mayor."

"He's okay with men. It's just women that make him shy."

"Not me."

"That's because you've been off-limits as long as he's known you. He hasn't thought of you as dating material. I don't think he asked a single girl out during high school."

"Get out your yearbook and think again. He was always running around with cheerleaders and beauty queens."

"He trotted around *after* cheerleaders and beauty queens, doing little favors, basking in traveling in their orbits. That's all it amounted to."

"I remember him coming home from Tech bragging to me about the great 'lookers' he'd met from Agnes Scott. The way he talked about them, he made me feel like chopped liver."

"But I'd bet he didn't date a single one of those lookers— or ask out any woman who might have accepted his invitation. Hubert was more naive about love than most twelve-year-olds."

"He's past sixty now," I pointed out, "and was married for years. He got married six months before we did."

"Because Edna set her cap for him after he came home from college, and maneuvered him into it. I don't think Hubert loved her, but he loved the notion that some woman liked him. And she loved the fact that he would own Spence's Appliances one day."

Hubert's wife had been a large, bossy woman with no softness or comfort about her. She never worked in the store, but was always telling Hubert how to improve it.

"They neither one got much joy out of the marriage, did they? The only thing they had in common was that they were both tighter than jeans washed in hot water."

"Hubert got that from his mother. She always acted like they didn't have a penny. And yet he can be generous when he thinks of it. Remember how he loaned us those televisions for my birthday party one year? And he always fixed our appliances for nothing."

"Well, Evelyn could have been good for Hubert. I'm sorry that blew up. Still, she doesn't need a cheapskate. She's not a spendthrift, but she likes nice things. And she needs somebody she can love who will love her back."

"You don't know that Hubert doesn't love her, Little Bit."

"Oh, really? After he tells a woman it's okay to share a room because he isn't interested in her that way?"

"I'd bet he was trying to reassure her that he's a gentleman, that he wasn't going to treat her like a woman of the streets. Wasn't that what she'd accused him of wanting? Poor Hubert. I'll bet he had no clue what she was really wanting."

I replayed the conversation in my head. "It's possible it was just a big misunderstanding, but he was still too cheap. Do you reckon he could be interested in her?"

" He's been squiring her around for several months."

"You think he's capable of love?"

"He fell pretty hard for that woman who was in town for her nephew's gubernatorial campaign, didn't he? She seemed to like him back, too. Hubert can be likable if he's not feeling threatened. That's when he gets on his high horse. On the other hand, his relationship with Evelyn has seemed to consist of movies, dinners, and walks so far, not unbridled passion."

That made me laugh, but I had to ask, "How do you know that?"

"Heck, Little Bit, the whole town would have known if Hubert was engaged in unbridled passion. The only folks who can get away with *anything* around here are folks without friends or relations."

That sobered me. "Like Robin Parker/Roberta Poynter."

❧ 23 ❧

After Joe Riddley took Bo and headed to the nursery, I spent a restless hour trying to shove Evelyn, Hubert, Robin's murder, Grady, Uncle Billy, three little kids who had lost their mothers, and one angry sheriff out of my mind so I could concentrate on my work. As I was finally buckling down to it, the sheriff strode back in without knocking.

"Where's Joe Riddley?"

"At the nursery."

"You've both got to get out of town at once."

"As in 'Flee, all is discovered'?"

"It's no laughing matter. I went by to talk to the guy from animal control who was on duty yesterday, the one who signed the dog out. He remembered something he hadn't put in his report. The man who picked up the dog said he'd really like to thank the people who rescued his pet, so the dummy gave him your names and told him he could find you here today."

Buster's hands were shaking and I wasn't breathing too good myself.

"You think he'll come with the dog—"

I couldn't even finish the thought.

"I don't know, but I want both of you out of town. Immediately."

"We can't leave town. Joe Riddley's got Session at church tonight, he's presiding at that breakfast benefit tomorrow for the work-release house for prison inmates, I've got the program at garden club tomorrow afternoon—it's not feasible."

"What's not feasible is for me to provide twenty-four-hour protection for the both of you. I'm investigating a murder here. I don't need complications."

We faced off like two angry schoolkids on the playground. Have you ever noticed how we tend to relate to folks the same way we did when we first met them?

Maybe one of us ought to act like an adult.

I tried. "Joe Riddley's down at the nursery, shifting sod around with the forklift, so he ought to be okay. Our folks wouldn't let a dog into the nursery."

His eyes narrowed. "There are things called rifles, Judge."

That took my breath again. I looked at the sheriff and knew we had the same picture in our minds: Joe Riddley happily lifting loads of sod (he loves working that forklift) while somebody got him in their telescopic sights.

He made a quick, impatient motion with one hand. "Get Joe Riddley on the phone and tell him to meet you at the house, pack yourselves a bag, and get out of town. Call me to say where you are, and I'll call you back when it's safe to come home."

Normally I'd be delighted to tell Joe Riddley we were commanded to take a vacation, but right then it wasn't possible. Not only did we both have a lot to do, but I had a promise to keep to four small children.

"How about if we go to Ridd and Martha's? Ridd left town this morning for a high school math competition, so Martha would probably like having other adults around. This Uncle Billy character won't be looking for us there. I don't know if I can talk Joe Riddley out of going to church tonight or the breakfast meeting tomorrow, but I'll try, and I'll definitely skip the garden club, since announcements about my program are plastered all over town. Evelyn can make the speech. It's about summer blooming perennials, so she knows everything I planned to say. We can instruct her not to tell anybody where we've gone. That would give you time to look for this character. You could even work out a system with Evelyn to get him if he shows up here."

The sheriff considered. "That could work. It may take longer than twenty-four hours to catch him, but if he doesn't come around here today, I'm pretty sure he'll leave the region. Call Evelyn in."

When she arrived, we put her in the picture.

She looked from one of us to the other. "Let me get this straight. We're expecting a man to show up at the store with a vicious dog, and I'm supposed to lie to him about where the bosses have gone?"

"Not lie." I corrected her. "Simply say you aren't sure where we are—we have left the store. You won't be sure where we are, exactly. I could be in Martha's living room, den, or bathroom, and Joe Riddley—"

"I get the picture, Mac, but I'm not crazy about talking to men with vicious dogs."

"I doubt he'd bring the dog into the store on his reconnaissance trip," the sheriff said, hoping to calm her. "He'll probably come in asking for the Yarbroughs, expecting you to point him in their direction. The important thing is that you don't tell anybody—and I do mean *anybody*, including Gladys—where they are. In fact, it might be better if you pretend you think Mac is here. If somebody you don't know comes in asking for either one of them, tell them you'll check the office to see if the judge is in, then come back here and call 911. We'll have somebody in the store within five minutes. You'll need to stall them that long. Can you do it?"

"Maybe. I could pretend to check the loading dock and the bathrooms, too."

"Good idea. Even ask for a name and phone number where Joe Riddley can reach him." He glowered at me. "Okay, Mac, hit the road. I'll head down to the nursery and explain the situation to your hardheaded husband. I don't want to see hide nor hair of either one of you until I give a green light. Stay down at Ridd's and don't show your faces in town. You got that?"

"Right. After I stop by the house to pack us both a few things. Tell Joe Riddley to come straight to Ridd's."

I was already grabbing my pocketbook. The thought of that dog on the loose was enough to churn my butter.

On my way home I called Martha to say she was getting a couple more guests for a day or two. "I'll explain why when I get there."

When I arrived at the house, our cook, Clarinda, was fixing to start dinner. We usually went home for our midday meal.

"Forget dinner," I called over my shoulder as I headed to our room. "We won't be here today or tomorrow. We've been suddenly called away. In fact, I don't know how long we'll be gone, so why don't you take a vacation? Go on home, right this minute."

She came to the bedroom door and propped both fists on her plump hips. "What you up to now?"

I didn't reply, being occupied with reaching my suitcase down from the top shelf of the closet.

"It's something about that murder, isn't it? You investigating it?"

I laid the suitcase on the bed and started filling it with clothes for two days. "No, I'm trying to keep from being the next victim. Joe Riddley and I went over to Robin Parker's house yesterday to feed a dog Martha thought might be there—"

She started to cackle. "I heard all about that. Dog was in the basement, but it got loose, so you jumped up on the fridge and the judge ran out the door and down the block." Joe Riddley would always be "the judge" to Clarinda. "I surely would have loved to see you scrambling up on top of a fridge with that animal nipping at your heels."

"That's not at all how it happened. Joe Riddley asked me to climb up on the refrigerator to watch the beast, and then he put drugged meat on the kitchen floor and threw a wad of raw meat down the basement steps to distract the dog in order to give himself time to get the basement door open and get out of the kitchen. He did not run 'down the block,' either. He heroically dashed across the kitchen a few steps ahead of the critter, and he stayed on the back porch the whole time while I watched the dog to see when it fell asleep. Joe Riddley would have stayed himself, but there wasn't any place he would be safe."

"Ha." Clarinda rocked back and forth, preferring her own version. "I can see you now, on top of that fridge, hoping that vicious animal wouldn't get up there to keep you company. Weren't you scared stiff?"

"There were moments. The problem now is that somebody told the owner of the dog where we work and he can find out where we live from almost anybody in town, so Buster's afraid he may come by to give the dog a second chance at my heels."

"Because of them drugs you all found?"

I gave her a short nod. Like I have said repeatedly, nothing is secret in Hopemore. I wondered how many versions of the story were floating on the breeze.

"Whoo-ee. No wonder you're leaving town. On sheriff's orders?"

"That's about it." I fetched our toothbrushes and other paraphernalia from the bathroom.

"I'm surprised he didn't put you in his cruiser and take you out of town his own self, if he thinks you're in that much danger. How come he let you drive home alone?"

"He had to go tell Joe Riddley. You know how he feels about Joe Riddley."

"I know how he feels about you, too."

"Yeah, he likes me, but he and Joe Riddley are halves of the same onion."

Clarinda made a rude noise. "They're tight, all right,

but if anything ever happens to the judge? Won't nobody but you be surprised when the sheriff starts hanging around here. I always did think he's as sweet on you as the judge is."

I packed our pajamas. "Don't be silly. Buster Gibbons is our best friend, that's all. Now hush a minute. I need to think what else to take." I added socks for Joe Riddley and panty hose for me. "Hopefully we won't be gone long, and I'll call you when we get back to town. I can't tell you where we'll be, but if you call Martha, she can find us."

"Oh. So you're goin' down there."

"I didn't say we were going down there."

"Didn't have to. After all these years, I can read you like a book."

I saw no need to protest. It was true.

"Don't tell a soul—and I do mean a soul—where we are. Okay? Say we had a hankering to get out of town for a few days."

By the time I finished packing, she had her coat on and was standing by the door. "Thought I'd see you out. In case something happened to you, I'd always regret it if I hadn't said good-bye." She grabbed the handle of the suitcase and took it to my car.

When I pulled out of our drive and headed toward Martha's, Clarinda pulled out behind me and followed me into town. Maybe she needed to stop by the Bi-Lo on her way home.

Down on Oglethorpe Street—the only four-lane road in town—I had to stop for the light. I wasn't paying attention to traffic around me until I heard an engine gunning on my left. I turned to frown at the driver of a dusty green Dodge pickup, and saw a huge black and tan head pressed against the passenger window. Beyond the dog, the driver had long blond hair and sunglasses.

When he saw me looking his way, he gave me an evil

smile and a small salute. Lulu saw the dog and sent up a vol-
ley of barks warning him away from her territory.

I had slung my pocketbook in the backseat so she could
ride up front, so my cell phone was out of reach.

What should I do?

I wasn't going to lead that fiend to Ridd's.

If only there was some way I could motion Clarinda to
get his license plate number and call the sheriff.

The light changed. I pulled away fast. The truck slid in
behind me, separating me from Clarinda. Next time I looked
in my mirror, the dog had its head lolling out the window.
His owner must have lowered the glass. They were having a
chilly ride.

I made a quick decision. At the next intersection, I turned
right. The truck turned right. Clarinda turned right.

I turned left. The truck turned left. Clarinda turned left.

One turn after another I wended my way out of town and
back toward the federal highway, leading my parade. I tried to
avoid deserted streets, not wanting him to speed around me
and cut me off. At the same time, I tried to keep my head
down below my headrest so he couldn't shoot me from behind. In a few minutes, I was so hot and clammy I had to
switch from heat to air-conditioning in the car.

Half a mile beyond the city limits, there was one more
turn to make. I turned left into a long drive at a blue sign:
SHERIFF'S DETENTION CENTER.

The truck went straight and roared away. Clarinda followed him.

"You dummy!" I yelled after her. "Didn't you see me
turn?"

What a quandary. Should I follow them to be sure
Clarinda was safe, or should I alert the sheriff's office?

I turned around in my seat and grabbed my pocketbook
from the back. "Not now," I told Lulu, who was ready for the
ride to be over.

I jerked my cell phone from my purse and backed into the
highway, startling an oncoming car. As I raced after

Clarinda, I punched the auto-dial for the sheriff's office. "Uncle Billy picked me up on Oglethorpe Street and followed me out of town, but when I pulled in your drive, he kept going, He should be about a mile farther than the detention center now, in a dusty green Ford pickup."

"Where are you?"

"Following him. Clarinda is right behind him. She was following me and he got between us. I'm terrified for her."

"Get yourself down to Martha's. We'll take care of Uncle Billy and Clarinda." When I didn't reply, he said sternly, "That's an order, Judge."

Reluctantly, I gave up the chase.

Martha and the children were in the kitchen getting ready to eat peanut butter sandwiches and apple slices. She and Cricket were delighted to see me and Lulu. The girls were delighted to see me, but pulled their feet up in their chairs when Lulu hopped in behind me. Now that I understood their fear, maybe I could do something about it.

I picked Lulu up in my arms and held her while she squirmed and protested. "Hush," I told her. "I want you to meet some friends of mine. Be nice, now."

She subsided and peered at the girls, whose eyes were like small terrified moons.

I went closer to them and squatted down so Lulu's head was lower than theirs. "I want to tell you something about dogs. They are like people. You know that there are some bad people and some good people, right?"

They hesitated, then nodded in unison.

"That dog at your house was a very bad dog. I saw him. I know."

Again they nodded. "He ate people up," Natalie said with an exaggerated shiver, enjoying the thought when the dog wasn't around to demonstrate.

"I think he would, if anybody got close enough. He nearly scared me to death, and I'm a grown-up. But not all dogs are that mean. Lulu, here, has lived with me since she was a tiny puppy, and there's not a mean bone in her body. She jumps around a lot because she's like Natalie. She has a lot of energy."

That got a flicker of a smile from Natalie.

"And she walks funny because she lost one leg when she got shot trying to save Pop. See?" I showed them the stub. "She's a very brave and loving dog. When she comes toward you, what she wants is to give you a dog kiss, like this." I lifted Lulu up to my face and she obligingly gave me a lick. "That's how she kisses people she likes."

"Cricket Dog does, too," Cricket contributed, not to be outdone.

"Do you hear Cricket Dog out in the dog pen?" I waited for the girls to nod. "He's upset because Lulu, his mother, is in the house while he has to stay outside. Both of them bark a lot because they are beagles. Can you say 'beagle'?" I waited for the girls to repeat it, then asked, "Who wants a kiss from Lulu?"

They cringed back in their chairs.

"I do," Martha said. I carried Lulu over to give Martha's cheek a lick.

"Me! Me!" Cricket cried, clapping. Lulu complied.

"I do," Anna Emily said softly, putting out her cheek. I held Lulu close and Lulu licked her. Anna Emily giggled. "That tickles." She put her cheek out for another kiss.

Natalie still drew back.

"If you don't want a kiss, would you like to stroke her head?"

She put out a tentative hand and I stuck Lulu under it. Gently she stroked the dog's fur. "She's real soft."

"I'm going to put Lulu down now and let her explore the house. She used to live here, so she has to make sure nobody has moved the corners."

That made them giggle. They giggled more when Lulu started on a sniffing tour of the kitchen, then headed for the den.

"What you here for, Me-Mama?" Cricket asked. He knew

as well as I did that I never came to his house in the middle of a workday.

"Pop and I need a place to sleep for a night or two. Do you all have a vacant bed?"

Martha answered. "Sure we do. Let me get these people fed. Then I'll show you to your room."

Not until we were upstairs and could hear the children piping away downstairs did I explain why I had come.

Her face went white. "He was actually in the truck beside you? With the dog?"

"Big as life and twice as ugly—both of them. I frankly never believed he'd come to town, but there he was. I sure hope Buster catches him."

The phone rang. Martha went to her room to answer it.

"It's for you. Clarinda."

"Does she sound all right?" I was already hurrying to the phone.

"I wanted you to know I'm okay." Clarinda obviously relished having taken part in our chase. "I followed the truck another mile down the road, and he turned at the crossroads leading to I-20. I didn't want to go that far, so I hung around the turn waiting to be sure he didn't turn around and come back. Then I came on back to town. I wrote down his license number, though. What should I do with it?"

"Call the sheriff and give it to him. Had his men caught up with you before the man turned?"

"Nope. I passed a cruiser on my way back to town."

"Then when you call the sheriff, tell him where the man turned."

"I will. But you might consider going somewhere else. If that man learns where Ridd lives, what's to keep him from coming down there to get you and the judge, and hurting Cricket and his parents as well? You only gonna be safe at Ridd's until somebody mentions you got a son down that road."

She was absolutely right. I hung up, shaking all over.

"Oh, Martha, he really is after us, and I may have led him straight down here. And Ridd isn't even home. What are we going to do?"

"Have some soup while we think about it." Martha is invariably practical.

⇥ 24 ⇤

We locked all the doors, but I felt very vulnerable as we sat down to eat. When I picked up a cracker, Cricket asked, "Why are your hands shaking, Me-Mama?"

Thank goodness for Natalie. Before I could reply, she had grabbed the conversation and run with it. "We were shaking a lot at our house, the night Uncle Billy didn't come. And crying, too. We were real scared, weren't we, Anna Emily?"

Anna Emily obligingly nodded, but there was no way she could get a word in.

"But Daddy angel protected us. Do you have a daddy angel?" That question was for me.

"I don't know, honey. What's a daddy angel? Is that like a guardian angel?"

She wrinkled her forehead. "I don't know a gar-jun angel. But our daddy died in the war and became a angel. Mama said so."

Anna Emily spoke softly. "Mama's a angel now, too."

Natalie reached over and patted her arm. "So now we have a daddy angel and a mama angel. Don't you have a daddy angel or a mama angel?" She was asking me again.

"I guess I do." I'd never thought of them like that, but I had felt their presence at important times in my life. Like on top of that refrigerator. The Bible calls the presence of those who have gone before us a "cloud of witnesses" or the "communion of the saints," but mama angel was as good a name for it as any.

"How did your daddy angel protect you?" Cricket asked Natalie.

Anna Emily finally spoke first. "He sat on the patio and kept us safe."

Natalie slapped a hand over her sister's mouth. "We weren't supposed to tell."

"That was that night," I comforted her. "He wouldn't care now." I was most interested in what she was saying. "How long did he stay?"

"Until the doorbell rang and the men started shouting, 'We're the sheriff. Let us in, by the hair of your chinny chin chin.'" Natalie had deepened her voice and was clearly enjoying her role as storyteller.

Anna Emily stayed focused on the main point. "Then he ran off to the woods."

"How did you know it was your daddy angel?" I felt like I was walking on eggshells. Interrogating children is frowned upon by a lot of people, including me.

Natalie resumed her role as family spokesperson. "He came to the front door and rang the bell, but I said we couldn't open the door for anybody except Uncle Billy. That's what Mama said. And he asked if Mama was there, and I said no, but she'd be right back. That's what she said to say if anybody came. He said he didn't want to come inside, but to look out the window and see if I knew him. So I looked through the blinds, and he looked like Daddy!" Her thin face lit up with more animation than I'd ever seen on it. "He went to war and died, but Mama had his picture in a frame, and I kissed it every night. I guess she lost it when we moved. We lost lots of things then—our books, our toys . . ."

She said that so matter-of-factly, it broke my heart. What kind of mother moved her husband's antiques and failed to bring her children's toys?

"What else did he say?" I wanted to get back to the angel.

"He didn't like us being there by ourselves. He said he'd sit in his car and wait for Uncle Billy. And I said Uncle Billy would be real mad if he came and found somebody there. Uncle Billy doesn't like people coming to our house. So Daddy angel said he'd take his car down the road and wait out back."

Martha was as interested as I was. "Did you see him out there?"

"Yep. He knocked on the kitchen door when he came back and I saw him through the window in the door. He asked if we had a blanket he could use, that he'd go down to the woods and wait for me to put it on the back steps. So I got a quilt from the living room sofa and put it on the steps. Then I locked the door again and he came back and wrapped up in the quilt and he said we could go on to bed, he'd stay until Uncle Billy came, so we would be safe. When Uncle Billy got there, I was to knock on the window in the back door so he would know to leave."

Anna Emily found her voice again. "We got in Mama's bed, so she could see us when she got home."

"I don't have any angels." Cricket's tone was envious. He slid Martha a look.

She tousled his hair. "I'm not going to heaven just to give you a mama angel, so don't be getting any ideas."

I was getting ideas. Ideas about a father who had searched all over creation for his wife and daughter, found two daughters, and found them alone. A father who would not ask them to violate their mother's orders about letting people in, but who would sit outside wrapped in one quilt on a frigid night to make sure they were safe.

"Excuse me," I said, pushing back my chair. "I need to make a phone call."

"I told you not to call me, I'd call you," the sheriff said when I reached him.

"I know, but this is important." I told him what Natalie

had said and my conclusions. "Ask Grady about it, okay? Tell him Natalie has been talking."

"I'll ask him why didn't he just tell us, if that's the case?"

"Would you have believed him? Without knowing a thing about him?"

The sheriff's brief hesitation was long enough for an answer.

"I wouldn't have," I assured him. "I'd have written him off as either a pervert—a Peeping Tom or worse—or a liar trying to exploit two grieving little girls. In my book, the fact that he didn't say a word that might expose those children to being interviewed about him points toward Natalie's story being true. Just ask him, okay? And on another subject, did you find Uncle Billy yet?"

"Not yet, but we found his license plate. He left it on a Toyota in a motel parking lot up near I-20. Clarinda called the number in—unless she got it wrong. We're running the number through DMV as I speak."

"Clarinda wouldn't get it wrong. I told her to call you."

"How did she know where you were? I told you not to tell anybody."

"I didn't. She guessed. Anybody could guess. I have to leave. Not only am I not safe down here, but these children aren't safe. I'm going to suggest that Martha take them to her mother's for the night, and I'm coming back to work."

The sheriff swore so rarely that when he did, people were so astonished that they capitulated.

I, however, had known him too long to bow down because of bad language. "Look, here's my plan. I'll hire an off-duty deputy to guard the store until you've caught the fellow, and I'll send Evelyn and Gladys home. I won't endanger them, but I can't stay down here endangering children, either. Who knows? Maybe my being in the store will lure Uncle Billy into town and your off-duty deputy can capture him."

He swore again. Before I could fuss at him, somebody spoke in the background.

He got back to me. "Got to go, Judge. They've checked with DMV and Clarinda did get the number right. They've also found the woman who owns the Toyota and gotten the tag number Billy's probably using now. I need to get people looking for it. Stay right where you are until I get back to you. You hear me?"

"I'm going to have Martha take the children to her mother's and —"

I was talking to an empty line.

As I hung up, I realized something: The girls were foster kids. Martha's mother lived in another county, and Martha couldn't take them out of the county without permission. That could take time to get.

I ran down a mental Rolodex.

Maybe Selena and Maynard would take Martha and the kids for a couple of nights. The big Victorian where they lived had at least five bedrooms upstairs. Besides, the girls knew and liked them. They would be safe there until we got Uncle Billy behind bars.

I sound a lot braver than I felt. The thought of meeting Billy face-to-face shivered my gizzard, and the thought of his dog . . . I was sure it would take a silver bullet to kill that beast, and I was fresh out. Besides, he could take me down before a bullet reached him.

Resolutely I put away concerns for myself and concentrated on getting the kids safe.

Selena had seen battered families at the hospital. A second after I'd explained that the Parker girls, Martha, and Cricket needed shelter because the girls' uncle was on a tear and likely to endanger them all, she was saying, "I'll go make beds right now. We've put a privacy fence around the backyard, too, so nobody can see in. The kids can play out there. I'll have Maynard run by Wal-Mart and get a ball and some toys."

Bless her heart. As heavy as it was about not having children of her own, it still expanded to take in girls in danger. I also had my first kind thought for the superstore. It used to be hard to buy toys in Hopemore—even toys for Lulu.

Lulu! I couldn't take her back to the office with me. I would not put her in danger any more than I would the children, and if the big dog came, she'd die trying to save me.

Selena couldn't take her. "Maynard is allergic."

I stood there feeling sick to my stomach. "It doesn't matter, honey. I have just realized that even if you could take Lulu, we would still be abandoning Cricket Dog and a pen of bird dogs to a potentially vicious man and a definitely vicious dog. Not to mention Cindy's horse, Ridd's new pig, and Martha's chickens. You couldn't possibly take all of them." The younger Yarbroughs had taken far more enthusiastically to animal culture than Joe Riddley and I ever had. "Forget the animals—that's not your worry. If you'll take Martha and the children, that will be enough."

"Couldn't you at least put the dogs and the horse in Hubert's barn for the time being? I'll bet Cindy and Walker would move them for you. It's her horse, isn't it?"

Hubert's house had been converted into a shelter for battered or homeless women and their families, but the barn still stood empty.

"A brilliant idea. Thanks. Martha and the children will be there as soon as they're packed." I didn't bother to tell her that Cindy and Walker and their kids were on a skiing vacation in Colorado. I could move a pen of dogs and a horse. Hubert wasn't likely to object, since he was out of town until Wednesday night.

I called down at the nursery and asked to talk to Joe Riddley. "He's right here. Just a second."

"You still down in our secret hideaway?" he asked.

"Only for a few more minutes. I have decided it's not as secret as we thought it might be. In fact, it could be dangerous for other people, too, including little people."

Why was I was talking in code? Nobody could hear me. "Martha and the kids are going to Selena's, and I'm going to

Myrtle's for dinner. We ought to be safe enough there, and I've given Clarinda a few days off. You want to meet me?"

"Yeah. It'll be half an hour, though. I have something I have to do first."

"Me, too." I didn't see any reason to mention horses or dogs.

Martha and I packed suitcases and hurried the children into her car. "We're going to spend the night with Selena and Maynard," she told the children. "She has a new backyard fence and some toys she wants you all to see."

Cricket was excited, but Natalie and Anna Emily were frightened. "Do we have to stay there?" they asked Martha. "Are you giving us away?"

"No, I'm going to stay there, too," Martha assured them. "This is a visit for all of us. Then we'll come back down here. Okay?" She turned to me. "We'll follow you out, Mac."

"Go ahead and leave. I want to move the dogs and Starfire to Hubert's barn, just in case."

I could see that she was about to say she'd help me. "Go on! You have a car full of kids. You take care of them and I'll take care of the animals. Go!"

Reluctantly, she went.

I went to the barn, saddled the horse, and managed to get up on him in only two tries. I wished Missy Sanders could see me, riding down the road. But my primary concern was that a man in a green truck *not* see me riding down the road. The rest of my ride, I found myself looking for a dusty green pickup and watching both sides for the glint of sunlight on a rifle barrel—especially when I passed the spot where Joe Riddley had gotten shot. I turned the horse in at Hubert's drive with a big sigh of relief.

One of the women in the shelter had grown up on a farm. When I explained that we had to leave our animals there for a few days, she offered to feed and water them. I walked back down to Ridd's and put food for the horse and dogs in my trunk, then bundled the five dogs into my car. Its interior would never be presentable again, but it was no more beat-up than the front, where I'd run into the tree to keep from hitting Anna Emily.

The woman and I put the dogs in another of Hubert's vacant stalls with food and water. Lulu and Cricket Dog were indignant at being treated like common yard dogs, but I promised I'd be back for them as soon as I could. "It's for your own good," I told them.

They had trouble believing me. I could still hear them objecting when I reached the main road, a quarter of a mile away.

I had to wipe tears away as I pulled onto the highway. I didn't know if they were tears of worry, fear, or grief that my hometown had turned into a place where I could not feel safe.

ॐ 25 ॐ

The Hopemore grapevine must have malfunctioned. Myrtle's was packed and looked blessedly normal, and the main topic of conversation was a rising wind that was bringing frigid air from the north and supposed to swoop our temperatures into the teens that night. Nobody seemed to have the faintest idea that a madman with a Rottweiler could be loose in the county, hunting me down.

Maybe he wasn't. Why should he hang around if he knew the meth lab had been discovered and Robin killed? Especially if he had killed Robin. If he was as smart as I thought he was, he had skedaddled out of the county and was halfway to somewhere else by now.

On the off chance that he wasn't, I passed up the empty booth by the window, where I preferred to sit, and took the empty one along the side wall in the back corner. I slid across the shiny new black bench and sat facing the door. I understand Al Capone used to do that, for much the same reason: I didn't want to be gunned down from behind.

Wylie Quarles was sitting at the table just beyond my booth. He looked happier than I'd seen him since Starr died. "Good to see you smiling this morning," I said in greeting.

"It's a great day, Judge. I just had a man come by and ask

me to mount a boar's head. Never did one of those before, and I'm looking forward to it."

"You all are open today?" I was surprised.

"Heck, yeah. Trevor wanted to close down in memory of Robin, but I didn't see any point in that. I told him I'll hold the fort until he feels like coming back."

He shoved back his chair, threw a dollar on the table, and swaggered to the register. I wondered where he'd been between eight and nine on Saturday evening.

"Clarinda sick?" Myrtle greeted me as she poured me a cup of coffee that cost a quarter more than it used to.

"Clarinda's taking some time off." I perused the new red menu. "How's the country-fried steak today? Tender?"

"Tender as always."

"I thought it might be tenderer, since it costs a dollar more. Bring me some of that with rice and gravy, fried apples, and collards. Vinegar, not pepper sauce, for the collards."

"I know you want vinegar. Redecorating nearly drove me crazy, but it didn't make me lose my memory. You eating by yourself? If you are, I'd rather you left the booth for a larger party and took that vacant table for two over by the restroom doors."

"I'm expecting a larger party. Joe Riddley will be here in a minute. Hold his coffee and my dinner until he arrives. I'll sit and sip until he gets here."

"Okay, but you only get one refill nowadays. After that, you pay for another cup."

"You're going out of business," I prophesied. "If folks can't come in here to sit and drink coffee, they'll find a place where they can."

She tossed her head and stuck up her nose. "I'm ready to retire, anyway. I only fancied up the place up so it will sell faster. I'm ready to play, baby." She flounced off to greet a new customer.

Hopemore without Myrtle's? I couldn't envision it. Her

mother had owned and run the restaurant before her, and she had been a Myrtle, too.

I sat there thinking about all the changes in town, happening so fast they made me dizzy. Was this how my great-grandparents had felt after the War Between the States, with everything turning upside down? Were some generations destined to live in earthshaking upheaval while others simply moved ahead? In spite of the Depression and World War II, my folks had firmly believed that the world in the twentieth century was marching onward and upward, getting better and better. In the twenty-first, one upheaval after another seemed to constantly throw us on our backsides and send us tumbling. Hope County was just a microcosm of what was happening all over—superstores putting local merchants out of business and eroding local economies; normal-looking people creating hellish concoctions in basements that maimed and killed other human beings; people retiring early so they could play, rather than devoting their lives, money, and considerable abilities to making a better world; developers bulldozing forests and farmland to build subdivisions with no concern for what future generations would eat or where they'd get oxygen to breathe.

I remembered something a writer had said at a library talk once: "When things get dull in a book, I do something surprising. Keeps my characters and my readers on their toes." Was that what God was doing in our generation? Had folks in the United States taken "better and better" too much for granted? Were all these challenges we faced simply another twist in the divine plot?

"I've been on my toes a while now," I pointed out to the great author upstairs, "and my toes are getting tired. I could use some peace and calm about now."

I did not consider the sight of Hubert coming in the door an answer to that prayer.

When he looked around and saw me, he turned his head real quick, like he wanted to pretend I wasn't there, but while

I expected him to feel lower than a pregnant dachshund's belly, he greeted everybody else like his normal perky self.

Unfortunately, Myrtle didn't have any more empty tables. I slid out of my booth and headed toward him. "Hey, Hubert, we've got an extra seat. Come join me. Joe Riddley will be here in a minute."

He sat down with obvious reluctance, but once seated, he adopted a hearty manner. "How you doing, Mac? Everybody treating you okay?" His ears were red. I didn't know if that was from embarrassment or because he hadn't worn a hat outside.

"Not particularly." I referred to the general state of the world, but when I remembered Uncle Billy and his dog, I had to add, "Not as bad as they could be treating me, though. Oh, I need to tell you something. We had a problem down at Ridd's and needed to put Cindy's horse and our dogs in your barn for a night or two. Will that be all right?"

"Sure. It's standing empty. I keep thinking I ought to sell the barn and the rest of the land, but I can't seem to get around to it. Truth is, I hate to get rid of my garden acre and that watermelon patch. It grows the best watermelons in Georgia."

"You got that right. I wonder if Ridd would like to buy it from you. You could put the right to all the watermelons you can eat in the purchase agreement."

"Now there's an idea. I'll think about it when I get over my jet lag. Just got back from New Orleans this morning."

"How was it?"

"Okay, I guess. I took in a couple of parades over the weekend, but I decided to come home early. You heard from Evelyn?" He wasn't looking at me. He was watching his forefinger trace circles on the red Formica table.

"She came to work this morning."

His head came up like a dog scenting game. "She did? When did she come back?"

"Yesterday, I understand. Wasn't it as much fun as you'd hoped?"

"Is that what she said?"

"She didn't say much of anything. I figured you all had a misunderstanding."

His temper hit the flash point and his face turned as red as Myrtle's Formica. "Misunderstanding, my foot!" He slammed the table with one fist. "That woman accused me of everything under the sun, then stormed out and never came back."

"Gracious! What had you done?"

"Not a thing. We'd barely got there. I don't know what her problem was. I got us a real nice room—it even had a view and a balcony. Cost a pretty penny, I can tell you that. But she left five minutes after we got there and I never saw her again."

I raised my eyebrows. "*A* room? Not two rooms? I didn't realize you folks were on that footing. Sounds like you were planning a racy time."

"I wasn't planning anything. I was being sensible. They stick you good down there during Mardi Gras. The room had two beds. Evelyn wasn't in any danger."

"Maybe that was the trouble. Maybe she'd have preferred that you get two rooms and then invite yourself into hers for a little danger."

He stared. "Two rooms? What a stupid waste of money."

"Nothing is stupid when you are trying to woo a lady, Hubert. If you like her, you need to let her know, and show her how special she is. What I'd suggest—"

Hubert pounded the table with both fists and shouted loud enough for everybody in the place to hear, "I don't need a woman in my life! Myrtle? Can you find me another table?"

Myrtle waved her table-wiping cloth. "One coming up over here, Hubert. Just let me clear it off for you." She threw me a smirk and started collecting dishes.

He stomped across the restaurant and didn't look back.

I hadn't noticed that Joe Riddley had arrived until he loomed up beside me, pulling off his cap and gloves. He wiggled out of his heavy jacket and piled his things in the other side of the booth before he took his seat. We get cold so seldom down here that none of the restaurants have coatracks.

"Were you proposing to Hubert, Little Bit? I heard him say he doesn't need a woman in his life."

I sighed. "I was proposing he learn how to treat women, but it didn't penetrate his thick skull."

"I presume it penetrated yours that he doesn't want your advice?"

I ignored that. "You took longer to get here than I expected."

"I stopped by the gas station to fill up a can and dropped it by the store. I called Evelyn about something and she said she was so upset when she got back from Atlanta yesterday, she forgot to watch her gauge. When she tried to go home for lunch, her tank was dry. I told her I'd bring her a few gallons on my way to dinner. She had walked down to Casa Mas Esperanza by the time I got there, but I left a can inside the back door. That ought to be enough to get her to a station on her way home."

"You've done your good deed for the day and deserve your dinner." I passed him the menu. "I've ordered country-fried steak."

Myrtle waltzed over and proceeded to flirt with my husband while she poured his coffee.

"Let me know when you need a refill," she cooed.

"But you only get one," I warned. "After that, you pay extra."

"For Joe Riddley I might make an exception." She batted her artificial lashes at him and wiggled away.

"Cow," I muttered.

Joe Riddley grinned. "Some of us have what it takes. Admit it."

He didn't seem real worried about Billy and his dog. I wished I could convince myself to follow his example, but my worrier was still in high gear.

Joe Riddley exchanged greetings with folks at nearby tables like it was a perfectly normal workday, but I soon discovered his cavalier attitude was all a big act. He motioned to Myrtle, she arrived within two seconds flat, and he announced, "I'll have whatever MacLaren's having."

He hadn't opened the menu, and he hated country-fried steak. He was more worried than he was letting on.

"Except he wants ham with sweet potatoes, and pepper sauce for his collards," I called after her twitching skirt.

"That's what I said," he said.

"Got it," she called back.

"The sheriff is really worried about that character and his dog." Joe Riddley rubbed the side of his cheek, another sign that he was disturbed.

"I know. I spoke to him right before I left Martha's. Billy stole somebody else's license tag up near I-20 and left his on their car. I'm hoping he's heading toward Atlanta about now. Or maybe Charleston."

"Buster seems to think he's still in the area, and he could be right." It was another sign how disturbed Joe Riddley was that he called the sheriff by his boyhood nickname right there in public. He added, "I want you to leave town for a few days—maybe go to the beach or something."

"It's February and freezing outside, in case you haven't noticed. Why would I go to the beach? And what would I do once I got there?"

"Then pick someplace else. Go up to Atlanta and shop or visit museums. You're always talking about how you want to go places."

"I'm always talking about how I want *us* to go places, preferably overseas. But we can't run from this thing, honey. Who knows when we'd feel safe to come back? The rest of our lives we'd be looking over one shoulder in case Uncle Billy showed up. Besides, who knows what he might do to our family or employees if he thought we'd left town to avoid him?"

"I wasn't talking about us leaving town, Little Bit, just you.

If something happened to you, Buster would never forgive me." He reached for his coffee and accidentally spilled it.

I handed him a wad of paper napkins from the dispenser. Myrtle doesn't run to cloth napkins or even the expensive paper ones, but as soon as she saw who it was who'd had the accident, she was there with a terry-cloth towel, a fresh cup, and a coffeepot. I didn't say a word until she was gone. Then I demanded, "*Buster* would never forgive *you*? The line is supposed to be 'I would never forgive myself.'"

He glowered like I'd said something stupid. "That, too, of course, but right now Buster's on my case. Back in sixth grade we had a little dustup over you. He felt I wasn't taking good enough care of you, and he said if I wouldn't, he'd be glad to take on the responsibility." Joe Riddley didn't even notice my jaw drop, he was so far back in memory. "I blacked his eye and he split my lip. Or maybe it was the other way around. In any case, I finally pinned him to the ground and he agreed he'd back off and let me have you, on condition that I kept you safe. But he's making noises these past couple of days like he thinks I'm falling down on my job. He may have a point."

I was incensed. "You two lugs thought a fight would decide who would 'have' me, like I was property you had a right to dispose of? I suppose you think if Buster had won back then, I'd be the sheriff's wife about now. Do you?"

He didn't say a word.

"I'll tell you something, Joe Riddley Yarbrough, and don't you forget it. I decided to marry you my first day of school, when you gave me the brownie from your lunchbox. Buster never had a chance after that. So you needn't worry about what Buster thinks or doesn't think about how safe you are keeping me. Besides, I can take care of myself. I've told the sheriff that I propose to go back to work this afternoon, but I'll hire an off-duty deputy to guard the store. If Uncle Billy is in the county, the deputy can deal with him. Meanwhile, I want to find out where Wylie Quarles was Saturday night. I think I've figured out Grady Handley's alibi. He was—"

Now it was Joe Riddley pounding the table. "You are not to get involved in this investigation! How many times do I have to tell you that?" He automatically moved his arm so Myrtle could set down his plate, but didn't even give her a glance. She slammed my plate down, glared at me, and swished off.

Myrtle's husband had died a while back after being puny for years. I had no doubt whatsoever that if I died before Joe Riddley, Myrtle would wear her best hat to my funeral.

We ate in what I think is called stony silence. My dinner certainly tasted like rocks and gravel. I tried a concession. "I'll dead-bolt the office door from inside, if you're worried."

"I'm not worried that Billy will come after you. I think that's nonsense. It wasn't our fault that the police found the meth lab. He ought to be grateful that we fed his dog. What I am worried about is that you'll go haring all over the county looking for a new suspect to replace Grady Handley, and you'll come on Billy unexpectedly. Leave the detecting to Buster. It's his job."

He turned down dessert for both of us, we shrugged on our coats and gloves, and he paid the bill while I waited at the door.

As he stood in line at the register, one of his friends who hadn't noticed me standing there said, "Tell your wife I said hello."

Joe Riddley nodded as he stepped up to pay. "As soon as we start speaking again, that is the first message I'll give her."

He took my elbow and led me to his car.

"Mine's right over there," I protested.

"We'll get it later. I'd rather drive you back myself."

"You don't even trust me to drive three blocks?"

He didn't answer.

Back in the office he called the sheriff's office to request an off-duty deputy. I booted up my computer. He sat at his desk reading seed catalogs.

It could have been a normal Monday afternoon. I settled down to work.

When the deputy arrived, I was fixing to tell him where to conceal himself in case Billy showed up when Joe Riddley spoke before I could. "I want you to sit right outside this office door and be sure my wife doesn't leave for any reason whatsoever—except to go to the bathroom or the Coke machine. Keep your gun handy, in case a man with long blond hair or a man with a dog heads this way, but that's unlikely. In that case, though, I want you to guard the judge, here, with your life. You got all that?"

"I got it, sir. I'll watch her."

The deputy dragged our wing chair out and I heard it creak as he settled himself in it.

"Looks like I've hired myself a jailer instead of a protector," I grumbled after we'd shut the door.

Joe Riddley didn't look up from his catalog. "You'd better behave yourself, or we might make it a permanent position."

The phone rang. "If anybody calls you wanting a magistrate this afternoon, I'd rather you stayed at the store," the sheriff told me.

"I've got a jailer outside my door," I informed him. "I'm not likely to be going anywhere. But it has occurred to me that you might want to look into the whereabouts of Wylie Quarles on Saturday night. He was pretty fond of Starr Knight, and when I saw him at Myrtle's just now, he sure wasn't grieving Robin. If he got wind of the fact that she and Billy were making meth and if he knew Starr was using meth, he might have decided Robin had something to do with Starr's death."

"It's an angle worth—"

I felt something at my ankle and heard a familiar *click!*

"Buster! Joe Riddley's cuffed me to my desk again!"

Joe Riddley took the phone. "I've got a deputy to keep anybody from getting in, and I've fixed it so she can't get out. You satisfied that she's safe enough?"

He held out the phone so I could hear the sheriff's reply. "She ought to be. But if you leave the office, be sure the dead bolt is on."

"Don't you tell me how to protect my wife! I'm perfectly capable of—"

I grabbed the phone back. "Stop it, both of you! I will not be treated like—"

Joe Riddley leaned down and spoke into the receiver. "Now buzz off and leave her out of this investigation. Good-bye, Sheriff." He pushed the button to hang up, then pinched the plastic button to disconnect the handset from my phone. He set it over on his own desk, out of reach.

Something moved outside our window at the edge of my vision. I looked that way, hoping it was somebody looking in who would see what Joe Riddley was doing and come to rescue me, but all I saw was the top of our tea olive moving in the rising wind.

"You can give me my phone back and take off the cuffs now," I informed him. "I've told the sheriff everything I know or suspect. That's all I plan to do about this."

"Heard that sort of thing before. As soon as I get down to the nursery, you'll think of one more thing and head out to help the sheriff a little more." He reached for his cap. "This is just to keep you here while I run down there to finish up a job. I'll be back in an hour."

"You've got a deputy guarding my door."

"Deputies have been known to go to the bathroom. It's not for long, Little Bit. I'll take it off as soon as I get back."

"But what if Uncle Billy comes, and his dog?"

"You have an armed deputy outside your door. No man or dog is going to get to you in the next hour. If it makes you feel better, I'll leave the deputy the keys to the cuffs and the dead bolt. But don't you try to make him let you out. He's incorruptible."

My ankle felt like it was weighted with iron.

I stooped to begging. "Please don't leave me like this again. Remember last time? I chafed my ankle so badly I nearly got an infection. I could have lost a foot."

"Exaggeration will get you nowhere." Joe Riddley moved over to the filing cabinet and took my lotion out of the top drawer. "However, because I'm a nice guy, I'll grease you up good. Didn't Martha say that would keep you from chafing?" He knelt beside me and put lotion on my ankle so thick I'd never get it out of my panty hose, even if they didn't tear.

I pummeled him on the back with both fists. He got to his feet and reached for a tissue from the box.

"First I was assaulted and now I've been robbed," I noted, glaring at him using my tissue to clean his guilty hands. "I'm going to throw the book at you this time."

"Not yet you aren't." He bent down and pinned my arms beside me while he kissed me. "I'll be back in an hour."

I pulled away. "I've heard that song before. I didn't like it the first time and I don't want to hear it again. Let me go. I hate being tied up."

"I know. I wouldn't do it if it weren't for your own good."

"Your verb tense shows you think it's a condition that isn't true," I pointed out.

"You always were better in English. See you in an hour." He settled his cap firmly on his head. He turned the key in the dead-bolt lock and, true to his word, left both keys with the deputy.

ᘒ 26 ᘓ

I checked my watch. One minute down and fifty-nine to go. I jotted the time on a slip of paper on my desk. So help me, if Joe Riddley wasn't back in one hour, I would pretend to be choking until the deputy came in; then I'd make him give me the telephone and I'd call Isaac down at the police station to go arrest the old coot for false imprisonment.

I fiddled with my right foot until I got the stool under my left. As comfortable as it was possible to get, I realized I wasn't really out of touch with folks. He'd left me my computer.

I sent e-mails to every member of our family who had an address: "I am being held prisoner in my office. Please notify the authorities or send help."

Immediately I had a reply from Bethany, but it made no sense whatsoever: "Thnx 4 tha jk. G2g to class. I <3 U. L8tr. B."

Five minutes later I had a message from Walker, out in Colorado. "Did he cuff you again? Looks like you'd learn your lesson."

I went back to Bethany's message and forwarded it to Walker. "Bethany sent this. Can you decode?"

About ten seconds later, our private office line rang—but of course I couldn't reach it. In another minute, I had another message from Walter. "Where are you? I called the office. Bethany said, 'Thanks for the joke. Got to go to class. I love you. Later.' You need to learn the language of text messaging. What was the joke?"

"No joke. She got the same message you did, and believe me, I'm not laughing. Your father also disconnected my desk phone. I am a prisoner, I tell you!"

"At least you ought to get a lot of work done. LoL, which means 'Lots of laughs.'"

Mumbling imprecations on irreverent sons, I tried to work, but all I could think of was Robin's death, who might have killed her, and why. I went back over everything I had heard about it and began to form some conclusions. I sent an e-mail to the sheriff. "Come see me, since I can't come see you. I think I know who killed Robin."

He didn't reply.

I sat there fuming, planning ways to get revenge on Joe Riddley for cuffing me again and revenge on Buster for inciting him to do it. First, I needed to get free. "Send me two hefty men," I prayed out loud, "and help me not to kill both Joe Riddley and Buster when I get out of here."

The deputy rapped at my door. "Okay if Trevor Knight comes in?"

"Absolutely." I was delighted. God hadn't sent two hefty men, but he'd sent one equal to two. Besides, I wanted to talk with Trevor anyway.

"What's with the dead bolt?" he asked as soon as the deputy had unlocked the door and locked us both inside.

"Joe Riddley's notion of a joke. It's too complicated to explain—and too stupid. I take it you haven't heard about our adventures yesterday?"

He shook his head. "Bradley and I holed up all day yesterday, and I haven't talked to many people today. Tell me about it. Then I want to ask you a favor."

"I'll tell you my story in a minute and you can tell me what's on your mind, but first, would you do *me* a favor? As part of his prank, Joe Riddley has cuffed me to this desk. I'm really uncomfortable. Do you reckon you could lift it high enough for me to slide the cuff down the leg?"

He shook his head. "Sorry, Judge, but the deputy told me if you asked me that, I wasn't to do it. Joe Riddley's orders."

"Why should Joe Riddley's orders supersede my wishes?"

"Us men gotta stick together."

"That's the dumbest reason in the universe for doing anything, but I can see I'm not getting any sympathy. You might as well tell me what's on your mind." I waved him toward Joe Riddley's chair. It would hold his bulk, even though he'd regained most of his weight since Christmas.

He settled in, shuffled his feet, and sat looking at his hands for so long, I wondered if he'd forgotten why he'd come. Joe Riddley used to do that while he was recovering from traumatic head injury. I thought maybe Trevor was suffering post-traumatic stress syndrome after Robin's death.

It was more than a minute by our office clock before he took a deep breath, let it all out, and said, "Wylie called and told me the sheriff has arrested Robin's husband for her murder."

"Not yet. So far he's just arrested him for trespassing and disturbing a crime scene. He was considering him for the murder, but I think we can prove where he was at the time."

"Oh. Does Sheriff Gibbons have any other suspects?"

"I think he has been leaning toward that fellow the girls call Uncle Billy—or possibly even Wylie."

"Wylie? He wouldn't kill anybody, particularly a woman."

"Anybody might kill with the right provocation."

"Well, you got this one wrong, Judge. It wasn't Wylie." His body slumped.

I recognized that posture. I'd seen it in the courtroom many times.

"You did it, didn't you? I figured that out this afternoon."

Startled, he asked, "How?"

"She couldn't have been in that elevator long, or somebody

else would have found her. The most logical suspects, then, were the folks who actually did find her. Somebody who went back to the parking lot and waited for somebody else to come along heading for the elevator, so he could tag along and pretend to find her. It had to be you or the man with you, who turned out to be her daddy."

That startled him. "Her daddy?"

"Yeah. Her parents had been looking for her for years, and had finally recognized the work she did on that fox. He certainly had cause to be angry with her, but he is a sick, frail man, without the strength to break her neck. Besides, he was so shocked by her death, he had a heart attack."

Trevor buried his face in his hands. "Dear, merciful God. And I was the one who let them find her."

"Bradley said you cried all night long after she died. I figured out you weren't crying from sadness, you were crying from remorse."

He nodded, his eyes pink. "I'll probably cry off and on for the rest of my life. I threw away so much. So much!"

I felt like somebody had taken a huge boulder and stuffed it into my middle. "Why?"

"I found out Robin and Billy were making meth and got Starry hooked. It was also Robin who arranged for Roddy and Slick to kill Starry, because she was going to rat on them." He didn't notice he'd reverted to her childhood name. He pounded his thigh with one huge fist. "She tried to tell me not to get mixed up with Robin. Why didn't I listen?"

There was no answer to that.

"How did you find out?"

"Roddy told me when I went to see him Friday evening."

It took me a couple of seconds to remember who Roddy was: one of the two men who had killed Starr—the younger one, who had put her in the truck and pushed it over the embankment into the kudzu. "You went to see him?" I was having trouble taking that in.

Trevor seemed relieved to discuss something else for a minute.

"Yeah. I've been going to see him every Friday for weeks. When the trial was over—well, I fell apart. Bradley got me back on track. He learned the Lord's Prayer in Sunday School, and he wanted to say it at every meal. You know that line, 'Forgive us our sins as we forgive those who sin against us'? It started working on me. I started thinking how I've been scum in my time. I've been forgiven a heck of a lot—not only by God but by this community. Heck, I probably understand those boys better than they understand themselves. I know how you can get so low you'll do anything for your next fix or a drink. I know what it is to believe nobody cares a thing about you. You get to the place where you aren't even yourself. It's like there's something in your gut that is bigger and meaner than you."

He was hitting his stride now. This was the Trevor we all knew and loved, the man who could address a bunch of high school kids or a bunch of well-heeled donors and hold them in his palm while he told his own story, then made a pitch for them to change their lives or give money to help others change. He could preach it better than anybody I knew.

I didn't need preaching right that minute. I needed wisdom. *Help!* I winged a prayer.

I motioned for him to stop talking. "I know your story. So you went to tell Roddy you forgave him. Did you go tell Slick, too?" I've been a Christian a lot longer than Trevor, but forgiving Slick—well, I was glad I hadn't been the one tapped for that assignment.

"I told them both, but Slick blew me off. Roddy cried. Told me he never wanted to hurt her, but the only way he could get more drugs was to do what he was told. He never would tell me who ordered him to do it, though. He kept saying that if he confessed or told anybody who they were, they'd get his sister, Charmaine, hooked on drugs. I kept pointing out that if they knew he had a sister, they'd try to hook her anyway. That must have gotten through to him eventually, because on Friday he told me. He begged me to help Charmaine before they get to her, since he can't do anything from inside. I promised."

Trevor smiled sadly. "Doesn't look like I'll be outside long enough to keep that promise, does it?"

We could deal with the question of Charmaine later. Right now I wanted him to finish what he'd come to say. "Roddy explicitly told you it was Robin and Billy who called in Roddy and Slick?"

"Billy actually called them, but 'his woman partner' was the one who told him when to call. Apparently they'd already suspected Starr was going to turn them in. They'd had Roddy and Slick watching her. When Starr called the shop asking to borrow Wylie's truck to drive to Augusta, Robin figured that was the day."

"Roddy named Robin?" I asked.

"When I leaned on him a little."

I was puzzled. "Looks like they would have said something at their trial—especially when she testified."

"I don't think they ever saw her. Roddy said Billy took care of the business end and his partner did most of the cooking. But Roddy did know that Billy's partner had 'some bird's name,' and she worked at the place where her truck was."

"Did Roddy say how they got Starr to take Robin's truck, or how he and Slick got Starr to stop the truck for them?"

"They didn't have to. They were the ones who took Robin's truck. Billy told them to go by Starr's and slash her tires, then come get Robin's truck, go back to Starr's place as if they were just riding by, and offer her a lift out to Trevor's to pick up Wylie's truck. Starr knew them. In addition to using drugs, Roddy and Slick were both selling. They were the ones who usually sold Starr her meth."

"So they drove her somewhere and killed her."

"Yeah. The woods near Robin's house, Roddy said. He swears he didn't have anything to do with actually killing her, but you can't believe everything an addict tells you. I've told some whoppers in my life. I remember . . ."

I didn't want us to get sidetracked onto Trevor's own story again. "Roddy put Starr in the truck. His prints were on the truck and on her body, while Slick's were only on the bat."

"They were both real upset about those prints. Billy had promised there would be latex gloves in the truck, but there weren't any. I've had time to think that over, and I have decided Wylie must have taken them earlier that day, to save himself a trip. We had run out and our order wasn't coming until Monday, so I'd told him to drive to CVS and get some. He came back almost immediately and said he'd found some in his cab. I think he took them from Robin's instead, figuring he could replace them before she missed them. Robin was out front talking to a customer at the time, so she wouldn't have known."

We sat quiet for a moment, imagining a series of actions unfold that would lead eventually not only to murder but to the discovery of it.

Finally Trevor resumed his story. "Roddy wanted to stop and buy gloves, but Slick was afraid somebody would remember who'd bought them. He told Roddy they'd get rid of the bat and wash the truck real good once they got it over with."

Trevor looked down at his hands as we both considered what "get it over with" had involved.

"They weren't supposed to send the truck off the bypass?"

"No, that was Roddy's mistake. Slick was in his own car by then, following, and Roddy drove the truck. Slick had told him to put the bat in a Dumpster and throw Starr off the bypass. Roddy decided to throw the bat in the kudzu, too. He put the truck in neutral instead of park when he got out to dispose of the bat, and the next thing he knew, to use his own words, 'that dang truck rolled off the edge before I noticed it was moving.'"

"An act of God," I murmured. Trevor looked up, startled. "Heaven only knows how long it would have taken to find her body in the kudzu," I explained. "Instead, the truck was found in a few days and the sheriff thought to look in the same place for the bat. It's all of a piece with the gloves not being in the truck. Things done in secret will come to light. We are promised that."

He nodded. "I believe it. Now, what I did in secret needs to be brought to light, too."

We had arrived at last to the moment we both had been trying hard to postpone. "Why didn't you tell Sheriff Gibbons what you knew on Friday evening and let him deal with it?"

"I planned to, but I'd made plans to meet friends for a drink and I was running late. Talking to Roddy took longer than it usually did, and driving was slow with the freeze. I figured, 'No sweat. I'll talk to the sheriff when I get home, or even tomorrow.' I didn't see that there was any hurry. Robin wasn't going anywhere if she didn't know I knew. When I started up to my friends' room, though, this lady in a fur coat was getting on the elevator up ahead. I yelled, 'Hold it!' and put on some speed. When I got inside, the woman was Robin, dressed fit to kill. Sorry, that's not what I meant to say."

"The language is full of violent images we don't usually mean. Go on."

"I said, 'I've just come from talking to your friend Roddy.' She shrugged and said, 'I don't know any Roddy.' I said, 'Odd. He said it was you who got Starr hooked on meth.' And she laughed and said, 'I don't know what you're talking about.' Then she moved closer to me and asked in this husky voice, 'You like the way I look all dressed up? We could have fun together sometime.' That's when I saw red— and it wasn't her dress. She had killed my daughter, and there she was, trying to vamp me."

I watched his color rise as the anger he had felt at the time surged through him again. He rubbed both cheeks with his hands and took several deep breaths to regain his composure. "I never meant to kill her. I swear it. I wanted to shake some sense into her. But once I started—" He looked down at his hands as if he couldn't believe what they had done. "I was back in Nam, with an enemy by the throat." He swallowed hard. "I'm not making excuses, but I was trained to kill. Once I started, that training took over and I broke her neck."

"You didn't consider calling the sheriff at that point?"

"Sure I did. As soon as she went limp I knew I had to call 911 and turn myself in. I reached for my phone, but I'd left it in the truck. I went back for it and was turning it on when the Poynters arrived. I got out to warn them not to use the elevator, and instead—"

I waved for him to stop. "I can guess the rest." Which of us has not chosen the easier way out of a difficult situation when it's offered on a plate?

We sat staring at each other for several minutes. Both of us were reluctant for him to take the next step.

"Speaking of things in the dark brought to light," I said, "did you hear about the meth lab the sheriff's deputy found in Robin's basement?"

"No, but Roddy said she and Billy were making the meth they sold at her house."

"Did he tell you Billy wasn't Robin's brother?"

"No. I didn't know Robin was supposed to have a brother, so the matter never came up."

"There's a possibility he's a man she ran away from home with seven years ago. She eventually left him and married somebody else, but they seem to have hooked up again recently and come to Hope County to make methamphetamine."

I shifted in my chair to get more comfortable. Outside the window I heard the crash of two automobiles hitting each other—or was that the crash of our world falling apart?

Inside my office, the only sound was Trevor's harsh breathing as he fought back sobs. "I cannot believe I let that daddy and mama find their own child's body. I am not fit to live. I gotta tell the sheriff, right now." He rose from his seat.

I let out a breath I hadn't known I was holding. "I can't think of anything else you can do. Not and remain the honorable man you are."

He gave a short, unfunny laugh. "I'm not honorable, Judge. For years I've been a man trying to do the best I could with what I'd got. This time, though, I really blew it. Blew it bad." He pressed his lips together and took several deep breaths. "What I really came about is Bradley. I want . . . I don't want . . ."

He broke down and spoke between sobs. "I don't . . . I don't want him to . . . to know that his T-daddy . . . his T-daddy is a murderer." He raised his face to me. Tears flowed down his cheeks and got lost in his beard. "Can you keep that from him, Judge? Do you think Ridd and Martha would take him again, tell him I got real sick and died? That's gonna be real hard on him, but not as hard as knowing the truth. And I can't stand to think of him coming to jail to see me. There's an evil spirit that pervades those places. I don't want it to contaminate him. He's so good, Judge. So pure. Can you all take care of him for me?"

Moved by his grief, I would have done anything he asked—except let him go free. "Sure we can, Trevor. We'll take care of Bradley. But we won't lie and tell him you died, because you won't be inside forever. It wasn't premeditated murder. You'll be home by the time Bradley is grown. You might even change your mind about seeing him before then."

He shook his head. "I don't want him to see me there. Don't bring him, even if he begs. Promise me."

"He couldn't come without your permission. You'd have to put him on your list. But seeing you paying for your mistake could be a powerful lesson in consequences. And you'd get to watch him grow up."

"No, Judge. I've given this a lot of thought. I went by the bank this morning and put all my money in his name, and I went to Jed's office and put the house and business in his name. I didn't tell anybody why I was doing it, but he'll be taken care of financially. All I ask is that you good people look after him for me."

I could hardly see him for a blur of tears. "We'll take care of him for you. And we'll tell him you are an honorable man who owned up to your mistake."

He shook his head. "It wasn't a mistake. It was a sin, but it was not a mistake. If I had Billy in my sights right now, I might do the same again."

"Leave Billy to the sheriff. He's looking for him as we speak."

"Then I pray he finds him fast. I need to go back home and get some last loose ends tied up. Then I'll go to the sheriff."

He stood and looked at me awkwardly, like he was waiting for something.

I put out my hand. "I'm proud to know you, Trevor Knight."

He gave me his big paw with a wry smile. "That makes one of us. See you later, Judge."

I didn't reply. We both knew where that was likely to be.

❧ 27 ❧

The deputy locked me in again after Trevor left. I returned to my computer and started printing payroll checks, afraid my brain was going to explode from overload.

When a siren shrilled up the street and wailed to a stop close by, I wondered if somebody had been hurt in the car accident. That was likely, because in a minute, through the glass in my office door, I saw Evelyn come rushing back to the deputy, waving her arms. I couldn't distinguish any words, but her tone was excited and she kept pointing to the street.

"I'll be right back," he called to me, and went with her.

I checked my watch. Forty minutes since Joe Riddley left. Twenty to go.

The first siren was followed by two more. What could be going on? We don't get many three-siren events in town. Normally I'd have been with everybody else out on the sidewalk. We'd share information as it reached us. It irked me that I had to sit inside and wait for Evelyn or Gladys to bring me the news.

They didn't come. Neither did anybody else. Our store was so dead you'd think I had wandered into Hubert's closed store by mistake. I strained to listen and couldn't detect a soul outside.

"Deputy? Hey, Deputy! Are you out there? Did you come back?"

He didn't reply.

I have never given much thought to the end of the world, but I began to get the creepy feeling that maybe all of humanity had been raptured and I alone had been left behind.

"Evelyn?" I yelled in the voice that used to call our boys to dinner from two fields away.

No response.

"Gladys? Evelyn?" We had a policy that everybody was never to leave the store at once.

Nobody came.

I picked up my dictionary and hurled it at the door to our office with all my strength. I thought it would make a racket as it hit the floor. Instead, it shattered the glass and went right through.

"Serves you right," I muttered to Joe Riddley. "You'll have to fix it."

It had made a lovely crash, but still nobody came.

"This joke has gone far enough," I yelled.

I heard soft footsteps. A tall form slithered toward my door.

Billy Baxter. He looked remarkably like somebody else as he peered at me through the broken glass. Probably Natalie. I'd seen a lot of her lately.

He turned the knob.

Thank God the dead bolt was locked.

He reached a hand through the broken glass, fumbling for the bolt on my side.

"It can only be opened by a key," I told him. "How did you get in?"

He spoke through the hole in the glass. "Easy. Nobody's here but us chickens. They're all outside, watching the fun. They's a big fire across the street." His grin chilled my soul. Looking at those crooked yellow teeth, I knew how Little Red Riding Hood's grandmother had felt.

I had to try twice before I could get out, "Fire?"

"Yeah, that old appliance store. Burning beautifully."

"Hubert's? It's empty. How could it catch on fire?"

Billy's satisfied smirk gave me one possible answer. A chill went up my spine. Had he created a diversion to empty our store?

He confirmed it. "Had me a little traffic accident that snarled traffic so bad the fire trucks had a hard time getting close enough, too. Wasn't that a shame?" When he smiled, I knew who he reminded me of. Not Natalie. Evil incarnate.

At least he couldn't know Joe Riddley had incapacitated me. How had he even known I was in the office?

I remembered the shadow at the window. Had that been Billy, peering in?

He was still feeling through the hole for a way to unlock the dead bolt. "It takes a key on both sides," I informed him.

"Some husband, locking you up like that and leaving you all by your lonesome."

I didn't correct his misperception. The deputy would be back soon. Billy couldn't get in. Maybe I could play him along until then.

"Did you treat Robin well?" I asked. "I understand you aren't her brother at all."

"You got that right. I'm gonna miss old Bobbie. Me'n her went back a long way. Been together for—let's see—must be seven years, except for three when I had to pay a small debt to society."

I wondered why they had ever let him out.

"Was that when Robin got married?" I spoke loudly. I wanted the deputy to hear us talking and approach warily.

"That wasn't what you think." Billy brayed a laugh. "We fixed that up between us, Bobbie and me. I told her to look for somebody who could finance a new start for us once I was free to roam. As soon as I walked, she dropped him and we took the midnight train to Georgia."

I believed it. What I had learned of Robin these past few weeks made me certain she would have married Grady to get her hands on his furniture and family silver, and left him as soon as Billy was free. My only question was what she saw in Billy. From the whiffs I was getting from the doorway, bathing was not on his list of favorite preoccupations.

He wasn't good-looking, either. *Weedy* was the word that came to mind. His face was sharp as a ferret's, his yellow hair limp and greasy on his shoulders. Had she been attracted to the air of bravado and danger that circled him like an energy field?

He leaned against the door, careful of the broken pane, and chilled me again with his next words. "I came in through the loading dock, but I lowered the grill back there and locked the other doors, so nobody can get in. We're all alone in here. You and me need to have a chat. You're the one sicced the cops on me, ain't you."

It was a statement rather than a question, and he didn't wait for a reply. "And let out my dog, got him drugged and carried down to the pound, and showed the cops our underground nest. Also thanks to you, now I got a cash flow problem. I got plenty of money, mind—Bobbie and I had been saving up, and we were about ready to split from Hope County and live high. But now the sheriff's confiscated it. Leaves me real short. I can't even use a credit card without setting off bells. But I'm getting powerful hungry, and my truck's low on fuel. Don't have enough gas to skip town, and I'm a wanted man. Heck, I can't buy food for my dog. He's getting real hungry again, and when he's hungry, he gets mean."

"Not as mean as what you did to Starr." That was what I wanted to say. What I would have said if the deputy had been standing beside me, as he should have been, and Billy was wearing cuffs instead of me. Courage, I discovered to my shame, is relative. Unable to run, I couldn't force a single word past my tonsils.

"So." He folded his arms and his face split in a wolfish smile. "It's payback time. I figure with a business like this, you'll be able to cover my expenses until I can get back on my feet again."

"I'd give you everything we've got, but I can't get to the register. The door is locked, I don't have a key, and I am temporarily disabled. See my ankle? My husband cuffed me to the desk to keep me from wandering off." I laughed, like it was a joke.

"You can tell me how to open the register. I'll write it down." He pulled a pen from his pocket and held out his forearm.

I gave him the steps and he wrote them on the whitest part of his skin.

"There won't be much," I warned. "We aren't doing much business in the store these days. Most of our work is with landscapers and developers, who pay by check through the mail."

He studied me like he was trying to decide whether I was bluffing. "I'll see what's there. And while I'm gone, you write me a check. Five hundred thousand will do nicely."

I laughed again. That time I couldn't help it. "We don't have that kind of money."

"Of course you do. You got a prosperous business here, a big nursery down the road—"

"And lots and lots of money tied up in inventory."

He pulled a gun from his waist and leveled it at me. "How much you reckon you got in the bank?"

"Maybe a hundred thousand. I was writing the payroll checks for this month when you came in."

"A hundred thousand will do for starters."

Now that I knew he had a gun, I didn't want Joe Riddley coming in on him unaware. *Dear God, let me get this man out of here before Joe Riddley arrives. If that's the last thing I can do for my husband, please help me do it right.*

I turned to my keyboard.

"Don't you be sending out e-mails. I said, 'Write me a check.'"

"I write checks on the computer. You don't think I write them all by hand, do you? Go get what you can from the register. I'll write the check."

As soon as he left, I switched to my e-mail account and wrote the sheriff. "Billy Baxter in my office. He set fire to Hubert's. Come fast! No sirens."

I returned to our business account and started writing his check.

Billy had no way of knowing that if anybody—including me or Joe Riddley—wrote a check for more than five hundred dollars on that account without a countersigner, a flag went up. We'd set up that procedure on the advice of an attorney who had seen too many supposedly happy marriages and business partnerships in which one partner cleaned out the bank account, then split. As soon as I wrote the check, the bank would get a notice that it should not be cashed. When Billy presented it, hopefully somebody would be around to arrest him on the spot.

He came back with a dissatisfied scowl. "There wasn't but forty-seven dollars in the register. Where's the rest?"

"That's all there is. I told you, we don't do much business in the store these days. Do I make this out to 'Billy Baxter'?"

"William Tecumseh Baxter—and no funny remarks about that."

I turned my head so he couldn't see my expression as I typed his name. What I was thinking wasn't the least bit funny: *General Sherman, you can be proud of your namesake. He's left a trail of devastation through our state that almost equals yours.*

So many lives destroyed to feed this man's greed and pride. What made him think he deserved so much?

I finished the check and heard the whir as my printer started taking in data. I automatically backed the data up onto our main computer as we watched the check print out.

"That thing isn't going to bounce, is it? There's money in the account to cover it?"

For the first time he sounded uncertain.

"Barely."

As I signed the check, I said, "Go get me a hoe. They're

on the aisle right behind you. I'll tape the check to one end if you can reach me."

He fetched the hoe in record time. He swore as his arm got cut when he thrust it toward me, but his desire for the check overcame his pain. By stretching as far as we both could reach, I managed to tape the check onto the blade. "There you go."

He folded the paper and tucked it into his shirt pocket. Then he stood looking at me with the gun in his hand. He pointed it at me. "To be sure you don't stop payment on the check, maybe I ought to . . ." He waved the gun up and down a couple of times as if considering his options.

If my life flashed before my eyes, I was too scared to notice. A voice in my head kept pleading, *This isn't what I meant by revenge on Joe Riddley. Don't let him blame himself for this.* I didn't know if I was praying or begging.

Again that wolfish grin spread over his face. "Nah, there's a better way they can't trace back to me. I noticed it on my way in. But first—"

He aimed his gun and fired. My computer monitor shattered. "Don't want you writing any of your friends. By the end of the week, I'll be lying on a sunny beach somewhere, drinking a toast to you." He made a rolling gesture with one hand like he was saluting royalty. "*Vaya con dios*, Judge. I think that covers the situation."

With a crablike sideways sidle, he left. I saw his shadow head to the back of the store.

I was still standing from handing him the check. I stretched as far as I could and managed to reach the button to lock the grill on the loading dock. That was the only way to lock or unlock it. He wouldn't be able to get out that way. But how could I let the others in?

I heard an unfamiliar *clunk*. Was he stealing fertilizer or plant food? Why on earth did he need either of those?

I didn't remember Evelyn's gasoline until I smelled it.

Dear God, he's going to burn the place down! How can I get out of here?

❧ 28 ❧

Rustle, whisper, crackle.

The outer walls of the building were brick and the roof tin, but the rafters and interior walls were pine. They'd go up like kindling. Besides, the back was full of chemicals. Would I burn first or be asphyxiated?

I jerked my leg, hoping the cuffs would give. They didn't.

I started to jettison everything on my desk. Books, papers, and what was left of my phone flew in a flurry. I heaved my monitor to the floor. In my desperation, I was strong enough to lift the desk, but I had to have both feet on the floor to do it, and couldn't wiggle my left leg enough to get the cuff to slide down the leg of the desk.

I bent down and pushed the cuff as far down as I could and tried again. Still I couldn't get the cuff off the leg of the desk. I grabbed my scissors and hurled them through the office window. It shattered, and they sailed through. *Please let somebody see them and come!*

Nobody came, but a breeze of frigid air whistled through the window. The flames crackled louder. I could smell smoke. Taste it. Feel the office growing warmer.

I heaved at the desk and dragged it a few inches, but I'd never get it to the window.

I fell back into my chair and laid my head on my desk. "Oh, God, I don't want to die like this. Please! Send help!"

I saw the wall dividing our office from the back of the store bulge and saw a dark pattern form over the filing cabinets. Would it take minutes or seconds for it to burst into flames? I heard crackling overhead and saw snakes of smoke coiling down through cracks in the punched tin ceiling. The rafters must be burning.

I left my chair and crouched beneath my desk, taking great gulps of still-fresh air into my lungs. How much longer before the air would be too smoky to breathe?

"Judge? Judge! Your building's on fire!"

Trevor Knight called through the window.

"I know! I'm under my desk. The door is dead-bolted again and the deputy's gone."

Through a haze of smoke I watched him rip off his jacket, wrap it around his hand, and finish smashing the window. He climbed in and lifted the desk. I slid the cuff off and my ankle was free.

He yanked me up as if I weighed nothing, carried me to the window, and more threw than dropped me out. I landed on my hands and knees on the asphalt below and moved just before he hurtled after me. Then he snatched me up and raced across the parking lot.

I took in great gulps of air. Trevor was winded. "I watched my best buddy burn to death in Nam. Nobody ought to die like that."

I breathed through my nose. Even full of the acrid smell of fire and cold as ice, the breeze was sweet. I raised my head to let it cool my face and ears. "Thank God you came back."

"Wanted to tell you I changed my mind. I do want Bradley to come see me. Will you bring him?"

"Of course we'll bring him. Don't worry."

Across the street, I saw the flames of Hubert's store shooting into the sky. I heard the hiss of steam as the fire department battled the blaze. I turned my head and saw identical flames coming from our store. They were raging along the side of the building and licking the roof, but folks standing on Oglethorpe Street had their backs to our building. Would anybody notice them before it was too late? The crowd was standing dangerously near.

I wriggled for Trevor to set me down. "I need to tell the firefighters that our store's on fire, too."

"Stay here. I'll tell them."

Tears rolled down my cheeks as I stood and watched my history and Joe Riddley's go up in smoke. That old store had supported four generations—five, if you counted our children—of Yarbroughs. I had met Joe Riddley in there, when I was four and he six. My daddy took me to his daddy's hardware store, and Joe Riddley hitched up his brown corduroy pants and asked, "You wanna go count nails?" We'd been counting nails ever since.

While we were counting, he had looked up and said, very seriously, "You are the cutest little bit of a thing I ever did see." That's why he eventually started calling me "Little Bit."

I had worked in the store during high school and every summer during college, learning the business from his mother and dad. When his parents retired, Joe Riddley and I had settled into their office at their desks and carried on in their tradition: honest prices, quality merchandise, and good service.

All of that was going up in smoke.

I stood there hugging myself and shaking like a blender. I didn't know if that was from the cold at my back or the disaster in front of me.

A wall gave way.

"Judge! Get back!" Trevor was coming my way again.

From the corner of my eye I saw movement. I peered through the flames and saw Billy Baxter heading toward the front of the store, frantically waving his arms. The place was full of flames. The back seemed clearer—there was less wood back there—but he couldn't get out the loading dock. He was trapped, and it was all my fault.

I took a step toward the flames. "Billy Baxter's in there! He started the fire!"

Trevor turned to look. "He's inside?"

I pointed. His figure could be seen battling flames as he tried to work his way forward.

Trevor lurched toward the side steps.

"No!" I yelled. "You can't go in! You'll never make it!"

"Nobody ought to die that way." A gust of frigid wind caught his words and blew them away as he plunged through the door and the wall of fire.

The same gust of wind circled back and hit the fire. In an instant the entire store was engulfed in flames.

I felt the breeze on my cheek while I watched Trevor reach Billy, saw them struggle together. Saw Billy draw back a fist. Saw Trevor catch the fist and use it to lever Billy onto his shoulder.

That's when the roof fell in, with a great *whoosh!* No one could get out after that.

I sank to my knees and cried, and cried, and cried.

If this were a fairy tale, Trevor would have been rescued. I like to think he was. His memorial service was larger than Starr's. I hope he knew how much he was loved.

The parking lot was getting so hot I had to move. The dangling handcuff clinked and caught on a root as I stumbled behind the thick trunk of an oak. I tripped and fell against the tree, skinning what was left of my palms after my flight through the window and my slide across the parking lot. The tree provided some protection, but when I peered around it, I could taste ash and feel my skin scorch.

Joe Riddley screeched around the corner and headed for the lot. I stepped away from the tree and waved, but he didn't see me. He slammed on his brakes, jumped out of his car practically before it stopped rolling, and headed for the blazing stairs. His cap blew off and he didn't even notice.

"Joe Riddley!" I more flew than ran toward him. I tripped on the cuff again and fell against his back. He grabbed me hard and held me so close I thought I'd smother. That would have been ironic, don't you think, after all I'd been through?

"I was so scared. So scared. So scared." He kept saying it over and over, like he couldn't stop. "I could have killed you. My God, Little Bit—"

I pulled back enough to catch my breath. "I'm fine. Trevor Knight showed up and got me out. But he died in there. He went back for Billy Baxter, and they—"

I started crying again and could not stop.

The heat was so intense that my face and hands were blistering. My tears burned as they rolled down my cheeks. Joe Riddley picked me up and carried me to the back of the lot and out into the street that ran behind the store. I buried my face in his shoulder and cried some more. Crying usually made Joe Riddley nervous, but he didn't seem to mind.

He finally set me down. Exhausted, we clung together and watched Yarbrough Feed, Seed, and Nursery go up in flames. The fire department had the good sense to concentrate their efforts on buildings nearby.

We were there a couple of hours.

At last, when the whole place was reduced to embers, we picked our way through the parking lot to see who was up on Oglethorpe Street. Evelyn, Gladys, and the deputy stood looking toward our store with stricken faces. When they saw me, it was like morning breaking after a storm. "We thought you'd burned up!" Gladys greeted me.

Evelyn didn't say a word. She just held me so tight I couldn't breathe.

Joe Riddley rested one hand on Evelyn's shoulder and another on Gladys's. "Everybody go home now. We'll call you tomorrow about what we're going to do."

We walked together toward his car. The paint was blistered, and I knew it would be too hot to touch. "I think you're gonna need a new car. Good thing we left mine at Myrtle's."

He gave a short laugh. "That's not all we're gonna need."

Glady's car, like his, was burned, but Evelyn had parked under the big oak at the back. She offered to take Gladys home.

As they pulled out, we waved, then stood staring at the ruin of the old building. Joe Riddley pulled me close and rubbed his chin on the top of my head. "What you thinking, Little Bit?"

"I'm thinking it was a good thing I persuaded you to let me network my computer with the one at the nursery. At least we haven't lost any records. What are you thinking?"

"I'm thinking we don't have to make the decision to close the store."

"And it won't ever be a real estate office, or an antique emporium, or a dollar store."

He gave me a squeeze. "Trevor saved the most valuable thing in there. The rest can go. Shall we walk home and get a bath? You smell like you need one."

❧ 29 ❧

When I woke the next morning, I didn't remember the fire for at least a minute. Then I felt the tight skin on my face and hands, and I smelled smoke. Although we had stripped in the garage and run stark naked to the shower—hoping the neighbors had the good manners not to look—the odor permeated our house. Joe Riddley swore I had the odor in the pores of my skin.

I lay there staring at the ceiling—the wonderful white, un-smoky ceiling—and thought about the mess we had to face. We had called Walker the night before, since he held the insurance policy on the business. He would be flying home that morning to start processing our claim. That hadn't made him a happy camper. We still had to deal with our own grief and with sadness from both our sons and their families. Neither son had ever wanted to take over the business, but they had grown up in the store and had seemed to think their parents would run it forever.

I had lost my pocketbook. Gladys and Evelyn probably had, too, leaving them behind when they dashed out to watch Hubert's fire. That meant that we'd have the hassle of replacing driver's licenses, credit cards, and things like insurance and library cards. I mourned pictures in my wallet I could not replace.

When I thought of all the suppliers I'd have to notify, out-standing bills that would still have to be paid, employees to take care of, I nearly pulled the covers over my head and stayed in bed. I would have to ask to be relieved of magis-trate duties for a spell. Heck. Maybe I'd retire!

Joe Riddley turned on his pillow. "Glad you can think of something to laugh about, Little Bit. Keep it up while we eat a quick breakfast and walk downtown. Let's see if there's anything we can salvage now that things have cooled down."

We arrived to find Oglethorpe Street closed off to traffic at each end of our block and full of people. Among the throng I spotted Maynard and Selena standing with Hubert. Hubert was frowning at his store and pointedly ignoring Evelyn, who stood with Gladys looking at ours. Jed and Meriwether were there, with baby Zach. Even Gusta was there, holding Otis's arm. From the door of the bank Vern, the security guard, eyed her warily.

Martha had brought Cricket, Bradley, and the girls. As soon as she spotted me, she asked Selena to watch the chil-dren and came to tell me privately, "They were going to hear about it anyway, so I thought it would be less traumatic to see it for themselves. But I've got a problem. Trevor called on my cell phone yesterday and asked if I could pick Bradley up from day care and keep him for the day. He dropped him off at Selena's around two and never came back. I've been trying to reach him, but he doesn't answer."

I took her out of earshot of little ears and explained what had happened. Her face went slack with shock. "I never imagined, when we trained to be foster parents . . ."

"Telling kids their relatives have died is not a standard part of the territory," I assured her, "but can you keep Bradley for a few days while we sort it all out?"

"Ridd's coming in this afternoon. I can ask—"

Before she could finish, Cricket spotted me and dashed over. "Me-Mama! Did you know your whole store burned down?"

"Looks that way, doesn't it?"

Together we stood and look at the charred skeleton.

Cricket tugged my hand and I bent down so I could hear him above the noise. "You didn't get hurt. That's what matters most, isn't it?"

"It certainly is."

I couldn't bear to look toward Bradley as I said those words.

Joe Riddley came back from talking with the fire chief. "He says we can't get into the building until tomorrow at the earliest—if then. We might as well go home." He looked tired, drawn, and gloomy.

"Let's all go to Myrtle's," Gusta suggested. "My treat."

That was such a rarity that everybody accepted.

All our lives, Myrtle's had been the meeting place after ball games and dances, movies and elections. That morning she had extra coffee on, expecting us. As she filled my cup, she leaned close and muttered, "I heard you nearly burned up. Glad to see you here, even if you do look a little singed around the edges."

"Glad to be here," I agreed. "Solid gold doesn't burn."

"Neither does wet garbage."

We glared at each other, then started laughing at the very same time. Myrtle raised her voice to be heard above the din. "Back to my old prices for the morning, folks. And as much coffee as you can drink, on the house."

Conversation was brisk, as if people needed to be cheerful after the previous day's disaster. The children had dishes of ice cream; the rest of us drank coffee with pie or doughnuts.

I sat there looking at the folks assembled and felt sad. Everything had changed for me, Joe Riddley, and Bradley, but nothing much had changed for most of them. Otis and Lottie still had to look after Gusta and Hubert. Evelyn and Hubert hadn't turned out to have a romance after all. Selena and Maynard didn't have any children. I hadn't been able to do a thing for anybody.

"Judge? Judge!" Somebody was calling behind me.

I looked and saw Grady Handley working his way through the crowd. "I heard what happened. I am real sorry. I came by to say thanks. They dropped all the charges."

"Daddy angel!" Natalie let go of Selena's hand and hurled herself at him.

"Nattie-boo!" Grady picked her up and tossed her into the air. She shrieked with laughter. I had never seen her so happy.

Anna Emily sidled over toward him. "Can I go home with you?"

He squatted down. "I certainly hope so. We just have to work out a few details. Who are you staying with right now?"

"That would be me." Maynard stood up. I had never thought of him as menacing before, but he seemed to grow six inches as he glared at the other man. "Who are you?"

"I'm these kids' father. We got—uh—separated for a while."

"He has a lot of antiques," I said quickly to Maynard, then added, to Grady, "Maynard is in the antique business."

Grady brightened. "Really? My folks were in the business. I grew up in it. We owned House of Handley, up in North Carolina."

The name meant nothing to me, but it did to Maynard. "No kidding? I have Wainwright House up the street. Come by and have a look." Something occurred to him. "You aren't planning to open a store in Hopemore, are you?"

"Hadn't planned to open a store at all. I'm a lawyer. But I might like to work in a store for a while until I pass the Georgia bar. This seems like a nice town in which to raise kids."

Next thing I knew, the two men and Selena were huddled at a table with Anna Emily on Selena's lap and Natalie on Grady's. I could hear snippets of the conversation.

". . . need to find a place to live."

". . . we've got lots of space in our house for the time being, and the girls know us."

". . . come see Wainwright House this morning, see what I've got."

". . . got a house full of stuff, as soon as I can establish my claim to it."

"Humph!" Gusta said to Jed and Meriwether, with a frown at Maynard's table. "I should never have sold that house. Pooh's isn't antebellum, and I can't see the courthouse from my window."

"What are you going to do now?" Myrtle asked Hubert as she refilled his cup. He had chosen a seat at Maynard's table with his back to Evelyn.

"Oh, get that mess cleaned up and see if I can put up something somebody will want to rent, I guess. After that? I don't know. Grow watermelons, maybe. I miss having my garden."

"What about you?" Myrtle asked Evelyn, moving over to pour her some coffee.

Evelyn darted a glance our way. "I might move over to Louisville and start a bed-and-breakfast. I've always wanted to run one, and now might be a good time to look into that."

"Sounds good to me."

Hubert turned in his chair. "You can't leave Hopemore, Evelyn."

She looked flustered. "Why not?"

He looked puzzled, as if he didn't know the answer, either. "Because . . . because . . . because I'm here! Why don't you move into our house and turn it into a bed-and-breakfast? It would be great for that. It's even got an elevator."

"What would Nana do?" Meriwether inquired. "Serve breakfast?"

"I'd move into that apartment upstairs in Wainwright House," Gusta told her. "I'd get my old room back where I could see the courthouse."

"Is that possible?" Jed asked Maynard.

"I don't see why not. She'd need to put in an elevator."

"I think I could manage that," Gusta said in the tone of one stretching her resources to their outermost limit. "Florine will come live with me," she warned Hubert. "You won't have her around to help with your bed-and-breakfast."

"Lottie might help with it," Otis volunteered. "But not right away and not living in. We've been thinking of getting our own place and taking a trip or two."

Hubert rubbed his hands together. "Wonderful! Then it's settled."

Evelyn was still staring at Hubert as if she hadn't heard anything for several minutes. "I can't move in with you."

"Why not? You want to run a bed-and-breakfast, and I've got a great house for one. I'll even help. I cook a mean breakfast."

"It's not . . . your house." She floundered around like she wanted to say something else.

"I'll buy it. Gusta, Jed, can I buy you all out?"

"Absolutely," Jed said, getting into the spirit of the thing.

"If I can rent Maynard's apartment," Gusta said, wheeling and dealing as usual.

"It wouldn't be proper!" Evelyn was as pink as a boiled shrimp, but she had her chin in the air and a spark in her eyes.

Hubert colored up. "Proper? I'll show you proper, woman! We'll get married." He slid his eyes my way. "The judge here will do it—won't you, Judge?"

"I did one wedding once," I allowed. "Married Valerie, the girl who used to live with Edie Burkett, and her biker friend.[8] But it's customary to have a proposal first, Hubert. That's the way things are done."

He looked over at Evelyn. She still had her chin in the air, but she nodded.

He took her hand. "I'm sorry about New Orleans, hon." His voice was husky. "You willing to give me another

[8] *Who Killed the Queen of Clubs?*

chance? I think we could have a lot of fun together, and like I said, I cook a mean breakfast."

Evelyn gave a choky laugh. "Okay," was the only word she managed to get out.

As we drove home to dinner (Clarinda having agreed to cut her vacation short), I said, "Here I've been so worried about Otis and Lottie, and Gusta, and Hubert and Evelyn, and Selena and Maynard, and they didn't need my help at all. They managed quite well on their own."

Joe Riddley gave a grunt. "Hold on to that thought, Little Bit. Worry ages folks terribly. Giving it up might net you a few more years. But I'd better tell you, the sheriff called while Hubert and Evelyn were billing and cooing a while ago. He said he'll meet us at the house around three. There's still some loose ends to tie up, he said."

That sobered me in an instant. "The biggest one is Bradley. You don't reckon Selena and Maynard would adopt him, do you?"

"That will be entirely up to them. You can't arrange everybody's life to come out right."

I sighed. "Heck, I can't even arrange mine to come out right." I was already wondering what I was going to do with all the free time I'd have now that the store was gone.

When Buster arrived, we sat in the living room. Although it was a gray, cold day outside, nobody suggested that we light a fire. We'd had all the fire we would need that winter. The house still smelled smoky, and I wondered if I'd ever get that odor out of my nostrils and my taste buds.

Clarinda brought in coffee and some of her pecan pound cake, and I curled up on the couch and told the sheriff about my two afternoon visitors the day before. I told him about Trevor's confession, and Billy's boasts. Then I told him how Trevor had tried to save Billy.

"Do we have to make it public that Trevor killed Robin?" I asked.

Joe Riddley asked from his recliner, "What is it the Bible says? 'Let the dead bury their dead.'"

The sheriff nodded. "I don't plan to say anything about it at all. However, if word gets around somehow that it was Billy, I don't plan to contradict the report."

"And I don't think Natalie ever need know he was her birth father, either, do you?" I asked.

"Not until she's grown, at least," he said.

"Poor Bradley. I hope we can help him remember what a fine man his granddaddy was."

We sat quiet for a few minutes of tribute to a hometown hero.

Joe Riddley looked at me over his cup. "Whose life you planning now, Little Bit?"

"Nobody's. Not even mine. I was just wondering what I'll do now."

Buster stood. "I'd better be getting on. Just wanted to finish up the case. Walk me out, Judge?"

I got up and walked him to the door. He paused on the threshold. "About what you should do next, well, I've been thinking. This is the slow time for your business anyway, right? Even if a fire hadn't wiped out part of it?"

I nodded. "Pretty slow for a few weeks now."

"I don't recall ever giving you all much in the way of birthday presents, anniversary presents, or Christmas gifts. So it seems to me I might owe you something for all the years you've put up with me." He reached into his pocket and brought out an envelope. "Consider this a partial payment on that debt." He handed it to me, then hurried down the steps.

I opened the envelope, and shrieked. "Joe Riddley, look! He's bought tickets for a cruise for two. In the Far East! Three weeks! Hong Kong, Singapore, Malaysia . . ." The words sounded like music to my ears.

Joe Riddley took the tickets from me with a sour look. "I see he got the nonrefundable kind."

From the kitchen I heard Clarinda. "Um-hmm. What did

I tell you? Judge, you better take good care of this lady, or I know somebody who will."

That's why we are heading off next week on an airplane to Hong Kong. Once he gets his feet wet on the cruise, Joe Riddley may like foreign travel. He may want to see India, Africa, the Middle East, and Europe. So if you don't hear from us for a while, picture us standing on a balcony in some distant place with smiles on our faces and the world at our feet. We'll send you a postcard.

MANY THANKS

One year we arrived at a family reunion to find a huge white bear on the back doorstep of our hotel. It turned out to be not an escaped polar bear but a taxidermist's form. That weekend we were invited to visit the exhibitors hall and competition exhibit of the North Carolina Taxidermists Association. After that, I knew that a taxidermist would have to figure in one of MacLauren Yarbrough's mysteries.

To get acquainted with the hands-on mechanics of taxidermy, I visited Artistry in Nature Taxidermy in Dallas, Georgia, where owner Mickey Wright and taxidermists Steve Blackstone and Chris Agan introduced me to their world. What I got right is due to their diligence in teaching. What I missed was my own fault.

Helen Machida and Shafer Gray helped me create an accurate text message, since I am as ignorant of the world of text messaging as MacLauren was. It is good to have knowledgeable friends from a younger generation.

Throughout this series, I have relied on Judge Mildred Ann Palmer as my inspiration for Mac. Anytime I need to remember how Mac sounds or help with a detail, she has been a phone call away. Thanks, Judge Palmer! I am also indebted to my editor, Ellen Edwards, who does such a good job of honing these books and helping me shape them. She is not only an invaluable editor, but a friend as well. I am grateful for my agent, Nancy Yost, who keeps the contracts coming and encourages me when I falter, and for Bob, who puts up with a wife who gets engrossed in a world that isn't there. Most of all, I'm grateful to you, the readers who have made this series not only possible but fun. Thanks to you all!

AVAILABLE NOW

TAMAR MYERS

AS THE WORLD CHURNS

A PENNSYLVANIA DUTCH MYSTERY

Magdelena Yoder may finally be married to
big-time Manhattan doctor Gabriel Rosen, but
she's still a small-town girl at heart, and thrilled
to be the emcee at the first annual Hernia
Holstein Competition. As a bonus, the
PennDutch and its barn are booked solid. But
then someone clobbers the contest's originator,
Doc Shafor, while he's admiring the cows, and
both Gabe and his daughter Alison go missing.
With the help of her best friend (and the
hindrance of her mother-in-law), Magdalena
vows to track down clues until the cows—
and her family—come home.

Available wherever books are sold or at
penguin.com